Dear Reader,

With its heartwarming blend of past and present, *The Light Over London* is a must-read for fans of *Lilac Girls* by Martha Hall Kelly and *The Nightingale* by Kristin Hannah. The charming prose transports us to World War II Britain through forgotten antique treasures, remembered triumphs, and fierce family ties.

This poignant women's fiction novel tells the present-day story of Cara, an antiques dealer who would rather bury herself in the past than confront the dilemmas of her present. So when she finds an old World War II diary from 1941, she delves into the life of Louise Keene—a small-town girl on the outskirts of the war, uninterested with the mundanity of her days. Desperate for a larger life, Louise defied her parents and joined the women's branch of the British Army in the anti-aircraft gun unit. As Cara journeys through Louise's life on the page and tries to figure out what happened to her, Cara just might uncover some truths about herself as well.

Brought wonderfully to life by critically acclaimed author Julia Kelly, these remarkable women reveal the power, love, and hope they have within.

I hope you love this novel where the past and the present collide, revealing truths and a sense of freedom that is applicable to every generation. Enjoy this early read, and, as always, I welcome your thoughts and can be reached at the contacts below.

All best,

Marla Daniels

Marla Daniels
Associate Editor
212-698-2127
marla.daniels@simonandschuster.com

THE LIGHT OVER LONDON

Julia Kelly

G

GALLERY BOOKS

New York   London   Toronto   Sydney   New Delhi

Gallery Books
An Imprint of Simon & Schuster, Inc.
1230 Avenue of the Americas
New York, NY 10020

First Gallery Books hardcover edition January 2019

GALLERY BOOKS and colophon are registered trademarks of Simon & Schuster, Inc.

For information about special discounts for bulk purchases, please contact Simon & Schuster Special Sales at 1-866-506-1949 or business@simonandschuster.com.

The Simon & Schuster Speakers Bureau can bring authors to your live event. For more information or to book an event, contact the Simon & Schuster Speakers Bureau at 1-866-248-3049 or visit our website at www.simonspeakers.com.

Interior design by Bryden Spevak

Manufactured in the United States of America

10 9 8 7 6 5 4 3 2 1

Library of Congress Cataloging-in-Publication Data
Names: Kelly, Julia, 1986- author.
Title: The light over London / Julia Kelly.
Description: First Gallery Books trade paperback edition. | New York : Gallery Books, 2018.
Identifiers: LCCN 2018010178 (print) | LCCN 2018014273 (ebook) | ISBN 9781501172922 (ebook) | ISBN 9781501196416 (trade paper : alk. paper)
Subjects: LCSH: Antique dealers—Fiction. | World War, 1939–1945—England London—Fiction. | GSAFD: War stories | Historical fiction
Classification: LCC PS3611.E449245 (ebook) | LCC PS3611.E449245 L55 2018 (print) | DDC 813/.6—dc23
LC record available at https://lccn.loc.gov/2018010178

ISBN 978-1-5011-9641-6
ISBN 978-1-5011-7292-2 (ebook)

For Anne, Judy, Sheila, and both my grandmothers

THE LIGHT
OVER
LONDON

1

CARA

It was the discovery Cara loved most: digging through the forgotten, the memorialized, the tossed-aside, and the cherished. Making sure that the treasures and trinkets left behind had the chance to tell their stories.

At Wilson's Antiques and Curiosities, it was her job to find out the where and when of every object that came through the shop's doors. But it was the why and the what that intrigued her most. When she answered those questions, she could give once-treasured possessions a new life with new owners.

When Cara couldn't unearth the history of a piece, she spun stories for herself. It was easier than thinking about her own mistakes and the regrets she carried. While she worked, she could escape into the comfort of someone else's life for a few hours.

Gravel crunched under her well-worn flats as she stopped to study the formidable house rising up before her. The Old Vicarage was a grand mansion of yellow Cotswold limestone, standing arrogantly against the dual ravages of weather and time, and punctuated by a pair of columns on either side of the white front door. A light wind rustled through the ivy that crept lazily between the first and second floors. Someone had pushed one of the third-story windows open, probably hoping to air out the house that had lain unoccupied since its owner had died almost six weeks ago.

The front door opened with a creak, and Cara's boss, Jock Wilson, stepped out with a blond woman in her early forties. Dressed in pale blue and white, all elegance and softness, the woman was a stark contrast to Jock's stiff tweed and polished leather brogues.

"Miss Hargraves, you're finally here," said Jock.

Cara glanced at the antique gold watch that Gran had given her upon Cara's graduation from Barlow University years ago. It was nine o'clock on the dot, the exact time Jock had instructed her to arrive—unless she'd misread his email.

A flush of panic heated her cheeks. She couldn't have gotten the time wrong. She'd been so careful since her first day two months ago. She'd had to be. This job was her chance to start again.

"Mrs. Leithbridge, this is my assistant, Cara Hargraves." Jock's hand swept out as though Cara were an early-nineteenth-century Limoges teapot he was presenting at auction.

She swallowed around her worry and crossed her hands behind her, hoping the gesture conveyed both deference and regret. "My condolences for your loss, Mrs. Leithbridge."

The client gave her a minute, dismissive smile. "Thank you. Let's get on with it then. I have a tennis lesson this afternoon."

As the lady retreated through the front door, her high-heeled sandals clicked on the mosaic tile floor, Jock raised his brows to Cara as though to say, *She's one of the types I warned you about.*

"I can't imagine how I got the time wrong," Cara whispered in a rush as they followed their client.

"You weren't late, but you weren't early either," said Jock.

Her step hitched. "What?"

"Better to be early and sit in the car than to leave a client waiting.

Now come on."Cara forced her shoulders down and breathed deep to soothe the sting of her boss's prickliness.

Focus on the job. Show him what you know.

The air in the entryway was cool and stale. It might've been unsettling except she could almost hear the echoes of children long since grown scuffing the floors as they tore through the place in their eagerness to play outdoors. It wasn't hard to imagine past proud owners standing at the huge white door greeting friends with two kisses and a warm smile each.

This was someone's home, not just a job site, she reminded, taking in the pale green paneling that climbed up a third of the wall before giving way to a familiar wallpaper of bold acanthus leaves on a deep-blue background. Immediately, her mind zipped through the categorization Jock had taught her.

William Morris. British. Mid-1870s.

When she'd first started working at Wilson's Antiques and Curiosities as an eighteen-year-old student, she'd thought she would have a natural advantage, having grown up surrounded by antiques in both her parents' and grandparents' homes. But Jock had been quick to show her just how little she'd known. Now that she was back more than a decade later, he'd made it clear that he expected her to become as knowledgeable as him in short order. That meant any time not spent visiting Gran in her nearby retirement village was spent reading up on the styles of furniture Cara would most likely encounter. But, standing next to him on her first trip into a client's home, she'd known the Morris wallpaper without the crutch of her books, notes, and Google searches. She could do this.

"Your brother mentioned on the phone that your great-aunt was a collector," Jock said.

Mrs. Leithbridge lifted a shoulder. "Great-Aunt Lenora was a pack rat. The whole house is jammed with clutter."

"Miss Hargraves, do you see anything of interest in this room?" Jock offered Mrs. Leithbridge a strained smile. "Miss Hargraves is currently training after some time away from the antiques trade."

"I see," said Mrs. Leithbridge as though she couldn't have cared less.

Determined not to be intimidated by her boss or by their apathetic client, Cara's gaze settled on a small bench pushed against the wall next to the front door. Its finish was worn where countless people had paused to pull on wellies and clip on dog leashes over the years. It might've been unextraordinary except for its back and legs, which were carved in an intricate geometric pattern.

"That oak bench," she said, pointing.

"Movement?" Jock tossed back.

"Arts and Crafts, likely constructed in the later half of the mid-nineteenth century."

"American or British?"

She walked over to the piece and ran a hand over the back, feeling for the smooth joins that held it together without the aid of nails. "The wood is in good condition, but there are a few dings and nicks. The finish is only fair."

"And what of the country of origin, Miss Hargraves?" Jock pressed, his formality making her feel like she was back in grammar school.

She stared hard at the bench. It was likely British, but people traveled, and collectors bought from abroad.

"Without searching for a maker's mark, I can't be certain," she finally said.

"Are you sure you don't want to hazard a guess?" asked Jock.

"Yes."

Her boss gave a small nod. "Very good. Better to be right than to guess."

"This is all fascinating, I'm sure, but is it worth anything?" Mrs. Leithbridge asked.

"With the right buyer, everything has value, but let's hope for pieces that are in better condition," said Jock. "Perhaps you could show us the drawing room?"

"Through here," said Mrs. Leithbridge, guiding them with a flick of her hand.

Always start in the drawing room, Jock had said when briefing Cara yesterday. *It's where people show off their best. And remember: F-S-P.*

Those were the two governing principles of his business. Furniture, silver, paintings. Find, sell, profit. F-S-P.

Yet for Cara, there was more to it than that. When she'd been at university, Wilson's had been a haven of sorts, a place to lose herself in the past. As she'd methodically catalogued each item in the storeroom, she'd felt like participant, witness, and confessor to little slivers of other people's lives. Now, thirteen years later, she'd finally have the chance to glimpse a fuller picture of the connection between antique and owner.

Jock stopped short in the drawing room doorway, nearly causing Cara to crash into him. But then she saw why he was rooted to the spot. The room was packed with furniture, with only little walkways weaving across the huge handmade wool-and-silk rug. There were at least five sideboards dotting the space, including two pushed flush against the backs of a set of massive roll-top sofas. A Gothic-style grandfather clock ticked away in a corner, and paintings were hung in the Victorian style over nearly every inch of the oxblood-painted walls, while a mess of photographs, vases, candy dishes, and other curios covered almost every surface. Yet it was the wood-and-glass monster opposite the wide, tiled fireplace that caught Cara's attention.

"Is that—?"

"A Collinson and Lock," Jock finished.

They approached the piece carefully, as though it were a skittish animal that might scare at any moment. Gingerly, Cara grazed her fingers over the edge of a cornice punctuated by a white scroll pattern.

"It's rosewood, and the inlay is ivory. The crosshatching is there," she said, thankful she'd just read about the furniture-making firm of Collinson & Lock that weekend.

"Very good, Miss Hargraves. The glass-fronted doors are also a key feature of the makers. But we won't have confirmation until we find the stamp." He opened the central cabinet door and made a show of craning his neck to look inside. "Not here. Would you look underneath? My knees are aching today."

Jock's knees seemed to be acting up quite a bit since she'd rejoined him, meaning it'd been up to her to do the crouching or bending around the shop. Nevertheless, Cara knelt on the floor and twisted to look up at the unembellished base of the cabinet's lower level.

Shifting to pull her penlight out of her back pocket, she clicked it on and illuminated the words "Collinson & Lock."

"It's here," she announced, pulling her head free. "Serial number 4692."

"What is it?" Mrs. Leithbridge asked as Jock jotted the numbers down in a small leather-bound notebook he kept in his breast pocket.

"A very fine piece, and a good indication of your great-aunt's taste. Perhaps," said Jock, turning on his most brilliant smile, "you might consider rescheduling your tennis lesson. We have a great deal of work to do."

~

Later that afternoon, Cara and Jock were in the dining room sorting through the contents of the late Lenora Robinson's china when her phone rang.

Her boss, who had been examining an Adams sugar bowl they suspected was from the 1850s, shot her a glare. "Miss Hargraves, will you turn that infernal thing off?"

Her grip reflexively tightened around the heavy stack of eighteen dessert plates she'd been pulling out of the butler's pantry. "I'm so sorry."

She slowly made her way to the dining table to set the plates down as the phone rang again.

"Miss Hargraves," her boss said again, crossing his arms.

She ripped the phone out of her back pocket, her stomach sinking as she saw Simon's picture filling the screen.

"Are you going to answer it or simply stare?" Jock asked.

She cleared her throat. "It's my ex-husband."

"Then I suggest you take this very personal call somewhere else. Far away."

"Yes, of course." She hurried out and picked up the call as soon as she was in the corridor. "What is it, Simon?"

His voice, as polished as it was judgmental, filled her ear. "Why are you whispering?"

She strode up a narrow flight of stairs that must've once been for the servants of the house. "Because I'm at work."

"With the antique owner of the antique shop?" He snickered.

"Yes, and Jock needs me, so if you'd just tell me why you called . . ."

Glancing around for Mrs. Leithbridge, she slipped into the first room she came to, kicking up a cloud of dust that swirled in the light from a single window. When she shut the door, an old, battered armoire creaked open.

"Come now, it isn't like you're performing surgery," he said.

God forbid he think her job was important.

"You should go back into events," he continued, his tone overbearing and snobbish. "I'm sure your old boss could find a spot for you, or you could start your own consultancy. Then you could make real money."

Of course Simon didn't think working for Jock was *good enough*, and it grated on her that, even though they were divorced, he still felt his opinion should matter.

"Simon, I hated working events and I should've quit long before I did."

"And I suppose that's my fault," he said, his voice sharpening.

"Part of it is, actually."

All at once, Simon's self-righteous bluster left him. "I'm sorry, Cara. I ruined everything. I'm going to get help, I just . . ."

She squeezed her eyes shut, waiting for the wave of guilt to come. Only now it had been long enough that it didn't crash down on her but rather lapped at her feet. They'd been down this path before. He'd first promised her when she'd told him she wanted a divorce that he would seek help, but he'd never gone. It had taken her considerable time with her own therapist to understand that her shoulders weren't broad enough to carry the full weight of her husband's narcissism, insecurity, or addiction.

"Why did you call?" she asked, weary to the bone.

He cleared his throat. "A bill was forwarded to me by mistake. It was for your parents' storage unit."

She slumped against the wall, the memory of the late-night phone call still fresh enough to leave her breathless. It had been a police officer, telling her with clinical dryness that a drunk driver in a Range Rover had hit her parents on a one-track country lane. They were being medevaced to a hospital in Cumbria. She hadn't arrived in time to say goodbye.

"Apparently the annual fee was paid out of our joint account. Since we closed it, it came back declined," Simon continued, oblivious or uncaring as to how his words hit her.

"Please forward it to my new address. I'll take care of it," she said, her voice cracking a little.

"You should clear it out and sell the lot. They've been dead for almost two years, Cara. You need to stop wasting money on this."

His callous disregard for the way she chose to mourn her parents' deaths might've felt like a slap once. Now it just left her with a deep, soul-aching sadness. "Send me the bill. I'll handle it."

"I'm only trying to help," he said.

"No, Simon, you're not, and one day I hope you'll see that." She swiped to end the call. Her divorced friends had told her that there'd be times when she'd be so angry at her ex she'd want to rage, but all she felt was sad. She could hardly remember why she'd fallen in love with him all those years ago.

She tucked her phone away, determined to focus on whatever Jock threw at her, but before she could, the glint of gold caught her eye from inside the partially open armoire. She moved to shut the door that had fallen open, but hesitated. Great-Aunt Lenora had proven canny about hiding things away in nooks and crannies. Who knew what was squirreled away inside?

The old hinges creaked in protest as she opened the door wide. Compared to the clutter of the house, the shelves were disappointingly bare. The gold turned out to be a hand mirror with an elaborate fleur-de-lis back wrapped in a sheet of newspaper from 1983, and next to it lay an old Scrabble set that looked to be at least two dozen letters short.

Not feeling particularly hopeful, she turned her attention to the two drawers on the bottom. Nothing in the first but a couple of dead moths. But when she opened the second drawer, she saw a biscuit tin molded to look like a shelf of upright books. She'd seen tins like this full of buttons and other odds and ends in Gran's house when she was a child. If she had to hazard a guess, against Jock's wishes, she would've said it was from the 1940s, possibly the very early 1950s.

Kneeling on the floor, she slipped her short nails under the top to rock the metal back and forth. It was slow work but finally the thin metal gave way, and her heart kicked up a beat at what she saw.

On top lay a small fat notebook bound in red cloth–covered cardboard and held together by a band. When she tried to open it, the elastic disintegrated in her hands.

"Damn," she cursed softly. She should probably set the book aside, but the damage was already done.

The notebook's first page was blank, but the next was covered in looping script written in faded blue ink. The date at the top read "14 October 1940."

The bombs fell again yesterday night. I'd just gone to sleep when the explosions started. They sounded so close I thought the ceiling might fall in. Dad says the Germans dropped six bombs on RAF St. Eval. We don't know yet how much damage was done.

I suppose that's why I'm writing in this diary. Dad has been saying for ages that I ought to keep a record of this war and of what happens to me.

Just last week Mum was horrid about the idea, saying, "What's she going to write about? Her job at Mrs. Bakeford's shop?"

Well, something has happened and I have to write about it, even if it is simply to spite Mum.

It was a diary. A World War II diary. Her curiosity piqued, Cara skipped ahead a dozen or so pages.

21 February 1941

For months I felt as though I didn't have anything to record in these pages. Everything stays the same here, but now things are different. Now it seems as though I can't stop writing.

Paul took me to the pictures in Newquay yesterday afternoon to see Freedom Radio. I told Mum I was helping Kate knit socks for the war effort, but instead I ran to the bus stop to wait for him. He was a perfect gentleman, buying my ticket and helping me to find my seat. We arrived at the theater just as the film was starting, and as soon as the title card came up he took my hand and didn't let go the entire time. I don't think I paid attention to a thing Clive Brook and Diana Wynyard were saying on the screen!

24 February 1941

Two days until I see Paul again.

I never thought I would be the type of girl to become all swoony over a man, but today at the shop I dropped a glass jar of boiled sweets. By some miracle it didn't break, but Mrs. Bakeford scolded me for having my head in the clouds. I wanted to tell her it wasn't my head but my heart.

With a smile, Cara flipped forward to a random section midway through.

25 September 1941

I said goodbye to Paul Paul this morning. He tried to talk me into staying in bed, but I told him that would be desertion.

Cara paged through the rest of the diary, looking to see how far it went. The writing stopped abruptly with a single line.

5 January 1942

Everything is over. I thought I loved him.

Guilt tugged at her as she closed the cover but, sitting with her hand still touching the journal full of another woman's most intimate thoughts, she couldn't deny that she was curious. Who was Paul and what had happened in those few months? Why was everything over, seemingly in less than a year? And whose diary was this in the first place?

When she tipped the rest of the tin onto the floor, out tumbled a tiny compass with a bent edge, a locket, a photo, a few pieces of paper, and a scrap of cloth. The cloth was easy enough to identify: a man's handkerchief, plain and serviceable, with a "P" stitched in one corner. One of the papers was bright coral and dry with age. She flipped it over. A cinema ticket to the Paramount Theatre in Newquay dated 23 February 1941, the day before one of the diary entries she'd read.

She set the ticket aside and examined the other scraps of paper. A small flyer with a torn corner for some sort of Valentine's dance at the generically named Village Hall on the fourteenth of February. An unused tube ticket for the Central Line.

She picked up the photo next. A woman wearing a uniform was looking over her shoulder, her hand raised to the cap that sat perched atop her swept-back, pageboy hairstyle. Her smile was bright and brilliant, as though the photographer had caught her at a moment of pure joy.

But that wasn't what made Cara pause. It was the uniform—she'd seen it before. Gran had been issued the same one when she'd joined the Auxiliary Territorial Service in 1943, and she recognized it from the two photographs Gran kept in her sitting room. One was a formal portrait taken on Iris Warren's first day of leave from the women's auxiliary branch of the army. In the other, she was lined up with four other uniformed girls, all linking arms and smiling.

"I met your granddad at a dance at the NAFFI," Gran had explained to her once. "Every few months, something official would be put on in the canteens with as good a band as they could scrape together, but more often we'd dance to music played on a gramophone. The Americans had brought the jitterbug with them, and we were all mad for it.

"Your granddad was an American GI, with his hair cut short and his sharp uniform. He did his best to woo me with chocolates and the promise of silk stockings."

But that was where Gran's reminiscences ended. The last time Cara had tried to ask about the war when she was just sixteen, Gran had abruptly clammed up and gone to lie down, claiming to have a migraine. Mum had scolded her, saying, "There are some things your gran doesn't want to talk about. Don't push her, Cara."

She traced her finger over the strong sweep of the woman's jaw before flipping the photograph over. On the back, in a different handwriting than the diary, someone had written "L.K. on the Embankment."

Setting the photo down, she picked up the simple gold heart locket, and eased her thumbnail between the clasp to open it. One side was blank but the other held a tiny photograph of a dashing man in a fleece-collared bomber jacket with a pair of goggles perched on top of his head. A pilot.

"Miss Hargraves!" she heard Jock shout from somewhere downstairs.

Quickly, she gathered the things into the tin and rushed downstairs to find Jock in the study with Mrs. Leithbridge.

"What have you there?" he asked with a raised brow.

"I'm not entirely sure." She set the tin down on a table. "Mrs. Leithbridge, did your great-aunt serve in the ATS during the Second World War?"

The lady lifted her brows. "I don't know what the ATS is."

"It was the women's service that supported the army during the war." When Jock looked over the top of his glasses, she added, "My gran served."

"Great-Aunt Lenora used to drone on about being an ambulance driver in London during the Blitz." Mrs. Leithbridge rose and click-clacked over to a desk near a pair of tall sash windows. Her hand wove through the air before plucking up one of the photographs that lined its edge. "Here."

There was no way the woman who stared out at Cara was the one in the ATS uniform. Even in black-and-white it was easy to see that Lenora Robinson, all sharp angles with high cheekbones and a thin, small nose, bore no resemblance to L.K. on the Embankment's youthful features and a strong jaw.

Still, Mrs. Leithbridge's great-aunt shared a first initial with the inscription on the back of the photograph.

Cara opened the tin and pulled it out. "Are you sure this wasn't her? The back reads 'L.K.' Maybe it was taken before she was married. What was her maiden name?"

Mrs. Leithbridge barely glanced at the photo. "Great-Aunt Lenora never took her husband's name. Quite modern, really."

"Oh." Cara glanced at Jock. "There was a diary too."

"There's a market for World War Two paraphernalia and diaries, but since it doesn't appear that Mrs. Robinson wrote it, we'd have to authenticate it and identify the writer," said Jock.

"I have a broker coming to look at the house in two weeks. Everything that can't be sold will be cleared out by a junk-removal company," said Mrs. Leithbridge.

"But shouldn't we do something with it?" Cara asked, holding up the diary. "Perhaps return it to the woman who wrote it?"

"Where did you find it?" Jock asked.

"In the back of an armoire in a small room off the back stairs."

"The box room?" Mrs. Leithbridge laughed. "No one's been in there for years. Throw it out."

"No!" Heat crept up Cara's neck as two pairs of eyes bored into her, but she refused to look away. She felt strangely protective of the diary, drawn in by the happiness and heartbreak she'd read and was now more determined than ever to get the answers she needed from Gran about her history.

"I'd like to keep it and try to figure out who it belonged to." Cara paused. "If that's okay with you."

"I don't care," said Mrs. Leithbridge. "I'll be in the drawing room if you need me."

When they were alone, Jock pinned Cara with a stern glare. "Miss Hargraves, we do not argue with clients."

"She wanted to throw it away," Cara protested.

"And that's her right. Mrs. Leithbridge can haul all of this to the back garden and set fire to it if she likes, but I'd rather persuade her to sell it and earn my commission. It would be helpful if my assistant didn't scold her."

"Aren't you the least bit curious as to who wrote it?"

"Given that I'm working and using up my client's valuable time, I'm far more interested in this writing box," he said, gesturing to a Victorian lady's lap desk that lay open on a table. "Or any other number of things that will actually turn a profit. F-S-P, Miss Hargraves."

She squared her shoulders, but before she could say anything, Jock sighed, took off his glasses, and rubbed them on a handkerchief from his pocket. "If it'll stop you from looking at me like I'm a philistine trying to destroy history, you can take the diary home. Go put it away, but hurry back. This is proving to be a larger job than I expected."

Cara kept her head down as she rushed to her car, but she couldn't help the little smile that touched her lips. She and Gran would have quite a bit to talk about after work.

2

LOUISE

Haybourne, Cornwall, February 1941

The bell above the shop door jangled, and Louise looked up to see a dripping umbrella fill Bakeford's Grocery & Fine Foods. It came down with a snap to reveal Mrs. Moss, who shook droplets of water all over the floor Louise had mopped an hour ago in a desperate bid for something to do.

"Good afternoon, Mrs. Moss," Louise said, pushing aside the account book she'd been working on.

"What a storm, dear. I was just telling Mr. Moss it'll be a wonder if we're not washed away one day," said the village solicitor's wife, touching her small purple hat that sat on a cloud of tight brown curls Louise knew she had washed and set at the beauty parlor in Newquay once a week.

"It's certainly keeping most of our customers away today," said Louise. "What can I help you with?"

"A pound of sugar and a pound of bacon, please," Mrs. Moss said.

"Do you have your ration books?" Louise asked.

"Oh yes." The lady opened her handbag and pulled out three of the little booklets. "Here you are."

Moving methodically, Louise flipped to the sugar coupons and set about detaching them.

"The rationing really has become ridiculous," said Mrs. Moss, *tsk*-ing her tongue as her eyes darted around the shop. "As though it wasn't enough after the Great War. What will it be next?"

Louise knew Mrs. Moss would be just as happy without her response as with it, so she focused on measuring out the sugar on the heavy iron scale with an exacting precision that had become second nature since the Ministry of Food had instituted rationing the previous year.

"And to think they called this the Phony War. Well, it wasn't so phoney after Dunkirk." Mrs. Moss crossed her arms over her purse and nodded to herself. "We had another letter from Gary. He mentioned you."

"Did he?" she asked, keeping her eyes down as she folded the sugar into a brown paper package.

"He doesn't know when his next leave will be. I told him he should've joined up with the navy, but the army was all he wanted.

"Have you been doing the accounts for the shop for long then?" Mrs. Moss asked, taking one of her abrupt changes of conversational tack.

Louise looked up and saw the lady eyeing the abandoned account book. "Yes, when Mrs. Bakeford hired me I mentioned I was good at maths in school. She's had me look over the books every week."

Mrs. Moss nodded approvingly. "That'll do well for you when you're married. Household accounts are at the heart of good housekeeping, I always say."

Louise winced and prayed the lady wouldn't begin her unsubtle campaign of nudging and prodding Louise about Gary. Neighbors separated by just a few streets, the two had grown up playing together, and while he was a kind man, he was also Gary. He had no greater ambition than to return from the war, read law, and go to work for his father just as he'd been told to do since birth. Gary would live in Haybourne for the rest of his life, a dull, predictable man well suited for a dull, predictable village. It was not the life Louise longed for—not that she knew exactly what it was she wanted.

Hoping to rush Mrs. Moss and her implications out of the shop as quickly as possible, she began to count out the bacon coupons. The first two ration books were fine, but when she flipped to the page where the bacon coupons should have been in the third, there were none.

"I beg your pardon, Mrs. Moss, but how much bacon did you want?"

Mrs. Moss toyed with a bit of string hanging off the cuff of her blouse that peeked out from under her coat. "A pound please."

"Mrs. Moss," Louise said slowly, "I'm afraid you don't have the right number of coupons. I can only give you half a pound with these."

Something flickered in the lady's eyes as she looked down at the coupons, but just as quickly Mrs. Moss flashed a brilliant smile that showed off the cracks around her mouth where her lipstick had settled. "You can overlook things this one time."

Louise closed the ration books, and slid them back toward Mrs. Moss. "I'm afraid I can't do that."

"I *beg* your pardon?"

The bite in Mrs. Moss's voice straightened Louise's spine even as she pressed her hands flat on the counter to keep them from shaking. "Mrs. Bakeford is very strict because the fines are so high."

"Louise Keene, your mother—"

The door crashed open and a figure wrapped in a bright yellow rain slicker and a matching bucket hat stomped in. "Lovely day for a stroll, darling!"

Kate. Louise could've run up and kissed her cousin, wet clothes and all.

"Oh!" Kate started when she whipped off her hat. "I didn't realize you had a customer. How do you do, Mrs. Moss?"

"Very well." Mrs. Moss sniffed. "My sugar please, Louise."

"Would you like the half pound of bacon as well?" Louise asked.

"Just the sugar."

Biting her lip, she wrapped the sugar in a second sheet of waxed paper to help protect it from the rain and handed it over. Mrs. Moss slipped it into her shopping bag, pulled her rain gear back on, and threw the door open to the storm.

A gust of wind swept in and banged the door hard enough that the shopwindow rattled. Kate sprinted over and slammed it shut. Pushing her hair back from her face, she laughed. "What was it that put that sour look on Mrs. Moss's face?"

"Kate . . ." Louise knew the censure in her voice would fall flat. It always did when it came to her cousin. Vivacious, bubbly, and just a touch glamorous, Kate was impossible to be angry with. For as long as Louise could remember, Kate had had a circle of friends orbiting her. In the spring of 1937, when both of them turned sixteen and Kate had transformed from pretty to beautiful, the ranks of her little group had opened to include most of the boys in Haybourne and some from the neighboring village of St. Mawgan.

"If Mrs. Moss doesn't want anyone to gossip about her, she shouldn't be such a busybody." Kate pointed at Louise. "And I won't hear a word of you defending her."

Louise pursed her lips and gave her cousin a small smile.

"Good. Now then," Kate said, spreading her hands wide on the shop counter, "what are you doing Friday evening?"

Louise blinked a couple times at the improbable question. "What I do every Friday, closing the shop down."

Kate sighed. "And after Bakeford's closes at five?"

"The accounts."

Kate flipped the account book around to face her and skimmed her finger down a column of numbers. "Looks as though you're a bit ahead of yourself this week."

"You're going to get it wet." Louise snatched the book out from under her cousin's fingers, snapped it closed, and shoved it under the counter.

"Come now, darling," said Kate.

"Do stop calling everyone 'darling,' Kate. You sound ridiculous."

"It's what all the film stars do."

"*American* film stars. Not girls who've never set foot out of Cornwall."

Kate twisted, draping herself over the counter so that her blond hair fell in thick waves over the polished wood. "Lord, what I wouldn't give to be in Hollywood." She flipped around again and leveled a look at Louise. "You never answered my question."

"What was that?"

"What are you doing after you finish the accounts, which you clearly have already started?"

"I suppose I'll go home and have dinner with my parents," said Louise with a shrug. It sounded just as uninspired as it felt.

Kate flashed her a grin. "Come to the dance with me."

"Oh, I couldn't," said Louise immediately.

"You don't even know where I want us to go."

Louise didn't have to know. Wherever it was, she could be absolutely certain that Kate would swan in, head held high, and immediately find herself swarmed by men. One would want to light her cigarette, two would push and shove to fetch her a drink, and four would fight each other for the first turn around the floor, showing off with a mock fox-trot danced with an imaginary girl in their arms. And through it all Louise would stand, hands clasped behind her back, too shy to initiate a conversation and feeling ridiculous for longing to be brought into their fold.

Louise probably should've resented her cousin for her ease with men, but that was impossible. Generous to a fault, Kate would be bursting with happiness if one of her admirers took a shine to Louise. But her cousin couldn't begin to understand what it was like to go through life without every door opening falling open. If Kate wanted, her feet would never touch the ground.

Louise, on the other hand, was decidedly earthbound. She'd been told all her life that she was quiet, reserved, *small,* until one day it became impossible to imagine how all of those things couldn't not be true.

"I don't need to know where you want to go," said Louise, sweeping imaginary grains of sugar off the scale with a cloth. "I just know that I'll find it a bore."

Kate scowled. "Don't be such a spoilsport. It's just a dance. A Valentine's dance."

"I don't dance," said Louise.

Kate laughed. "I know for a fact that isn't true. I've seen you waltz before. You were quite good at it."

"With your brother. It was hardly thrilling."

"That's only because you haven't had the chance to dance it with the right partner," said Kate with a grin. "Come with me."

Louise shook her head, her hand shooting up to push back in one of her plastic tortoiseshell combs that was threatening to slip out of her hair.

"Please?"

Louise narrowed her eyes. "Why are you being so insistent?"

"Because you deserve a bit of fun, darling." Kate dropped her gaze. "And Mum said I could only go if I was with you."

"Why?" Louise asked, warily.

"Oh, who knows for certain." Kate sighed, waving her hand about.

"Kate . . ."

Her cousin huffed. "Mrs. Lovell saw Geri Parker kissing an airman on the road out of Saint Trebelzue last Saturday. Now Mum won't let me go anywhere with Geri or anyone else. She says my judgment is compromised."

"And is it?" Louise asked.

Kate turned her nose up and said primly, "I might kiss the boys, but if they think there'll be any more than that, they're sorely mistaken."

"And why am I acceptable to Aunt Claire?" Louise asked.

"Because you're you." Kate shrugged.

Because they all know I would never do something as daring as kiss an airman on a lane in full view of who knows who.

The thought was thoroughly depressing.

"Okay then."

Kate looked up with a start. "What?"

Louise crumpled the rag she'd been clutching and threw it on the counter. "Fine, we'll go. Where it is?"

"The Village Hall in Saint Mawgan. Oh, darling, you won't regret it one bit!" her cousin gushed.

"Saint Mawgan? We'll have to take the bus," Louise said.

"It's best to cycle," said Kate with great authority. "At least if it's not raining. That way we don't have to stand by the bus stop for an age. We can leave whenever we want."

"And stay as long as we like?" Louise asked.

"Exactly. Now, what will you wear?"

Louise shoved the errant comb back into place again. "I don't really know. My green wool is probably best."

Kate wrinkled her nose at that. "You wore that to the concert at the village hall two months ago and it was a full two inches too short in the hem then."

"I'm nineteen. I doubt I've grown since then. Besides, how many people from Haybourne will be there to notice that I've worn it again, and will any of them really care?" she asked.

"No, but there will be airmen there."

"Who will spend the entire evening looking at *you*."

"Don't be silly," said Kate. "I promise you more partners than you can dance with."

Louise laughed, knowing full well that her cousin was only being generous.

But if she expected Kate to relent, she was sorely mistaken. Instead, Kate snapped her fingers. "That's what we'll do."

"What?"

"Find you an airman."

"I don't want an airman." But it was too late. Louise could tell the idea had already taken root in Kate's mind and would no doubt be impossible to shake free.

"Come to my house at six on Friday. You can wear my red crepe with the buttons down the front. It'll look far better on you than on me anyway. I've become too busty for it."

Knowing that to argue any further would be futile, Louise let her shoulders sag while her cousin stuffed her hair up under her hat and buttoned up her slicker.

Twiddling her fingers in the air, Kate trilled, "We're going to catch you a pilot, darling."

Louise laughed into her sigh. Friday was bound to be a very long night.

$\sim$

Louise lifted the latch to the garden gate and hurried through the rain to the front door. On either side of her, the ground lay cold and mostly bare except where her father had erected a cloche to protect his winter vegetables. Digging up the family's front garden nearly two years ago had been the first big battle of her parents' war within the war. Her mother, house-proud and keenly aware of the image the frontage projected to the rest of the neighborhood, hadn't understood the need to pull her roses, geraniums, and hyssops out at the root. Her father, never an avid gardener, suddenly went mad, buying seed for all number of vegetables and insisting with great authority that the back garden facing the open sea was too harsh to cultivate enough food in case of rationing. The argument was finally won one spring day when Louise had returned from a bicycle ride to find her father knee-deep in the mud, ripping out just-flowering plants, while her mother stood in the front window, arms crossed and face pale.

Her father, it would appear, had been right, Louise realized as she let herself into the house. Now, a year into rationing and well into the war, no one knew how far it would reach or when it would all end. Louise wasn't entirely sure that the fact that every other garden on their street had been given over to vegetables in an effort to "dig for victory" was a comfort to her mother.

"Louise, is that you?" her mother called from kitchen.

"Yes, Mum," Louise shouted back, shucking her mac and sitting down on the stairs to work off her wellies.

"Don't you tread mud into this house. I've already cleaned up after your father once."

Louise looked down at the thick layer of earth encasing the boot in her hand. Toeing the other boot off as carefully as she could, she tiptoed in the thick socks she wore to protect her precious stockings to the hall cupboard and wrestled free the mop. It was still damp from its last use.

Creeping back to the front door, she gave the floor a wipe as her father stuck his head out of the door of the front room.

"You're home," he said. "Good day at the shop?"

She shrugged, scrubbing away the dirt. "Hardly anyone came in."

He grunted and then retreated, happiest sitting in his usual armchair until the meal was on the table. He would have his paper in hand and be plotting on his huge atlas the new troop movements that had been reported, just as he always did after coming home from his job as the local postmaster. She knew he couldn't help but feel left out of this war, having fought in the last but being too old to be of any use this time around.

Upstairs in her room, Louise ran a brush over her hair and reset—hopefully for the last time—the comb that hadn't stopped slipping all day. Looking in her mirror, she noticed that the postcard she'd tucked into the plain wood frame had slipped to a drunken angle, a slight on her normally tidy room. She recentered it, her fingers trailing along the printed rows of brashly colored orange groves, lush under the California sun. She'd bought the card for threepence at a junk shop in St. Ives she and Kate had stolen away to when they were fifteen. Her mother thought junk shops were common, and going had seemed like the height of rebellion at the time. Kate, obsessed with Hollywood, swept up an armful of publicity stills cut out of a fan magazine and pasted to pieces of cardboard. But the promise of glamour hadn't captured Louise's attention the way the promise of a warm California day and soaring mountains so different from pokey little Haybourne had.

Downstairs, Louise set the table as she did every night. Spoon, knife, plate, fork, napkin folded once, twice, three times, water glass. Her father occasionally had a whiskey before the fire, but only after dinner. Her mother rarely joined him in drinking alcohol except when there were guests in the house. Then she'd take a little bit of sherry, "to be polite."

Supper arrived on the table just as the mantel clock in the parlor chimed seven. Louise's mother placed a casserole that, thanks to rationing, was more vegetable than meat in front of her father, who picked up the serving spoon and began to help himself just as he did every night. There was something so unfailingly normal about the whole ritual. Outside, in the rest of Britain, families might be carrying their bedding down to air raid shelters or wrestling with the constant fear of an invasion, but here in the Keene household time marched on almost uninterrupted by war.

Louise focused her gaze on a faint gravy spot on her mother's otherwise flawless white tablecloth, every ounce of energy repressing the urge to scream, to run, to do *something* unexpected.

"Please pass the mashed potatoes, dear," said her mother in her deceptively soft voice.

Louise unclenched her fists from in her lap to hand the warm blue-and-white patterned bowl to her mother.

"Mrs. Moss called on me this afternoon for a cup of tea," said her mother. "She mentioned she'd stopped at Bakeford's."

The faint hint of disapproval at the idea of her daughter working in a shop was unmistakable, but there was little Rose Keene could do about it when Louise had her father's support. That particular battle had been lost more than three years ago when Louise had turned sixteen and was still smarting from the news that her parents thought her headmistress's suggestion that she sit a university entrance exam to read maths a preposterous waste of time and money.

"Mrs. Moss mentioned some confusion about the ration books. Apparently one of hers was issued without the full complement of tickets," said her mother.

"That seems unlikely," said Louise's father.

"It's what she said," said her mother.

Father's and daughter's gazes met for a moment before sliding back down to their plates.

"She also said Gary asked after you in his last letter. Have you written to him yet this week?" her mother asked.

"I haven't had the time," Louise said as she cut a piece of parsnip in two.

In truth, she hadn't wanted to write Gary back. What did you say to a boy who'd taken you to one dance and to the pictures twice but who seemed to have little interest in you? Gary's letters were polite but uninspired, as though he wanted to write those battlefield letters as little as she wanted to receive them.

"You be sure to make the time," said her mother in her too-polished voice. "Good young men like Gary Moss don't come by the dozen in Haybourne. If you're smart, he'll come back and ask you to marry him. His prospects are the best in the area, with him set to take over his father's business one day."

"Leave the girl alone, Rose," said her father.

"Arthur—"

"He's fighting a war, not attending a garden party. Louise can't be hanging all of her hopes on him, even if he does manage to come back."

"What a perfectly wretched thing to say," said her mother.

Her father shrugged. "It's the truth. There's no telling who might be killed out there."

Her mother huffed. "Well, I for one don't understand why they can't simply send more soldiers and have it done with."

"Perhaps you should tell the generals that," said Louise's father with a laugh.

"Perhaps I should. It really is a disgrace. Just think of all the girls left behind like poor Louise."

Louise dug her fingers into the flesh of her thighs as the familiar urge to scream roared back. *Poor Louise.* That was who she was here. All she'd ever be. She had to find a way to leave Haybourne and this house where her future was lined up neat and orderly and inevitable without a word from her.

"Kate wants me to go with her to a dance in Saint Mawgan on Friday," Louise said, hoping the change in subject would keep her mother from prodding her about Gary any further.

"Saint Mawgan?" her mother said. "But that's two villages over."

"We'll ride our bikes. They'll be more reliable than the bus," Louise said.

"Who is invited?" her mother asked suspiciously. "Will there be servicemen there?"

"Of course there will be," her father interjected. "The entire county's crawling with them."

"I really don't know if that would be entirely appropriate," said her mother.

Her father lifted his brows. "We met at a tea dance. Was that appropriate enough for you?"

Louise's mother opened her mouth, then shut it again. Her mother never spoke of it, but over the years Louise had gathered enough of the details to know the story. Rose Wilde, daughter of a local fisherman, had gone to the dance in her one good dress. Her father, Haybourne's newly appointed postmaster, had caught her eye. They'd danced all night and three months later they'd been married. Louise had always thought her parents had married in August, but once, when her father had indulged in three whiskeys instead of his usual one, he'd let it slip that they should really celebrate their anniversary at the start of October. Louise had been born seven months later, on the eighth of May.

"I just think that with Gary serving, Louise could show a little deference—"

"She's nineteen," her father cut in. "She wants to go out and have a bit of fun with her cousin."

"Kate asked me just this afternoon. I haven't spoken to anyone else about it and I don't know who else will be there," said Louise, trying to soothe the tension in the room.

"Go," said her father, before her mother could protest again. "Enjoy it."

The rest of the meal was held in strained silence, her mother punishing her father for overruling her objections, and her father no doubt basking in a meal without the constant interruptions and observations of a difficult wife.

∽

Louise wiped the last plate clean and set it in the cupboard to the right of the sink. She was just folding up the dishtowel when her father shuffled in.

"This could do with a wipe," he said, holding up a glass.

Louise took it, wiping it inside and out.

"Thank you, Lou Lou."

"You're welcome, Da," she said, using the pet name she'd used for him until she was five and her mother had decided it wasn't proper.

He made as though to turn but then looked back over his shoulder. "About this dance—do you want to go?"

She shrugged one shoulder. "Kate wants me to go."

"That's not the same thing as wanting it yourself."

"Sometimes it feels like it should be when Kate's pushing," she said. He smiled.

"I suppose it will be a change," she said with a sigh.

"Do you know what I think, Lou Lou? You should go and dance with every man who asks you."

"And what if they don't ask me?" Her tone might have been light, but there was no mistaking the little quaver in her voice.

Her father reached over and tugged a lock of her hair gently. "They will. If you let them."

She watched him leave and touched her hair comb, not minding that it had slipped once again.

13 February 1941

The Spitfires are flying again today. I can see them from my desk, where I write this, but it's impossible to tell whether they're engaging in exercises or patrolling for submarines.

It's strange to think that in such a short time, we've all learned how the different engines sound and we're all able to pick out a bomber or a Spitfire. Children playing in the street still stare up at them or chase the planes down the road, but the rest of us hardly stop what we're doing. Da says that people can become accustomed to anything, and I believe him. Our gas masks hang on hooks by the door, half forgotten about even though it sometimes feels like most the village has gone off to fight.

We shouldn't be so complacent in thinking we're safe. St. Eval was hit several times last summer. The worst was in August. From my room you could see the flames when the Germans hit one of the pyrotechnics stores. Betsy, who works near the base, said it looks like they're still repairing the damage to the hangars from the October hit. I asked her if it bothers her being so close to a place that the Luftwaffe is trying to bomb, but she simply shrugged and told me it's nothing compared to what those poor people in London are experiencing in the Blitz.

I wonder sometimes if we shouldn't all be a bit more like Mum. She might fight the entire German army herself, if only over the rationing of tea, sugar, and butter. She says that when eggs go, it'll be the beginning of the end. Those aren't rationed yet, but it's so difficult to find them that we heard Mr. Nance at Bolventor Farm has taken to locking the chicken coop at night and standing guard at the farmhouse window with a shotgun in case anyone comes to steal from him.

I asked Da why Mum is so bothered by the rationings, and he said it's just because she remembers it from after the last war and that reminds her of her older brother who died. It's strange to think I had an uncle Monty whom I never met and only know the sight of because Mum keeps his picture on top of the piano in a silver frame she polishes every Saturday.

The one thing we can't ignore even in our sleepy little village is the soldiers. There are rumors that as soon as the Americans join the war— God willing—they'll be four deep on the streets of every town from St. Eval to St. Ives. But until then, it's just our boys. A truck painted olive green and covered in canvas rolled down the high street today. I rushed out of Bakeford's just in time to catch a glimpse of the soldiers out of the open back of the truck. They weren't at all like the men you see in the newsreels, all scrubbed clean with rosy cheeks and a wink for the girls. They stared off into space, not quite seeing us, even though Mrs. Latimer's boys ran out after them, shouting and trying to earn a wave.

The men in uniform are, of course, a topic of great interest among my friends. We may've all left school, but they still laugh and twitter and touch up their lipstick like schoolgirls whenever they think a serviceman might be near.

Kate can't contain her excitement over the dance tomorrow. Sometimes when I tell people that we're cousins, I can see them trying to work out how we could be so very different. Blond and brunette. Bubbly and shy. Tall and short. I would hardly believe it myself if I didn't know Uncle Jack was Dad's brother.

Mary Hawkley once asked me how I can stand having a cousin so popular. "Doesn't it just kill you that the boys all talk to Kate?" But then she stopped herself and laughed. "It's a good thing you have Gary, isn't it?"

She flitted away before I could say anything.

3

LOUISE

"Oh, my hair is an absolute wreck," said Kate as she stared into the mirror of the village hall's powder room and rewound one of the pin curls that had become crushed under her hat.

Louise stopped plucking at her cheeks and glanced at her cousin. "Stop your nonsense. You look like Betty Grable."

Kate rocked back on her black patent leather heels and dropped her hands to her sides. "Do you think so?"

With Kate's hair piled on top of her head sharpening her cheekbones and her mouth painted vermilion, it wasn't too outrageous a jump to make, so Louise nodded and then squinted at herself in the mirror. "The best I can hope for right now is Bette Davis."

"Don't be ridiculous," said Kate, but she'd gone back to twirling curls to reshape them.

Louise pulled her lipstick out of her purse and applied it to the bow of her lips. When she looked down, Kate was holding a tissue out. She took it and blotted.

"Ready?" Kate asked.

Not at all, but she nodded nonetheless.

They dropped their coats off and walked into the hall. Although it was only quarter past seven, the dance floor was already crowded with couples. There were a few very young men in sweaters and collared shirts, but most were in uniform, just as her mother had feared.

"Kate!" A handsome man with short blond hair who wore the navy service dress of the Royal Air Force gave a wave as he called out from near the pinewood bar.

"Come on," Kate said, snatching up Louise's hand and pulling her through the crowd.

"I've been waiting all night for you," said the man with a crooked grin.

"Is that right, Tommy Poole?" Kate asked with a toss of her head.

"Of course it is."

"Then what's this I hear about you using your leave to take Irene Walker to tea last Tuesday?"

"Looks like she's caught you, Poole," said another man with a Lancashire accent who'd turned to watch their approach. "Where's Geri, Kate?"

"Not here," said Kate primly.

"And who's this?" asked a third man, who had a redheaded girl named Joanne whom Louise recognized from school hanging on his arm.

"This," said Kate, pushing Louise slightly forward as though Louise were a trophy on display, "is my cousin Louise Keene. You should all dance with her tonight if you want to make me happy."

"Come on then, Louise Keene," said man who'd asked after Geri, offering her his arm. "You've a much better chance of making it around that dance floor without having your toes stepped on with me than Poole or Davidson."

"We haven't been introduced," she said, cringing immediately at how like her mother she sounded.

"This isn't an audience with the queen. No need for introductions," he teased. "But since you asked, I'm Sergeant Martin Taylor."

"A pleasure," she said, taking his hand and feeling slightly ridiculous at the little laugh he gave before gamely shaking it. "Shouldn't we wait until the next song?"

"We'll just shove our way in. More's the merrier," he said.

She glanced at Kate, who nodded slightly, excitement shining in her clear blue eyes. A few moments in the hall and already Louise had an invitation to dance. Perhaps the night would be a lark after all. Taking a deep breath, Louise placed her hand in the crook of Martin's elbow and let him lead her to the edge of the dance floor.

It took them a few moments to find a gap in the fox-trotting crowd large enough to squeeze in, and when they did she could feel herself pressed uncomfortably close to him. She looked up, wondering if he'd noticed, but his gaze was fixed on a point somewhere over her shoulder. She craned her neck and spotted Kate.

"She's lovely, isn't she?" Louise asked.

Martin smiled sheepishly. "Your Kate has half the men at Saint Trebelzue in love with her."

"It was the same way in school."

"What about you?" asked Martin, shuffling them around a couple counting cautious steps.

"Me?" asked Louise.

"Come on then, no need to be coy."

"I'm not being coy. I'm not the type of girl who attracts that sort of attention."

Martin laughed. "I bet you are and you don't even know it."

"I hardly think so. I spent most of my childhood sitting in an apple tree in the front garden with a book."

"Well, that's it then. Probably had all of the boys in the neighborhood walking by and wondering if you'd ever look at them."

The idea was so ridiculous, she had to laugh, her shoulders coming down from around her ears as she did.

"There we are," he said. "No woman should look so serious when dancing with me."

"Do you have such a high opinion of your dancing abilities?"

"The Charmer of Chorley, that's what they call me. Fastest feet in fifty miles."

"I'm sure they do."

"You're a good one, Louise Keene."

She dipped her head in thanks. "It's a shame then that you're in love with my cousin."

"Ah well, everyone's in love with the wrong person during this war, I reckon. Maybe you'll find one of those neighborhood boys getting up the courage to ask you dance tonight."

"I doubt that very much," she said as the music ended. "Most of them are off fighting like you."

"An airman then," he said with a wink. "Plenty of us here."

She blushed. "I don't know that a uniform would suit me."

"A uniform always suits so long as the right man's wearing it. Come on then." He threaded her hand through his arm and led her back to Davidson and Poole, who were watching mournfully as Kate danced with a man with officer's stripes on his sleeve. Next to them another man stood lighting a cigarette, yet, despite his proximity, he seemed to hold himself somehow apart.

"Who's that with your friends?" she asked, watching as the man dropped his long, elegant fingers from his lips and let the cigarette smolder at his side.

"That's Flight Lieutenant Paul Bolton. He's a flier. A pilot, but he's all right. Doesn't give off too many airs like some of the officers. Lucky lad has all the girls after him."

"Do you fly together?"

Martin shook his head. "He flies a Supermarine Spitfire. I'm on a Bristol Blenheim, a kind of bomber. I'm a gunner and wireless operator," he said, pointing to a cloth patch on his arm embroidered with lightning bolts as proof, "and Poole's our observer. Davidson's ground crew. I'll introduce you to Bolton."

She was about to protest, but Martin surged forward, taking her with him. "Flight Lieutenant Bolton, this is Kate's cousin, Miss Louise Keene. Dances like a dream."

Flight Lieutenant Bolton flicked his gaze over to her. He straightened and put out his hand. "How do you do?"

He had a lovely voice, as deep and sophisticated as a film star's, and when she took his hand, her whole body went warm.

"Do you live in Saint Mawgan, Miss Keene?" he asked.

She shook her head. "Haybourne, just down the road."

"Then how have I never seen you at one of these before?" he said. "I'm sure I would've noticed you."

She blushed. "Kate brought me because her usual friend couldn't come."

He leaned over and put out his half-finished cigarette in a tin ashtray on a high-topped table. "In that case, I'll have to thank Kate's absent friend. Would you care to dance?"

This time there was no hesitation as she nodded and took his proffered hand. She glanced back and caught Martin's eye. Another wink. Another blush.

The small band on a makeshift stage at the far end of the room began to play "All I Remember Is You," and Flight Lieutenant Bolton wrapped his arms around her.

"I like your dress very much," he said, pulling her so close that she could've rested her head on his chest if she'd dared.

"Thank you," she said, sending a kind thought Kate's way.

"You look cheery as a summer's day."

"That's hardly fitting for February," she said.

"I've had enough of grays. A red dress on a pretty girl is just the thing." Her feet missed a step, but if he noticed, he was polite enough not to mention it. "Tell me about living in Haybourne."

She licked her dry lips and started hesitantly. "There isn't much to tell. I live in the same house I was born in. I work at the same shop I've worked at since I was sixteen."

"What do you do there?" he asked.

"Everything. Restock the shelves, help customers, do the accounts."

"You've a head for numbers then," he said.

"I suppose I do," she said.

"I'll have to be careful then."

"Why?"

He pulled her a fraction of an inch closer. "I lose my head around smart girls."

"Flight Lieutenant Bolton—"

"Please call me Paul if you're going to scold me." His smile warmed his eyes in a way she hadn't seen when he was around his fellow airmen, as though dancing was somehow thawing a frozen core.

"I was going to tell you that teasing a girl isn't very nice," she said.

He smiled. "It isn't teasing if it's true."

"You're a terrible flirt," she said.

"I'm not terrible, surely."

"Terrible," she said firmly, while struggling to keep a grin from bursting out over her features.

"Then I won't flirt with you, Miss Keene. Not if you don't want me to."

She chewed on her lower lip, hardly trusting herself enough not to blurt out how very much she wanted him to continue flirting with her. It was far and away the most thrilling thing that had happened to her in ages.

"What would you do if you weren't working in a shop in Haybourne?" he asked, the conversation veering back to respectable small talk.

She sighed. The little spark of something between them that had flared bright for a moment seemed to have died out.

"Haybourne is my life."

"Doesn't every girl in every small village have secret dreams of leaving?" he asked.

She looked up sharply. "You can tease me all you like, but there's no need to be cruel. I'm not a silly girl."

"No. I expect you're far too practical to have silly dreams." She started to pull back, but he dipped his head a little to draw his lips closer to her ear. "I promise I'm not teasing. I've never wanted to know the answer to a question more seriously in my life."

The softness of his words, achingly intimate over the music, and the stomping sound of the dancers' feet wrapped around her even as she pressed her lips tight to keep back the urge to answer. She was acutely aware of the heat of their hands pressed together. Of the faint growth of dark whiskers coming in on his chin. Of the sensation that swooped through her stomach when he spun her, almost as though she were falling.

And then the music stopped and the shuffle on the dance floor became less ordered. Couples broke apart and streamed around them as the musicians flipped pages on their crooked stands.

"Our song's over," the pilot said with a rueful smile. He offered her his arm and led her back to their little group. She kept her head lowered, unable to meet his eyes yet. The dance had somehow left her raw and exposed, as though every fundamental part of her had been taken apart, rearranged, and put back together again.

"Two dances in and I already feel like I'm standing on a sand dune in the Sahara," said Kate, fanning her face with her hand as they approached.

"Would you like something to drink?" Flight Lieutenant Bolton asked.

Louise shook her head, but Kate smiled brightly. "A squash for me please."

Out of the corner of her eye, she watched him bow his head, the old-fashioned gesture making Kate giggle, and then he was gone.

"Doesn't he look just like Clark Gable?" Kate asked.

Louise watched his broad back weave through the crowd until she lost him as the floor filled up again. "Maybe in a certain light. If you squinted."

"He's very handsome, and he seems to like you," said Kate, wiggling her thin-plucked eyebrows.

"He was only being kind."

Kate put her hands on her hips and lifted her chin. "Martin, what sort of girl does Flight Lieutenant Bolton usually dance with?"

A smile cracked over the gunner's face. "He doesn't dance. Not usually."

"See," said Kate, turning back to her with a raised brow. "You're *special*."

Now that the men were watching her, everything was too close. The music was too loud, the room too hot, the attention too intent.

"I need to step outside for a moment," she said.

Kate took a step forward. "Louise?"

She waved off her cousin's concern. "Just a little fresh air. I'll be back in two ticks."

The entrance was all the way on the other side of the room, but, having helped a friend's mother set up a jumble sale here three years ago, she knew there was a back door. Louise darted between men holding pints and girls sipping delicate glasses of sherry, ducking her head in case someone from Haybourne recognized and waylaid her. Any other time she might not have minded, but not that night.

She hit the handle of the heavy metal door with the full force of her body and it swung open, leading her to her refuge. The door clattered closed behind her as Louise sucked in deep breaths of cold, damp air. *We'll be lucky if we're not caught in in a rainstorm riding home*, she thought as she leaned against the white plaster wall, relishing the cold that seeped in through the thin fabric of her borrowed dress.

Although the music bled out through the cracks around the door, the night was peaceful. She tilted her head back, looking up at the stars. When she was a child, she'd loved going into the back garden with Da as he pointed out the constellations to her. She still thought them beautiful, but they were the same ones she'd been gazing at her entire life.

Her breathing had slowed to a normal pace, and she closed her eyes a moment. Inside, Paul would be talking to other women, sophisticated ones with long red nails and hair in proper sets who didn't have to borrow a nice dress. Worldly, sharp, and wise women who knew what to say to a man. How to idly flirt. How not to place so much hope on one short dance and a few scraps of conversation.

The squeak of unoiled hinges snapped her eyes open, and she let her head roll to one side so she could see who her fellow escapee was. He looked to his left, his face shadowed, but she knew in an instant. Paul.

Her foot scraped against the concrete, her instinct to shrink away into the dark and hide. He must have heard her, for he turned, his face illuminated now, and smiled.

"There you are," he said.

He had a lit cigarette in one hand and held a pint of ale in the other. No squash.

"Did Kate send you?" she asked.

"Kate's dancing with someone."

Then why are you here?

As though reading her mind, Paul said, "Your cousin's good for a laugh and nice enough, but she already has enough men chasing after her. She doesn't need me."

They stood in silence for a moment, him sipping his ale and her shifting from foot to foot. Finally, desperate to smash the awkwardness, she asked, "Why did you join the RAF?"

"My uncle was a second lieutenant in the Royal Flying Corps during the Great War. He was killed while training. Never saw action." He flicked his cigarette away. "It broke my mother's heart when her brother died."

Louise watched the cigarette's burning orange tip slowly fade against the cold pavement.

"My uncle was killed in the war too," she said.

He shook his head. "Too many families with too many sad tales. You must think me horribly rude, not asking if you'd like a drink."

She looked up. "I don't mind."

"Let me find you something. Or you can steal sips of mine."

He lifted his glass toward her, but she shook her head. "My mother says ladies don't drink ale."

He leaned across the gap and nudged her shoulder with his. "Then we won't tell your mother, will we? Go on, Louise Keene. Be just a little daring."

"That won't work, you know. My mother claims there's never been a more stubborn girl than me," she said.

"Your mother says quite a lot of things."

"She has many opinions."

"Do you always do what she says?" he asked.

Setting her jaw, she stuck her hand out. A flicker of something crossed Paul's face when he handed her the glass. She raised it, wondering for a brief moment if her lips would touch where his had been, and drank. More than a sip. Less than a gulp. A perfectly respectable amount of a drink that respectable young women didn't drink.

She handed him the glass back and licked her lips, the bite of bitterness and a touch of caramel lingering on her tongue.

"First ale, then what? Life outside of Haybourne?"

"You're teasing me again." She wrapped her arms around her waist, wishing she'd thought to pull on a cardigan over her dress.

"I'm not." But he grinned when he said it.

She pushed off the wall. "I'm going back inside."

His hand shot out to stop her. "Louise, wait."

She looked down at where his fingers had fallen, gently pressing her forearm. "What is it?"

"I couldn't let you go without asking something," he murmured. He gave her arm a little tug, and she took a step forward, her body moving of its own accord.

She swallowed down the rising mix of anticipation and fear and lust that surged up in her. This was the closest she'd been to a man since she'd let Gary kiss her behind a hedge just to see what it would feel like. It hadn't felt much like anything, as it turned out.

"What do you want to ask me, Flight Lieutenant Bolton?"

Rather than answer, he dipped his head and kissed her. And *oh,* now she understood what her first kiss had been missing. Paul's lips were soft but full, playing over hers as though he had all the time in the world, just for her. His free hand slipped into her hair, combing through her waves and twining them around his fingers. She gripped the lapels of his uniform, trying with all her might to hold onto this moment so tightly that it might never slip away.

He pulled back, his lips lingering on hers until at last they were no longer one.

She stood there, breath coming fast, eyes cast down. Anyone could've come upon them and seen. Then it would be her and not Geri everyone was gossiping about. But in the back of her mind, a tiny voice whispered, *Good*.

She had no obligations to anyone, had made no promises, no matter what her mother might hope. She wasn't Gary's wife or fiancée or girlfriend. She was nineteen and trapped in a tiny village on the edge of a country at war, target enough to know what bombs sounded like when they fell but removed from any hope of doing anything about it. Her life felt insignificant, and Flight Lieutenant Paul Bolton was quite possibly the most thrilling man she'd ever met.

"I thought I told you to call me Paul," he said.

She hadn't realized she was chewing on her lower lip until he lifted her chin with one finger and ran his thumb over it.

"Paul," she whispered, still a little dazed.

"I should like it very much if I could see you again, Louise. Would you like to walk with me Monday afternoon? I have a few hours leave from base due to me."

He was asking to call on her, to court her as though she was a lady in a Victorian novel. The idea, antiquated as it might be, charmed her.

"I would like that very much," she said.

"You won't be working?"

She shook her head, knowing she could ask Mrs. Bakeford if she might work that morning instead. Louise asked to change her shift so rarely, she was almost certain the woman would be willing.

"Good. Then perhaps you'd do me the honor of this next dance," Paul said.

With her hand tucked into his elbow, she walked back through to the dance floor. No one would know it looking at her, but everything had changed.

4

CARA

"Are you going to tell me what's weighing on you, or shall I guess?"

Cara started at the realization that Gran was examining her with narrowed eyes.

"What makes you think there's something on my mind?" she asked, sitting up a little straighter and lifting her brilliantly colored teacup to take a sip of fragrant Earl Grey.

"You keep staring off into space, and you haven't once complimented my haircut," said Gran, touching the pin-straight bob that just grazed her jaw. Regular visits to the salon she'd been going to for more than twenty years had been one of the conditions Gran had placed on moving to Widcote Manor last year. Iris Warren might be in her nineties, but she intended to maintain the sort of independence she'd enjoyed since leaving her parents' home in 1943.

"I don't want to be fussed over any more than I want to be stuck in a corner to fade away," she'd told Cara.

Cara couldn't imagine Gran allowing anyone to forget about her. Chic to the core, the woman refused to wear anything she deemed too "old mumsy," opting instead for brilliant colors and clean lines. She wore white gloves and pearls to church every Sunday, and her diamond earrings to dinner. She said exactly what she thought with the relish of a woman who knew she was old enough that people wouldn't try to hush her.

"Your hair looks smashing, Gran," Cara said.

Gran shot her a sly smile. "Now you're just patronizing me, but thank you all the same. Tell me that I'm wrong about your preoccupation."

Cara laughed. "You're not wrong. I actually wanted to ask you about something I found at work today."

"In Mr. Wilson's shop?" Gran asked. A lifelong patron of Wilson's Antiques and Curiosities, she'd been the one to suggest to the crotchety Scotsman that he might want to take Cara on for a few hours a week while Cara was at university.

"At an estate we were clearing out. It's a diary from the war."

Gran sat back in her pistachio-and-white wing chair, saying nothing.

"I think the writer was in the ATS." Cara rose, crossed the room to the sideboard cluttered with mementos, and lifted up the portrait of Gran at eighteen. "There was a photo with the diary. It was of a woman wearing the same type of uniform you're wearing here."

"Is that so?"

A long pause stretched between them while Cara weighed her next move. Finally, she said, "I'm planning to read the diary."

"Why?"

"I thought the woman who owned it would want it back if she's still alive. Or one of her family members could take it."

Gran set her teacup down on the coffee table. "Then I hope she's an entertaining writer."

Cara knew she was in danger of being shut out. When Gran didn't want to talk about something, her lips thinned and her eyes danced around to look at everything but the person she was speaking to. It had been like this the first time Cara had tried to ask about Gran's war work. And it had been like this when she had tried to ask about the phone call between Gran and Mum just three days before the crash that had claimed Mum's life.

She swallowed hard as she remembered letting herself into her parents' house with her spare key on a break from the office. Both Mum and Dad were supposed to be at work, so she'd though she'd just drop the book she'd borrowed off with a note. But when she'd opened the door, she'd heard her mother's voice.

"I can't believe you've kept this from me for so long," Mum was saying.

Cara froze, thinking she'd walked in on a fight—all the more disturbing because her parents rarely quarreled. But no one responded. Instead, a pause lingered on, filled only by the sound of Mum treading across the parquet drawing room floor.

"I do have a right to know, Mother."

Gran. Mum was arguing with Gran. Cara had known to expect some tension as they all worked to sort through Gran's house in order to ready her for her new home at Widcote Manor, but this was something else. Something weightier.

"I don't care that it was during the war."

Another pause. Cara could imagine Mum, hand pressed to her right temple as she tried to stave off a headache.

A sharp laugh echoed out into the hall. "Well, it's too late for that. I'm not sure I can forgive you lying to me since the day I was born."

Something clattered on the floorboards. Cara was pretty sure it was Mum's phone tossed down in frustration. Slowly she backed up, closing the door softly behind her. She'd return the book another day. Only another day didn't come because three days later, Mum was dead.

After the funeral, when all of the mourners had finally left the house Cara had grown up in, she'd asked Gran what the fight had been about. Gran had shut down, her face blank and drawn and her hands twisting in her lap around a handkerchief. Cara had meant to press again, but she'd been swept up by her divorce. She hadn't wanted to risk losing Gran's support by dredging up the fight. But now it was time to try again, and the diary was the perfect entry point.

"Will you tell me what it was like serving?" she asked now.

Gran waved her hand. "It'll just bore you. I never left the south of England."

"That doesn't matter. I want to know more about the family past before . . ." She swallowed, unable to bring herself to talk about a day when Gran, her last living relative, would no longer be with her. Fresh from the divorce and with the sting of grief still catching her at unexpected moments, Cara was struggling to reconcile herself to the idea of that.

Gran's expression softened, but still she said, "There's not much to tell."

"Why . . . why did you and Mum fight over the phone before she died?" When she saw Gran flinch, she hurried to add, "I'm not angry. I just want to know."

Even from across the room, she could see the older woman's eyes begin to well up. "Why would you want to know about a petty fight?"

"Because it didn't sound petty," Cara said softly.

Gran shook her head, her silver hair swinging clear of her shoulders. "We'll talk about this another time. It's been such a trying day. Beatrice from the fourth floor came for tea. I adore her, but she does overstay her welcome and I'm exhausted. I'm sure you're tired too."

Cara tried to push through her disappointment at being dismissed and forced a brightness into her voice. "That's fine. I'll be back on Sunday."

"Don't forget to bring the tea cakes," Gran said.

Cara nodded, making a mental note to add a box of Tunnock's marshmallow-and-chocolate treats to her shopping list. "I won't, Gran."

She leaned down and kissed Gran on her soft, cool cheek. She was about to pull away, but Gran stopped her with a birdlike hand on her wrist. "You know I love you, don't you, dearest?"

Cara smiled. "To the moon."

Gran squeezed her hand. "And back."

～

Gran's evasion nagged at Cara during the entire ten-minute drive home from Widcote Manor. While she could understand why the fight weighed on Gran, she *needed* to know what it had to do with Gran's military service. Just like another family deserved to know the story of the woman whose diary was tucked away safe in the back seat of her car.

She was so caught up in her thoughts that she barely registered the white moving van parked in front of the house next to her little thatched cottage on Elm Road until she was nearly to her drive.

"Oh, you can't be serious," she muttered, pressing the brakes. The van was half blocking her drive, making it impossible for her to park on the already-packed street.

She killed the ignition and climbed out of the car. Her keys jangled against her granddad's dog tags she kept on her key ring as she tucked them into her purse. The van's doors stood open, showing off to the street two stacks of boxes, a dark green armchair, and a bed frame that leaned in parts against the vehicle's metal wall. She walked around to the cab and called out, "Hello!"

Somewhere nearby a dog barked sharply, but no one appeared in the wide-open front door of the cottage that had been vacant when she'd left that morning.

Sucking in a breath, she steeled herself to do something completely at odds with the particular brand of British politeness her mother had bred into her. She let herself through the little wood garden gate, walked up the path, and stuck her head into a complete stranger's home.

"Hello," she called again.

In the twilight of the autumn night, the entryway blazed with light from a pair of glass sconces. An old-fashioned hatstand with carved hooks stood haphazardly in the middle of entryway next to a rolled-up rug. Piled up in a corner sat a stack of boxes with "Books" written on them in bold, black marker. An oil portrait of a woman with shingled hair wearing a black bias-cut dress and swathed in a gauzy white shawl was propped against a wall.

Interwar period. Maybe British. I like her dress.

"Is anyone here? I'm afraid the van's blocking my drive," she called.

There was a great crash somewhere nearby and a clatter of nails on hardwood. She stepped back hard into the door handle with a yelp as a lanky red Irish setter burst into the entryway and leaped up on her, planting one paw on each of her shoulders and sending the contents of her purse scattering to the floor.

She gave a little laugh as the dog's long tongue slurped at her neck, nudging up under her arms in an aggressive display of affection.

"You're quite the handful, aren't you?" she asked as she tried to ease the dog back down.

A pounding of a pair of feet against the wood floor sounded through the house, and a man with sandy-colored hair flew around the same door the dog had sprung from.

"Rufus, come here!" The man lunged, but Rufus danced behind Cara's legs.

"It's all right," said Cara, stooping to scoop up her wallet and a lipstick.

Rufus barked his approval as he looked out from behind her legs.

The man grimaced and pushed a pair of black-rimmed glasses up on his nose. "He's hopeless, I'm afraid. He's already failed obedience school once."

"What did he do?" she asked.

"It's what he didn't do. The trainer called him 'unmotivated by food,' which is ridiculous because he sits and stares at me all through dinner." The man shot her a concerned look. "Are you sure you're really all right?"

Her back ached a little where she'd collided with the doorknob, but she didn't want to make a fuss. "I am. I'm sorry to intrude while you're moving, but—"

A door opened and a beautiful woman with a long blond ponytail swept in wielding a leash. In one smooth move, she snapped it onto Rufus's collar and straightened, graceful as a ballerina.

"Meeting the neighbors already?" the woman asked.

"I think so." The man dusted his hands on a pair of faded jeans that looked like they'd seen better days and grinned. "I'm Liam McGown. This is my sister, Leah." He laughed as Cara raised a brow. "We don't know what our parents were thinking either."

"They've never been able to keep our names straight," said Leah, as she stuck her hand out.

Cara shook Leah's hand, strangely relieved to find out that the pair were not a couple. Not that she cared.

"Cara Hargraves. I live at number thirty-three," she said.

Liam grasped her hand with both of his as though meeting her was the greatest honor. "A pleasure to meet you."

When they'd been living in the big house in Chiswick, Cara had had a habit of spending lazy summer days when Simon was out playing endless games of tennis lounging on a cushioned chaise in her backyard, a stack of romantic books at hand. In nearly every one, the author described the moment of first contact between the hero and heroine as something electric. Tingling skin. Lightning bolts of awareness.

It surprised her, then, that when Liam enveloped her little hand in both of his it was hardly electric. Instead, an awareness of him slid through her like fresh honey dripping from a comb. His touch wrapped around her, soothing her, and for the first time since filing for divorce she had the mad temptation to curl her body against a man's chest just for the comfort of it.

She tugged her hand away, breaking the connection. She'd just untangled her life from Simon's. There was no room in her life for another man. Not yet.

Liam nodded to her cottage. "Isn't number thirty-three just next door?" His eyes widened. "The van. It must be blocking your drive."

"It is a little, yes," she said.

"I'm so sorry." He starting patting his jeans pockets, a lock of his hair falling over his forehead as he looked down. "I have the keys around somewhere."

With a sigh, Leah pulled a set of keys from the pocket of her zip-up jacket. "These?"

He grinned and snatched them out of her hand. "I'd be lost without you."

"You usually are!" Leah shouted, as he ran down the path and through the garden gate. She smiled at Cara as Rufus settled at her feet with a huff. "The stereotype about absentminded professors is sometimes so true it's comical."

They watched with Rufus as Liam started up the van and backed it into the street before pulling into the slope of his drive behind a little blue Ford that was already parked there.

"There you are," he called as he climbed out and strode up the path to join them again.

"How long have you lived in Barlow?" Leah asked Cara.

"I went to university here, but I was in London for years. I just moved back over the summer," she said.

"So I'm not the only one new to the neighborhood," said Liam.

"Maybe you two should have dinner. To celebrate your moves," said Leah, glancing between them.

"Oh, no, I don't think so." The words rushed out of Cara's mouth before she could think of how rude they made her sound. Quickly she said, "It's just that I'm still settling into my new job and we already have a project that's going to be keeping me at work late. I don't know when I'll be free."

"Well, that's a shame," said Leah with a sigh, and Cara couldn't help but feel that she'd somehow disappointed the woman.

Liam just shrugged. "I can understand. Lectures start in two weeks, but I'm sure we'll see each other around. We are neighbors, after all."

They said a quick goodbye and then Leah gave Rufus's leash a tug. "Come back inside, you wonderful pain of a dog."

Cara watched as Liam laughed and brother, sister, and dog disappeared into the house.

She returned to her car and pulled the wheel hard to the left, swinging into her drive and parking. Reaching into the back seat, she grabbed the biscuit tin from the old Barlow University sweatshirt she'd wrapped it in. When she looked up, she saw Liam and Rufus standing at the bay window. He raised a hand in a little wave. She smiled tightly, ducked her head, and hurried into her house.

The tart she'd baked for her dinner had turned out beautifully: it was golden brown, flaky perfection. Soft goat cheese melted around thick lardons of bacon nestled in a bed of sweet leeks. This was the sort of self-care she liked. Taking the time to cook for herself properly felt like the ultimate indulgence, a declaration that it didn't matter whether Cara ate alone or not. She was worth the effort.

She picked up her half-empty glass of minerally Spanish wine and pushed back from her kitchen table to wrap up the rest of the tart for the next day. The Old Vicarage was just down the road from a park, and she planned to bring her lunch and eat it on one of the benches she'd spotted.

With the leftovers in the fridge, she set about washing the dishes and lining them up neatly in the bamboo rack by the sink. There wasn't a dishwasher in the cottage's tiny kitchen—one of the landlord's eccentricities, the leasing agent had told her—but she liked the meditative practice of dipping, scrubbing, and rinsing.

Simon hadn't understood that.

"Why don't you use the dishwasher?" he would ask on the rare weekday evenings their jobs allowed them to be together.

"I like cleaning up," she'd say. "I started the meal and now I'm clearing it away. It brings everything full circle."

He would grunt at that and go back to sipping his port. She would smile at how much her eccentric refusal to use a dishwasher unsettled him; they could afford a Miele dishwasher, so she should use it. But she wasn't Simon. She couldn't make herself care about that sort of thing.

From the day they'd left uni, Simon had been obsessed with keeping up with his friends. While Cara had grown up comfortably affluent in a big, five-bedroom brick house in Hans Place, he'd come from a modest suburb of Manchester and was eager to shake off all the middle-class markers of his childhood. He'd worked hard to reinvent himself, making the right friends at uni and taking the right job in the right industry. He'd wanted the big house in Chiswick, an expensive neighborhood of West London, because it was where his friend Sam lived. He'd become a member of the same club as Theo and Jasper, paying the exorbitant fees to join. He'd bought a Porsche 911 for himself and a Lexus SUV for Cara—even though she hated London traffic and rarely drove—because Edward had mentioned he was buying one for his wife. One summer, Simon had even tried to take up polo after Claude had invited him to play, but he was nothing more than an average rider and resigned himself to drinking champagne on the sidelines instead.

Now Cara suspected she'd just been another marker of status—the right kind of girl with the right kind of background—but she couldn't deny having been a bit dazzled by Simon from the moment they'd met in a Barlow pub as students. Smart and charming, he'd painted a picture of his own brilliance so seductive she'd believed it for years. When his redundancy came, seemingly out of nowhere, she'd assured herself he would find another job at another hedge fund quickly. But weeks had stretched into months and he'd stopped boasting of the interviews he was setting up. The headhunters he was certain would call had never materialized. He'd spend nights out, telling her that he was networking, but networking shouldn't have ended so often with him snoring through his drunkenness on the sofa.

The sponge slipped from her fingers, splashing into the water and sending a soapy spray into her face. She wiped her cheek, the last traces of the day's makeup coming off on her fingertips, and sighed. Life was better without Simon than with him. That afternoon's phone call was evidence enough. After everything that had happened, all of his promises that he was getting better, he was still patronizing and self-important. Talking to him had left her feeling drained and sad at the thought of how long she'd lived in denial of the problems that were right in front of her. She'd focused on working twice as hard to try to keep their bank accounts from slipping into overdraft because it was easier than admitting that her seemingly brilliant husband wasn't who she thought he was—a truth that pressed hard on the tenderness in her heart.

But it was the lying that had hurt the most. An application for a second mortgage on the house he'd tried to convince her to sign without reading it through. Credit cards taken out in both their names that she hadn't known about. The gambling debts. He'd been sinking for years, and when it became obvious that he was drowning them both, he'd refused to change.

Her eyes drifted up out the kitchen window. It looked out into a narrow side return the last tenant, a talented gardener, had done her best to spruce up with pots of sculptural bay trees. Cara had brought the worn wooden bench that had stood outside of her kitchen in Chiswick and arranged her pots of herbs on it. In several weeks, she'd have to bring the tender plants inside to protect them from the first frost, but for now she liked being able to look at them as she cleaned.

Across the brick wall, she could see the top of a window in Liam's house. She wondered how he was spending his first evening on Elm Road. The lights were on downstairs, and she could hear the faint strains of guitar and drums drifting through the air.

She should've been friendlier, taking up his sister's suggestion that they have dinner together. He was just a neighbor, nothing to be fearful of, but her scars still tugged uncomfortably.

The doorbell sounded, startling her.

She shut the faucet off and dried her hands on the tea towel as she walked barefoot to the front door. The bell sounded again.

"Coming!" she shouted. When she opened the door, her breath caught in her throat. "Oh! Liam."

He smiled, warm and open. "I'm sorry to bother you, it's just that I think you dropped this."

He held up her phone in its purple-and-teal flowered case.

"Thank you," she said, taking it from him. "It must've fallen out of my purse."

He rubbed the back of his neck. "I apologize again. Rufus is a constant cause of embarrassment in my life, but I love him."

"As you should."

"Is that an Elkes tin?" he asked.

She followed his gaze to the biscuit tin sitting innocently on the sideboard where she'd dropped her keys and her purse.

"Huntley and Palmers." She picked it up and tilted it to show him the name painted on the top.

The corner of his mouth hitched up. "Is it meant to look like a bookshelf?" he asked, leaning closer but not stepping forward—almost as though he knew the cottage was her sanctuary.

"Yes, it is."

"Extraordinary. When do you think it's from?"

"Probably the forties or fifties, but I haven't authenticated it yet," she said.

"Authenticated it?"

"I work for an antiques dealer. I found it when I was clearing out an estate today."

"Extraordinary," he said again as he rocked back on his heels. "I had no idea we shared a common interest. I'm a lecturer of history at Barlow University."

So that was what his sister had meant about absentminded professors.

"What's your area of specialty?" she asked. Maybe he could help her figure out who the author was.

"I'm a medievalist."

Not his era, then.

"Well, I should finish cleaning up," she said.

"Yes," he said, sniffing the air. "Whatever was for dinner smells delicious."

The opportunity to invite him in hung in the air. She could easily pull the leftover tart out of the fridge and pour him a glass of wine. He'd just moved. He might want company.

Next time, she promised herself. A day when Simon hadn't called and her muscles weren't aching in places she'd forgotten she had. A day when talking to Liam didn't make her feel quite so thrown off-axis.

"Thanks again for returning my phone."

"Of course, of course. Anytime."

As he walked out of her yard, she shut the door before she could see whether he'd turned to wave again.

She carried the tin back to the kitchen table and pried it open. She'd left it in the hall because she hadn't wanted to risk the possibility of something spilling and destroying the diary before she'd even had the chance to read it. First, she pulled out the photograph of the woman. A corner of it had been bent at some point and folded back into place, and she smoothed her thumb over it now.

"'L.K. on the Embankment,'" she mused as she pulled out the diary and flipped open to the front cover. There was no name or initials or address. That would simply be too straightforward an end to this mystery. She would have to figure out who the diarist was the hard way.

She thumbed past the first entry and began to read

15 February 1941

Kate's wish was granted. I went to the dance dressed in her crepe, which really does suit her better even though she said it fit her too tightly in the chest three times before we'd even left her house. But I went and, would you know, something actually happened ther. A real, honest-to-goodness exciting thing. I hardly know where to start, but I'll try, for I think this was one of those nights I'll want to remember for the rest of my days.

I met Paul. He's an officer and a pilot. I thought at first he was one of Kate's admirers, but then he hardly looked at her all evening. Instead he danced with me. At first he overwhelmed me, as though he could see straight through to my soul and know exactly what it was I was thinking. I've never felt that before.

When he returned me to Kate and her airmen, she wouldn't stop asking questions, and I became flustered. How do you explain something you can't seem to understand yourself? But when I stepped outside for some air, he followed me. We talked, and he kissed me. It was sweet, all butterflies and heat. When we went back inside, all I wanted to do was dance with him, and we hardly left each other's side all evening.

We danced and danced, as though there was no worry and no war. I could see Kate watching us, wondering what it was that had happened when we both disappeared outside. When she and I finally had to pull our coats on to cycle home, she tried to ask what had happened, but I pretended the wind made it too hard to hear. By the time we made it back to the village, the edge of a storm had caught us up in the wind and rain, and she had to pedal home or risk being soaked through. I've never been so happy for rain in my life.

I'm not ashamed of having kissed Paul, although Mum would be horrified if she found out. She is so determined that Gary and I should be married after the war, no matter how many times I tell her I could never think of him that way. To me he'll always be the little boy tumbling over his undone shoelaces as he raced around at the back of the pack of neighborhood children.

There was always something different about Gary. The solicitor's son. The most well-off boy in the village. While we ran wild in cotton smocks and knitted wool sweaters always threatening to burst at the elbows, he had little navy sport coats and crisp white shirts. He was a Moss, and we all knew that meant he was better than us, even if he never made us feel it. Perhaps because he knew that it really didn't matter what his father did or that he lived in the big white house with a stone gate around it at the edge of town. He was never going to leave the village either.

I know Mum worked hard to become friends with Mrs. Moss, although it's strange, because surely Mrs. Moss sees that Mum only wants to be friends with her because she has the largest house in the village. Still, I know Mrs. Moss encourages Gary and asks him in every letter if he's written to me, which is why I receive one a week like clockwork, bland enough to make it through the censor with hardly a mark.

Paul is the very opposite of bland. Handsome and erudite, he seems worldly in a way no one else here does. He told me he comes from London and went to Cambridge for university. He dances beautifully, and he's easily the most handsome man I've ever seen. I still wonder why he chose me out of all of the girls at the dance, but when he kissed me, it was as though it was the only thing he'd ever wanted to do.

That is what I couldn't explain to Kate as we rode home. To her, the airmen are nothing more than a constantly changing buffet of admirers. From time to time, she'll allow one of them to buy her an ice cream or take her for a walk along the beach, but she knows better than most how to keep them at arm's length. When I asked her about it once, she told me it isn't wise to become too attached. They're bound to be sent away from Cornwall at some point, and knowing that they're out there on the battlefield when we're at home safe is too difficult.

5

LOUISE

It was so easy for Louise to slip out of the house undetected while her mother hung out the washing on Monday afternoon, she wondered why she hadn't tried it before.

She'd worked earlier that day at Mrs. Bakeford's, nipping home to have a lunch of a sausage, a shredded bit of one of the cabbages from Dad's vegetable patch, and some bread Mum had baked fresh that morning, spread with a scraping of margarine. She'd choked down her glass of milk, which had been reconstituted from a powder that the Ministry of Food claimed tasted no different from the real thing. Louise would gladly have forsaken it, but her mother still set it out for her at every meal. It was easier to simply drink it than to argue.

The breeze off the Atlantic played with Louise's brown hair as she stuck her hands into her dark green wool coat and buried her chin a little deeper in her muffler. The rains of the previous week had given way to a gloriously crisp day, the brilliant sun breaking through the winter gloom, but there was still a wicked bite in the air.

As she rounded the bend in the lane, she spotted Paul, tall and handsome in his dark uniform. Her heart leaped up when he turned, his eyes brightening. He threw away his cigarette and grinned. "There you are."

He moved to kiss her on the cheek, but she pulled back, glancing around.

"We mustn't. Not here," she said. No one was out digging for victory in their vegetable patches, but that didn't mean they weren't watching.

"Nosy neighbors?" he asked.

"You've never lived in a village. Give me your arm. That's safe enough."

He held out his arm for her like a gentleman but leaned in close enough that she was wrapped in the warm reassurance of intimacy. "All right, but I plan on stealing a kiss from you the moment we're out of sight."

Louise swallowed. "Only if I let you."

A pause stretched between them, and Louise felt a flash of worry that she'd gone too far. She'd meant to walk the fine line between cautious and flirtatious, but she was hardly an expert. Her cousin or any number of girls would've known what to do, how to walk and talk with a man who'd kissed them. They wouldn't feel awkward, as though their limbs were somehow moving without their permission, their entire bodies outside of their control.

Her worried gaze flicked up to Paul's, but then he threw his head back and laughed long and hard, pulling her closer into his side.

"I do like you, Louise Keene," he said, as though it was a confession and a revelation all at once. "You say exactly what's on your mind."

Did she though? Her brow furrowed as she examined that thought from all sides. She'd never been the sort of girl to speak up, rarely drawing attention to herself whether at school or home. Yet with him she wanted to ask herself why not?

"Where are we going?" she asked as they turned toward the shore.

"A spot one of the other pilots in my unit told me about. He said it was a secret and I'll never have seen anything like it."

She allowed him to lead her on, even though the likelihood of him showing her something new in Haybourne was slim. They wound their

way down the cliff path to the rickety wooden steps someone had in-
stalled years ago to get down to the little white sand beach that lay
below.

"Nearly there," said Paul.

"I used to bathe on this beach when I was a little girl," she said,
her hand hovering over the rough wood banister. She wished she'd worn
gloves to protect her hands from splinters.

"Did you have a pail and a spade to build sandcastles?" he asked with
a laugh.

"Yes, and my mother made me wear a wool cardigan over my bathing
costume some days when the wind was too high."

When they reached the bottom of the stairs, Louise's short leather
heels sank into the sand and she looked around at the beach, just the
same as it had been her entire life save for a few new pieces of driftwood
that had been tossed up during the last storm.

"Is this it?" she asked.

He clucked his tongue. "I can't expect to impress a Haybourne girl by
taking her to the very spot she used to go bathing."

He pulled something out of his pocket. It was a little compass, smaller
than the divot at the center of his palm.

"How sweet," she said, touching the brass instrument with one
finger.

"You call it sweet, I call it lifesaving." He handed it to her, the needle
trembling a little as it swung north. "It's an escape compass. Fliers like
me carry them on our missions in case we're shot down behind enemy
lines and need to navigate our way over unfamiliar territory. But this one
is . . . more than that."

"What do you mean?" she asked.

"Every time I go up, I know it could be the last time. And every time
I land, I'm grateful. I've carried this on every mission, and I never fly
without it. Maybe it's what's keeping me safe."

"Paul . . ."

"That must sound silly to you," he said.

"It doesn't."

He raised his head, a lock of hair falling over his forehead. "Are we always to talk of sad things, you and I? What's the line from *Romeo and Juliet?*"

"'A glooming peace this morning with it brings. The sun, for sorrow, will not show his head. Go hence, to have more talk of these sad things,'" she recited.

"I think, Louise Keene, that if my masters at Rugby had had you in a class, they wouldn't have paid any attention to us boys."

Louise blushed at the compliment. "But you went on to Cambridge."

"Trust me when I tell you that has no bearing on the intelligence of a man." He tugged on her arm. "This way."

They made their progress across the sand slowly, Louise stopping once to empty her shoes of sand, letting each bare foot hover for fear of ripping her precious stockings. Paul offered to carry her, but she declined, telling him he was going to have to work harder than that to sweep her off her feet. He laughed, and she felt braver for having said it.

When they reached the spot where the bottom of the cliff met the easternmost stretch of sand, she realized where he was taking her.

"The Smugglers' Cave," she said.

"You guessed."

"We're nearly out of sand to walk on," she said with a smile.

"I was told we'll have a couple hours before the tide comes in and blocks off the pathway back to the beach. Have you been before?" he asked.

"Not in a very long time. A boy from the neighborhood tried to lead us all on an expedition to reclaim smugglers' gold and we nearly were stuck because the tide started rushing in. Da and Mr. Itzler had to come round with a rowboat and get the last of us out."

It had been Edward, Mr. Itzler's son, leading their little band, with Kate and Mary Hawkley in the front and Dea Wells and Gary trailing behind with Louise. They'd had a grand time, each of them armed with sandwiches wrapped in waxed paper packed by their mothers. Edward even had a torch, and the more intrepid children had ventured from the first cavern through a tunnel to another. Louise, however, had hung back with Dea, content to stay in the light spilling through the mouth of the cave.

It had been the perfect afternoon until they'd lost track of time, none of them being old enough to wear a watch. Dea had been the one to shout that the water was rising. The froth of the churning sea that had seemed magical only a couple hours before suddenly felt sinister, advancing on them more rapidly with every passing moment.

She knew now that they'd never been in any real danger. The adults of knew that if children seen playing on the beach hadn't returned home by the time the tides rose, they were likely in the Smugglers' Cave, but it had been terrifying as a child. She would never forget the relief of seeing her father, solid and steady, jumping off the rowboat's bow and wading in to scoop her up.

"I promise to keep a close eye on the time. I'd never live it down at the base if we had to be rescued," Paul said. "Why is it called the Smugglers' Cave? I always thought most of their hiding places were in the cliffs to the south, facing France."

She shrugged. "That's always been its name."

"Well," he said, stopping at the bend around the rocks lining the bottom of the cliff, "are you ready?"

She nodded. She thought he might give her his arm again, but instead he picked up her hand, twining it in his.

He tugged her into a run across the damp, hard-packed sand and shouted, "Come on then!"

She let out a surprised laugh, the tails of her coat flapping behind her as they sped along. She could feel the combs sliding from her hair, but rather than try to shove them back into place, she ripped them out, stuffing them into her pocket as Paul slowed to a stop before the slash in the rock that was the opening to the cave.

"Just like Mickey said it would be," he muttered before turning to her. "Would you like to do the honors?"

She nodded, eyeing the gap in the rock. It had seemed so large when she was a child, but now she could see that it was little more than eighteen inches wide, although it was more than tall enough for Paul to enter without having to stoop. Turning sideways, she breathed in and shuffled into the cave.

"I can hardly see," she said, any light from the entrance blocked as he shimmied through the gap behind her.

"Close your eyes."

She did, listening to the scrape of his boots against the sand.

"Now open them," he said, his voice coming from close to her right shoulder.

Her eyes flicked open, and she gasped. Now that Paul was by her side, the entire cave shimmered with the light streaming through the entrance. The walls glinted as she slowly swung around in a circle, as though she was standing inside a jewel.

"I can't believe I don't remember this," she said.

"Mickey says it only happens during the winter months at certain times of day. The sun has to be low enough that it comes in through the entrance and hits the crystals in the walls at the right angle."

"It's beautiful," she whispered, her eyes still fixed on the shimmering walls.

"Then it's a surprise?"

She offered him a smile. "It is."

He took a step forward. "Then would you allow me . . . ?"

She nodded and turned her cheek to him to permit him the kiss she hadn't wanted anyone to see in the lane. His lips brushed skin, warm and soft. But he didn't stop with a kiss on her cheek. He brought his lips to her cheekbones and then just to the side of her ear. Under her jaw and to the side of her mouth.

She shivered, her hands flexing by her sides, hardly knowing what to do for the wanting of him. But when he pulled back an inch and breathed, "Louise," instinct took over. Her fingers wrapped themselves in the crisp lapels of his uniform, and she turned her mouth, bringing her lips to his.

He kissed her, long and sweet, with just a touch of pressure. His hands spread wide on her back, holding her to him and arching her body so it matched with his. Her lips opened, and she lost herself in the depths of an unhurried kiss for the first time in her life.

With a sigh of contentment, his hands stroked up her back, and he carefully, slowly pulled away. She felt almost drunk, unable to blink away the haze of pleasure that had settled over her in this extraordinary cave with this extraordinary man.

"Is there another man?" he asked quietly.

She shook her head.

He breathed out a sigh of relief. "Good. In the lane—"

"My mother hopes I'll marry the village solicitor's son, Gary, when the war is over."

"That sounds very grand," he said.

"It's not. I promise."

"And what would Gary think of you kissing me?" he asked.

Drawing her shoulders back, she looked at him square in the eye. "It doesn't matter what he thinks."

"Good. I shouldn't like to steal a soldier's girl."

"I'm no one's girl."

He picked up her hand, toying with her fingers and turning them over as though memorizing every line of her knuckles. "Perhaps then, Louise, you might consider being mine."

∼

Louise floated home. Her shoes would need a good brushing to rid them of the damp sand, and she'd done her best to wrestle her hair into order on the beach, using Paul's comb to scrape her set into place, but she had no doubt she looked something of a mess—a blissful mess.

The afternoon had been wonderful. They'd explored the cave as far as they'd dared, using a torch Paul had liberated from his base, and then settled down on a low, flat rock to split a Crunchie bar he'd bought in the NAAFI shop. True to his word, he'd kept an eye on his watch, and they'd made it out of the cave while the water was still low.

He'd walked her back to the bottom of the lane again, stealing kisses when they were sure they were out of sight. He squeezed her hand good-bye, but it wouldn't be for long. He'd asked her to the cinema in Newquay later that week, taking advantage of a scheduled night of leave. He would meet her at the bus stop and they would go see *Freedom Radio* with Clive Brook and Diana Wynyard.

She suspected Kate would be more than happy to provide an excuse for her to miss the meal with her parents. In all likelihood, her cousin would insist that Louise borrow something else from her wardrobe, and perhaps dress her hair as well, insisting that an updo would look far more adult than her misbehaving waves.

Louise let herself through the garden gate, prepared to answer any of her mother's inevitable, pointed questions about her afternoon. She'd gone for a walk with a book. (That would account for the time.) She'd decided to go to the beach. (That would account for the sand on her shoes.) It certainly was a windy day, but it had felt good to be outside in the sun after a dreary winter. (That would account for her windswept hair and rosy cheeks.)

With a little smile, she pushed open the unlocked front door of her parents' house and shrugged off her coat.

"Louise, is that you?" her mother called.

"Yes, Mum. I'm just hanging up my coat."

"Come join me in the parlor."

Her hand stilled halfway to the hook. There was a pleasant sweetness to her mother's voice that she only used when they had company.

"Just one moment," she called back.

With her coat hung up, she smoothed her hands down the front of her jumper and straightened the collar of her white cotton shirt. Then she straightened the seams of her fawn-colored skirt, stretched a smile over her lips, and went through to the parlor.

Louise has been right. Her mother was perched ramrod-straight on the chintz chair, and to her left, sitting on the rose patterned sofa with antimacassars covering the arms, was Mrs. Moss.

"Louise, how are you?" asked Mrs. Moss as she replaced the teacup she held in its saucer.

Louise clasped her hands behind her back, fingers twisting as she glanced from Gary's mother to her own. "I'm very well, thank you."

"Louise, won't you join us?" her mother asked in a way that told her there was only one correct way to answer the invitation.

"If you don't mind, I'll just wash up. I was at the beach." She edged to the door. "Perhaps I can bring you more hot water for the tea."

"Louise, you will sit." This time her mother's voice brooked no argument. Louise sank into a chair. "Now, will you please explain why I received two telephone calls today asking me the name of the RAF officer you were with?"

"I—"

"Now, Mrs. Keene," said Mrs. Moss, leaning her considerable bulk toward Louise's mother, "I'm certain Louise meant nothing by it."

"Then why is it that Mrs. Chalmers said he was waiting at the bottom of the road for her? What an utterly common thing to do. If he had any manners, he would've called on you," said her mother.

The very idea of Paul having to do something as old-fashioned as "call" on her so that her mother might scrutinize him and find him

lacking in this parlor surrounded by lace curtains and bowls of pot-
pourri made Louise recoil. But the real reason she'd asked him to meet
her away from the house was so that she could avoid this very conversation.

"And then you were seen walking the steps from the beach with him,"
her mother continued.

"Who was it who saw us?" Louise asked.

The question brought her mother up short, and she blinked at Louise
a couple times. "Mrs. Dorsey spotted you from the road. She was walking
back with her shopping. She said she was so shocked that Gary's girl was
with another man, she nearly dropped her string bag."

I am not Gary's girl. The words lodged on her tongue, but Mrs. Moss
was leaning over to pat Louise's mother on the arm.

"This is all just the idle gossip of housewives. Louise has never been
anything but a good girl," said Mrs. Moss.

"I will not have my daughter gallivanting around with some officer,"
said her mother.

"He's a friend," said Louise before she could stop herself.

"A friend?" Her mother might've snorted if Louise had ever heard her
make such an uncouth noise.

"Of course he is," said Mrs. Moss. "It's to be expected, with so many
young people about. What's his name, dear?"

"Flight Lieutenant Paul Bolton. He flies Spitfires for Coastal Command out of RAF Saint Trebelzue," Louise said reluctantly, for resistance
would only encourage suspicion.

"And how did you meet him?" asked Mrs. Moss kindly. Except Louise
had known Gary's mother for long enough to know not to mistake kindness for empathy. Where her mother was all hard edges and flint, Mrs.
Moss could pretend at softness, smothering people until they did or said
whatever it was she wanted.

Carefully, Louise said, "He's one of Kate's friends. He wanted to see the Smugglers' Cave, so I told him I would show him." A half-truth and a little white lie, but she hoped it would be enough to squash her mother's distrust.

"See, Mrs. Keene? There's nothing more to it than that. Louise would never do anything to hurt Gary. Not while he's being so brave, fighting for his country," said Mrs. Moss.

There it was, the particular brand of crushing guilt that Mrs. Moss specialized in. Louise had told Paul the truth when she'd said that she was no one's girl, but that didn't account for the expectations of the two women sitting in front of her.

Setting her teacup aside, Mrs. Moss rose to her feet. "I really must be heading home or Mr. Moss won't have a thing to eat for supper tonight."

Louise's mother shot Louise a look that told her the conversation was far from over, but busied herself showing Mrs. Moss out.

When the front door shut, Louise sucked in a breath, waiting for the inevitable. It came as soon as Rose Keene walked back into the room.

"I cannot believe that a daughter of mine would do anything so disgraceful," her mother hissed.

"There was nothing disgraceful. I explained—"

"You were *seen*, Louise. Mrs. Dorsey saw you kiss that man on the steps leading away from the beach."

Louise's gaze fell to her hands. She knew there was no way she would be able to keep up the charade that she and Paul were simply friends. Not that her mother had believed it for one moment.

"Now," her mother said, arranging herself primly in her chair, "you can understand why I chose to withhold that particular revelation from Mrs. Moss. I should hate to think that a mistake like this would make her think you had been untrue to Gary."

"Mum . . ."

"That boy intends to ask you to marry him, mark my words. I will admit, I'd once hoped my daughter would set her sights higher than a small village solicitor's son. If only your father would've shown some ambition, he might've been the postmaster at Truro and you would've met an entirely different class of person, but that wasn't to be."

The thumbnail of Louise's left hand bit hard into her palm. She'd heard this story so many times before, but over the years it had been edited down. Gone were the mentions of her mother's less-than-modest upbringing as a fisherman's daughter. Gone were the tales of having just two dresses and one pair of shoes a year. Her mother had recast her history to suit her purposes, and now she intended to mold Louise's future to further her frustrated ambitions.

"It's clear that I cannot hope to keep this from Mrs. Moss forever," said her mother. "You know how life in a village is. You should prepare yourself for her disappointment and hope that she chooses not to write to Gary about it."

"Gary and I are *not* engaged to be married. We saw a film or two and went to a dance. That was all," she protested.

"He was courting you, and if it hadn't been for the war, you would've been engaged by now," said her mother firmly.

The surety of her mother's words choked her. Louise didn't want to become her mother, her domain a small house in a little village with four hundred people, all of whom she'd known from birth. She wanted *more*—California skies and thrilling dances and handsome men asking her to be theirs—and meeting Paul had made it all seem somehow more possible.

"I don't even know if Gary *likes* me," she said.

"Gary adores you. Not that you deserve it, carrying on with officers," said her mother.

"And what of what I want?" Louise asked. "You and Mrs. Moss have just decided that we were going to marry. No one ever asked me."

"Enough!" her mother shouted. Placing a hand to her throat as she composed herself, she continued in a quieter voice, "This is not a matter for discussion, Louise. Now, go peel the potatoes. I will not have your father's supper late to the table due to your selfishness."

Louise's lips pursed as she fought to hold back all the words she wanted to say, all the years of things she wanted to shout at her mother. But she knew better than most that trying to drive through an immovable mountain was impossible. Instead, she would somehow find the path around it.

6

CARA

When Cara's phone pierced the silence of her house with its ringing, she lunged for it with a gasp of relief. She'd been hunched over her laptop at her kitchen table reading up on French verdure tapestry because Jock had sent her a scathing look that said, *Not only am I annoyed, I'm disappointed,* after she'd drawn a complete blank identifying a large tapestry she'd discovered rolled up in one of the Old Vicarage's hall cupboards. It had been the low point of her Friday, a sign that her progress in getting up to speed was beginning to plateau.

When she flipped her phone over, a photo of her best friend, Nicole, grinned back at her. Swiping to answer, she said, "Hello, stranger. Fancy you calling me."

"Not a stranger," said Nicole over what sounded like her car's hands-free system. "International business traveler of mystery."

She laughed. "How was Switzerland?"

"Breathtakingly expensive. You wouldn't believe how much a bottle of wine costs."

"Sounds like you need to bring your own if the agency decides to keep sending you," Cara said.

"Don't think I haven't considered bringing another suitcase. If I did my job well and the bank chooses to pick up my ad campaign, I'll be spending at least a few months on-site. Speaking of wine, have you looked around the new neighborhood? Any good drinking establishments where you could take your oldest friend?" Nicole asked.

Cara traced one of the knots in her wooden kitchen table with the tip of her index finger. "There's a pub just a couple blocks over on Church Road, and a few other places around."

"How are they? I can't believe how long it's been since we were at uni. I'm sure everything's changed except for the pubs."

"Pubs never change. I can't say for the other places. I haven't been yet."

"Caraaaa." Nicole drew out her name in mock disapproval that probably was also half-serious.

"I've been busy! I moved my entire life."

"Oh please. I know you. You were unpacked within three days of moving. Try another excuse," said Nicole.

Actually, it had been more like two days, but Cara wasn't going to give her friend any more ammunition.

"I'm also in a job that makes me feel like an idiot at least three times a day. I'm trying to study as much as I can, but Jock keeps throwing me questions I can't answer," Cara said.

The constant pressure of knowing that she should eke out just a little more study time had forced her to set the diary she'd found aside after that first night. But curiosity kept tugging at her. Cara knew wartime romances could burn hot and fast—Gran had met Granddad and been married in the space of two months—and already she could tell the girl in the diary had been swept away by the handsome pilot who'd taken her to the Smugglers' Cave.

"You only feel like you don't know everything yet because Jock has been in the antiques business for decades and you're just starting out," said Nicole, pulling Cara's attention back to the present.

"Maybe." She sighed. "It's just that he took a chance on me and gave me a job—"

"He gave you a job, not a kidney. And from what you used to tell me, the man sounds like he can be an ass."

"He's not an ass," Cara said, surprising herself at how quickly she rose to Jock's defense. "He's particular and very, very good at what he does. He wouldn't have taken me on if he didn't think I would be a benefit to the business, but that means he expects me to be able to do my job well *now*. Not in six months. Hence the studying."

She could hear Nicole's phone come off speaker, meaning her friend had arrived at her destination. Their call would be cut short and Cara would have to go back to more tapestry. Even she had to admit that didn't exactly make for a thrilling Saturday.

"Well, I plan to make sure you take at least a little time off," said Nicole.

Cara smiled. "I promise I will when my head's above water."

"And when will that be exactly?" Nicole didn't wait for a response. "And no, seeing Iris doesn't count, as much as I love her."

"She says hello and wants to know when you'll be visiting, by the way."

"Tell her I will as soon as I make you take a day off."

Cara laughed. "As though you've ever been able to make me do anything I didn't want to. Remember that stupid dare after our last exams?"

"I still say you should've skinny-dipped in Barlow Pond. It's practically tradition," said Nicole.

"Then you wouldn't have had anyone to come collect you, Gemma, and Pete from the police station." She remembered all too well the sheepish grins on her friends' tipsy faces when she'd shown up to talk the local constables into letting them out of the holding cell without booking them. Simon was supposed to have been with them but had been conspicuously absent, having drunk himself into a stupor a few hours earlier—a sign of things to come, if only she'd known to pay attention.

"Well, I may not be able to boss you around over the phone, but I can do it in person," said Nicole.

"Right, like you can take the time out of your busy schedule flying all over the Continent," Cara teased.

The doorbell rang.

"Well, I'm free now."

"You didn't . . ."

Nicole laughed. "Why don't you go answer the door and find out?"

Cara dropped her phone on the table and raced to the door, ripping it open to find her best friend on her doorstep.

"You're here!" Then, for no good reason at all, Cara burst into tears.

Nicole wrapped her up in a hug, and the familiarity of it dragged another sob from Cara. Nicole had been a constant for so long, grounding her with their shared past while standing by her for the future unknown. Next to Gran, Nicole was the closest thing Cara had left by way of family, and somehow seeing her brought everything to the surface—the divorce, the grief, the move, the anger, the rejuvenation. But mostly it allowed Cara to admit to the loneliness that had crept into her life in Chiswick and hadn't dissipated in Barlow.

She pulled back, shaking her head as she wiped away tears. "I don't know what's wrong with me. I just can't tell you what a relief it is to see you."

"Good. I like to be wanted," said her friend, tossing her long, straightened black hair over her shoulder. "Now, here's what's going to happen. You're going to show me around the cottage I've heard so much about and then we're going down to the pub so I know that at least you have a decent local. Okay?"

Cara laughed, sniffing a little. "Yes, of course. Come on."

∽

An hour later, Cara had pulled on black skinny jeans and a silky green top that were far more appropriate for going out in public than the sweats and camisole she'd been wearing. She was tucked into a wide wooden booth at the Hollow Crown across from Nicole, a bottle of pinot grigio and two glasses sweating on the table between them as Cara told her the story of finding the World War II diary.

"There's just something about it," she said. "It starts like any other diary you might imagine a nineteen-year-old would write. She loves her father. She has a difficult relationship with her mother. She works in a shop."

"That could've been me writing it when I was a teenager," said Nicole with a snort.

"Exactly. But then this man walks into her life and sweeps her off her feet."

"The pilot. Do they get married?" Nicole asked.

"I have no idea. I haven't had a chance to read much because—"

"You're studying for Jock. I don't think you put this much work into your degree exams," said Nicole.

"This is important."

Her parents' deaths had changed everything. Rushing up to Cumbria and finding out she had been too late to say goodbye had been a constant physical blow in the days, months, years that followed, like being hit hard in the stomach over and over again, the nausea building until she could hardly take it. She'd simply put her head down and escaped into work because it was better to be there than at home with an unemployed, spendthrift husband who drank too much, gambled, and disappointed her in a thousand different ways.

When she'd finally let herself admit that she wanted a divorce, it was as though a fog had lifted. She could at last see the giant compromise her life had become—one she constantly seemed to lose out on. She'd lived in a house she hadn't really wanted in the far west of London, isolated from Nicole and her other friends until she rarely saw them. In a moment of youthful uncertainty, she'd let herself be pushed into the job Simon had picked for her so that they could afford to live together at twenty-two. And then there'd been her marriage, which had deteriorated until she'd hardly recognized the man she shared a life with.

She'd promised herself, as she'd numbly sat her in her solicitor's office learning about the steps it would take to untangle her life, that there would be no more losing compromises. She wanted her own life of her own choosing. Barlow had been the last place she'd truly felt at home, so she'd returned, a decade after graduating, to start again.

"So now you're going to figure out who wrote the diary. Any ideas?" Nicole asked.

"No, except her initials might have been L.K., and she might've been in the ATS, but I'm not sure yet."

"Wasn't that the branch Iris served in?" Nicole asked.

"Yes, but when I asked her about it she brushed me off. I don't know why she refuses to talk about it."

"Maybe something bad happened to her," said Nicole.

"Maybe."

"Well"—Nicole picked up her glass of wine and tilted it toward Cara—"it sounds to me like you need a private investigator."

Cara laughed. "To track down a woman who hasn't mentioned her hometown or anyone else's last name yet? I don't know where they'd even start."

"Cara?" Her heart jumped into her throat. Liam stood at the bar a few feet away, pint of ale and notebook in hand.

"I'm sorry to interrupt, but I thought that was you," he said.

Nicole craned her neck to look over her shoulder, and when she turned back her dark eyes were sparkling with delight. Cara's stomach sank. She knew that look. It was the one her friend used to wear when they'd go out and Nicole would try to introduce her to every single-looking man in the pub, including, on one particularly memorable evening, Cara's art history tutor.

"It's good to see you," she said. "Nicole, this is my neighbor, Liam."

Nicole stuck her hand out. "Pleased to meet you."

Don't ask him to sit down.

"Likewise," Liam said.

"What brings you to the pub?" Nicole asked.

He lifted the notebook. "I was tired of sitting at home going over my lecture notes, so I thought I'd come in and have a pint while I work. I haven't been to the Hollow Crown before."

Don't ask him to sit down.

"This is Cara's first time too," said Nicole with a smile.

"A happy coincidence," said Liam.

Don't ask him to sit down.

"Would you like to join us?" Nicole asked.

Dammit, Nicole.

Liam's eyes flicked over to hers. "If you don't mind."

"No, of course not," she said, bracing herself for an evening of heading off Nicole's best intentions. "How are you settling in?"

"Everything's still in boxes, but I can never seem to finish unpacking entirely. There's always one box of books sitting in the garage."

"Have you moved a lot?" Nicole asked.

"Life of a visiting lecturer," said Liam with a smile. "I've taught at Bristol and Exeter, and was in the States as a visiting professor at Reed College in Oregon for two years."

"So you're a professor?" Nicole asked.

"At Barlow, I'm technically a reader in the history department. Professorships are rare."

"Will you be staying?" Nicole asked, shooting Cara a significant look.

"Yes. For the first time in my career, I've found a permanent placement," said Liam.

"Congratulations," said Cara, lifting her glass.

While they all toasted, Cara took the chance to study him. He was handsome in an endearing, academic sort of way. He had a good smile, and his hair always seemed threatening to flop over his forehead and brush the top of his glasses. The sleeves of his washed-out blue Henley were pushed up to his elbows, exposing ropey forearms and a plain steel watch on his left hand. He was too old to be boyish, but there was something youthful about the curious energy that seemed to pulse around him. She was sure he was one of the professors students gossiped about, speculating about his private life as he assigned pages or reading, no doubt oblivious.

"I wanted to ask, has Rufus's barking bothered you?" Liam asked.

"I haven't heard him at all," Cara said.

"Rufus is my dog," Liam explained to Nicole. "He seems to be adjusting now, but the first day he barked every time the church bells rang."

Cara laughed. St. Luke's marked every hour, regardless of the time of day. "You poor man."

"He also keeps escaping. I had to chase him through one of the neighborhood's yards yesterday."

"Whose?" she asked.

"The big brick Victorian on the corner," he said.

She winced. "Not Mrs. Wasserman's?"

The grim set of his mouth told her it had indeed been Mrs. Wasserman, the tyrannical octogenarian who patrolled the street. "I barely survived the tongue-lashing. She has a remarkably expansive vocabulary for a woman who looks so sweet."

"You have my sympathy. I've already had a run-in with her over not taking my rubbish bins in by four in the afternoon on collection days," she said.

"There's always one in every neighborhood, isn't there?" he said with a rueful laugh.

Cara toyed with her wineglass, stealing another glance at him. Attractive, seemingly kind, and willing to laugh at himself. A few years from now, when her divorce was well behind her, he might be just the sort of man she'd go for.

"Liam," Nicole said abruptly, "maybe you can help us with a dilemma Cara has."

"Nicole," Cara said sharply, not trusting her friend not to say something mortifying like, *Cara hasn't had a date since she was twenty-one. Want to take her out?*

"What?" Nicole tipped her head to one side innocently. "He could help with your discovery."

The diary. Of course.

"What's this?" he asked, looking between the two women.

"Cara has a historical mystery she's trying to solve," said Nicole.

"It's just something I found. The diary of a woman from World War Two."

"Really? Did you find it in the cottage?" he asked.

She shook her head. "At a property I'm helping clear for work. It was in a biscuit tin in the back of an armoire that looked as though it hadn't been touched in decades."

"The tin you showed me earlier this week?" he asked.

A grin slid over Nicole's face, showing her to be no doubt concocting all sorts of reasons why Cara had conveniently left out mentioning that she'd done more than just introduce herself to her cute neighbor.

"What is it that I can help with?" he asked.

"Cara wants to find out who wrote it," said Nicole.

His eyes twinkled. "Then it really is a historical mystery. Do you know where your author was from?"

"A village in Cornwall. She mentions riding her bicycle to attend a dance in Saint Mawgan, so she couldn't have been too far."

"There was an RAF base around there," he said. "Actually, there were a couple."

She nodded. "The writer mentions the planes and a raid when the Germans bombed a storage building on a base. And she also talks about going to Newquay to the pictures. She went out with a pilot, Paul, who was stationed in the area for a brief time."

"A wartime romance. Do you know how it ended?" he asked.

"Not well, I think, but I'm still reading."

"Paul the pilot," he mused. "We could check the records of the local RAF bases against the dates in the diary to see how many pilots named Paul there were, but it's a common name."

The mention of "we" sent a tingle of excitement through her.

"Do you think I could see the diary?" Liam asked.

"Sure," she said slowly.

"Cara, you should make Liam dinner and show him the diary then." Cara nudged her friend with her foot, but missed as Nicole turned to Liam. "She's a wonderful cook and a fantastic baker. You should've seen the cakes she used to make in our terrible student kitchen. They were incredible."

Cara was going to kill her friend. "Nicole, I'm sure Liam's busy with the new start of term and—"

"I'm not, actually." He gave her a sheepish grin. "And I can barely warm up a tin of baked beans, so I'll never turn down a good meal. If it's on offer."

She blinked. How had she gone from sitting at home on a Saturday afternoon to being at a pub planning a dinner she hadn't intended to give? And yet, somehow she found herself saying, "Does Thursday at eight work for you?"

"It's a date." Liam frowned. "Or rather, not a date. An academic exercise? A historical puzzling?"

"A diary inspection," she suggested, oddly comforted by his floundering.

He rubbed the back of his neck. "We'll call it that. Well, I'll leave you ladies to talk, and I'll see you on Thursday, Cara."

Cara and Nicole watched him push away from the table and retreat to a booth on the opposite side of the pub.

"He's so charming," said Nicole.

Cara sighed. "In a bumbling, academic sort of way."

Nicole shot her a look. "Which is the complete opposite of Simon, which, I'll remind you, is a good thing."

"It doesn't matter whether it's a good thing or not. My divorce was only finalized a few months ago. I just uprooted my entire life. I'm not looking for anything right now."

"I know the last couple years have been tough, but you can't just pull up the drawbridge behind you, Cara. You need to see people."

"I see people," she said. "There's Gran, and I've met a few of my neighbors. Charlotte, who lives on the other side of me, seems nice." She made a mental note to invite Charlotte and her husband over for a drink one day, if only to quash any future needling from Nicole.

"Then tell me truthfully that you aren't lonely," said her friend.

Cara opened her mouth to protest but shut it again. She was lonely. She didn't notice it so much in the routine of the day, when she had work and errands to keep her busy, but at night and on the weekends it washed over her in waves. It was why she'd cried when Nicole had appeared on her doorstep. It was why, in a strange way, a tiny part of her was looking forward to the idea of cooking for someone else.

Nicole covered Cara's hand with hers. "Start with dinner with the hot professor."

"Nicole, it's not a date."

"Oh, right, a diary inspection." Nicole laughed. "You two are made for each other."

Cara scowled as Nicole laughed, but she couldn't help but be excited. Whether it was because she might be one step closer to finding out who wrote the diary or because it was Liam who was going to help her, she couldn't really say.

26 February 1941

I'm becoming talented at subterfuge. Today was my day off from Bakeford's and I convinced Mum that I was going to have lunch with an old friend from school. Instead, I boarded the bus and got off at St. Mawgan, where Paul was waiting for me.

"Hello, darling," he greeted me. (I don't mind it when he calls me "darling." It sounds so much less silly than when Kate says it.)

He took my elbow and led me around a corner. He stopped and touched my lower lip with his knuckle. "We're out of sight. May I kiss you?"

I nodded, and so he did.

I don't know if I'll ever become used to Paul kissing me. His lips are soft and he can make my legs feel as though they're about to crumple beneath me.

He took me to lunch at the Star Inn. At first I was worried. St. Mawgan is so close to home that there was a risk someone might recognize me, but I felt sophisticated sitting at a table in one of the big bay windows, a glass of hock at my hand. We spoke about our lives. I asked him to tell me about his time at Cambridge, and he made me laugh with stories about nearly falling into the Thames at the Boat Race and stealing a friend's car at midnight on a wager that he couldn't drive from Cambridge to Trafalgar Square and back in under two hours. (He won.)

He's fascinated by my life in Cornwall, even though I can't imagine how anyone could find it anything but dull. I tried to explain how sometimes my life seems so small I almost want to scream, and he leaned over the table and took my hand.

"Where would you go?" he asked.

"Go?"

"If you didn't have to be here."

"But I do," I said. "My parents would never let me leave."

"But what if you didn't have to worry about any of that? If you could go wherever you wanted in the world, where would it be?"

"California." When his brows shot up, I explained about the postcard and the trees and how the sun seems to always promise to shine.

"Then you should see the orange groves for yourself," he said.

I almost told him that it isn't just seeing them. I wanted to live there, an entire world away from everything I've known. But instead I said, "It's silly to wish for something that will never happen."

"Why not?" he asked.

"So many reasons. There's my job at the shop."

"Mrs. Bakeford could find another girl to work behind the counter and do the accounts." He smiled. "Although she'd never be as pretty as you."

I tutted at him because no one calls me pretty, but I was more pleased than I could say.

"What about Kate and my friends?" I asked.

"They'd write."

I shook my head. "My mother would never let me."

"Darling, one day you'll stand up and think to yourself, 'I'll just leave and no one will stop me.' And then you'll wonder why it took you so long." His voice held such conviction—as though he knew it would come to be.

I want to believe that he's right.

5 March 1941

I saw Paul again today. He took me for a walk along the water in Newquay. He wanted to buy me ice cream, but I laughed and told him no one would be selling it in the winter, when the wind is still so biting.

We talked about everything, as we always seem to do when we're together. He told me about Christmas in London with his family. They always have champagne before their dinner, and once, when his father was carving the goose, it flew off the plate and onto the floor! His mother burst out laughing. She sent it back down to the kitchen—they have a cook named Mrs. Dunn who comes every day which does sound grand—and it came back with all of the good meat sliced and bread to make sandwiches. They called it their Christmas picnic.

After our walk, I was shivering so much that Paul insisted we stop at a hotel that had been commandeered by the Royal Marines to billet its officers. He joked that it was a shame it would be so long before we could celebrate a Christmas together and drink champagne. I was so happy that he might want me to meet his family that I let it slip that I've never had champagne. He immediately ordered a bottle even though it was three *o'clock in the afternoon. I was shocked that they had any at all because good alcohol can be scarce these days, and I tried to tell Paul I didn't want it because of the expense. He just laughed and told me that I was worth it.*

The champagne was delightful, all bubbles and fizz, and I drifted back to the bus stop in a daze.

7

LOUISE

"Rationing jam? What's next?" Mrs. Bakeford muttered, locking the shop door as a fog rolled down the high street.

Louise couldn't help but agree with her as she buttoned the last button on her coat. Despite the signs they'd put in the window and at the counter, the entire day had been spent explaining why the housewives of Haybourne couldn't purchase more than their allotted portion of jam and preserves. She'd been cajoled, importuned, and even yelled at by old Mrs. Harper, whom she'd never particularly liked anyway.

"It'll be better in a few weeks' time. They'll be used to it then, just like they were with tea and meat," she said, reassuring herself as much as Mrs. Bakeford.

"Let us hope so. I'll see you tomorrow, Louise."

"Good night, Mrs. Bakeford," Louise said, hooking her handbag over her wrist and starting the short walk home.

If the day had left her tired, at least there was the prospect of seeing Paul that week to lift her spirits. He hadn't been able to tell her exactly when he'd be able to secure an afternoon's leave—he was flying a series of exercises—but he was confident he'd be able to steal away at some point. He'd let her know through Kate, who had been more than willing to act as a go-between, but that didn't mean her cousin was entirely silent about the arrangement.

"People will find out at some point, you know," Kate had said the day before after church.

Louise had glanced around, but her mother and Kate's were chatting, both with folded arms, their handbags hanging off their arms and swaying slightly with every punctuated point. Their fathers had rushed out as soon as the service had ended to stand with four other men from the neighborhood, each with a pipe or a cigarette clamped in his mouth.

"No one's paying us any mind," said Kate, nudging her with her elbow.

Louise blushed. "You can never be too careful in Haybourne. Everyone always seems to know everyone else's business."

"And they all have an opinion to go along with it. But that's why you need to think about this. Otherwise you'll wind up with your mother and Mrs. Moss in the parlor all over again."

"I know, I know. I just . . . I just want a little more time."

Once she'd explained to him the difficulties she'd faced after their trip to the beach, the last few weeks with Paul had been blissfully uncomplicated as they'd avoided meeting in Haybourne again. She liked that he leaned in when she told him stories about growing up in the village because he hadn't heard them all before. And she loved when he spoke about his family, his travels, his life. He was different from any other man she'd ever met. Raised in a mansion flat in Kensington, he doted on his mother and revered his father, a prominent barrister and Master of the Bench at Lincoln's Inn. Paul had read history for his degree with a mind to entering politics, before the war had broken out. He'd been one of the first men from Cambridge to join up.

It seemed extraordinary to her that this man who belonged to a glamorous world so removed from her own had chosen her, a girl who'd hardly ever ventured out of Cornwall save for the few times she'd visited her mother's sister in Bristol. Louise hadn't even seen London, while Paul kept a bedsit on what he called a bohemian street in Chelsea for when he was home from university, even if he'd told her it had nothing more than a gas ring for making tea and an electric fire to keep him warm.

"You'll have to write to Gary too," said Kate, her voice sympathetic.

"Why should I?" Louise asked, suddenly angry. "It's our mothers who've gone mad, not us."

"Because when you tell your mother that you're in love with a flier, you'll be happy to know that Gary has backed away quietly. Even Aunt Rose can't shame a man into marrying a woman whose heart's already taken."

Her lips parted, ready to deny that she was in love with Paul, but something stopped her. "I'll think about it," was all she had said before her mother beckoned her over to say hello to Pastor Egan.

Kate's words still echoed as Louise let herself in through the garden gate. Maybe all it took was a month to find the man who made her heart quicken when she saw him. She should think the entire idea barmy, but wasn't she always reading newspaper articles and seeing movies where couples fell madly in love, the pressure and uncertainty of war only accelerating declarations that were inevitable?

Inside, she unknotted the scarf she'd tied over her hair to protect it on the wet evening. She was just hanging up her mac when her father appeared in the parlor doorway. One look at his grim expression, and her blood froze. Quickly, she ran through the list of men she knew who were fighting. Kate's brothers, Harry and Michael. George, John, and Richard from school. The vicar's son. Euan, the butcher's assistant, who'd only been called up two weeks ago, even though he'd put his name down for the navy as soon as he turned eighteen. Gary.

"What is it, Da?" she asked. "Has there been bad news?"

Her father's lips thinned even further, but he just said, "You'd better come join us, Lou Lou."

She followed him, fear tingling through her, but when she crossed the threshold into the parlor, she understood. Sitting in a spindly chair, his cap in hand, was Paul.

"What are you doing here?" she asked, taking a step toward him. Her mother's voice stopped her.

"Flight Lieutenant Bolton has come to call on you."

"Louise . . ." Paul made to rise from his chair, but her mother coughed, sending him back down again.

"You can only imagine our surprise to open the door and find him standing there, given that we've never been introduced," said her mother.

"Rose." Her father's voice sliced through the air, drawing all three of them up straight. "I'm sure the gentleman has his reasons for coming." He turned to Paul. "You fly Spitfires?"

"I do, sir," said Paul. "I'm a pilot. I was stationed at RAF Saint Trebelzue."

"'Was,'" her father said. A look of understanding passed between the two men, and her father nodded. "We'll leave you for a few moments."

Louise's mother's lips pressed into a thin line. "Arthur, I don't think—"

"Come along, Rose," her father said, standing at the door to the parlor.

Her mother hesitated, her reluctance easy to read, but she followed her husband nonetheless. With one last look back, her father shut the door behind him.

The ticking of the mantel clock counted off the seconds as Louise stared at her twisting hands, unable to unravel the emotions warring in her. Thrilled to see him. Shocked that he was in her parents' home after she'd done so much to uncomplicate this part of her life. Worried about what his presence really meant.

"Louise." He choked on her name as he said it.

"Why are you here?" she asked again.

"My unit just received orders. We're leaving Cornwall tomorrow."

Her head jerked up. "No."

"I'm not supposed to be here. We weren't granted leave. I jumped base."

"Paul, what if anyone finds out?"

"Whatever the RAF wants to do with me, they can." He rose now, crossing the room and dropping to his knees in front of her chair. "I had to see you."

Tears pricked at her eyes, and he gathered her hands in his, the press of his warm skin comforting her.

"Where are you being sent?" she asked.

He shook his head. "You know I can't tell you that."

"But when will we see each other again?" The first tears had begun to fall, but her voice, though soft, was still steady. They *would* see each other. They had to.

He lowered his forehead to their clasped hands. "I don't know. When I can next get leave long enough to come here."

But Louise knew that could be months.

He lifted his eyes to hers. "Will you write to me?"

"Oh, Paul, I'll write to you every day. How could you think I wouldn't?"

Lifting her hand, he kissed her knuckles. The sweetness of the gesture made her ache.

"I know I don't have the right to ask it, but I'd hoped you would say yes. These last weeks . . ." He cleared his throat. "These last weeks have been everything to me."

She placed a gentle hand on his jaw, cherishing her last few chances to touch him. "Me too."

Pushing up on his knees, he kissed her. Hot tears slipped down her cheeks, and for the first time she hated the war not as a far-off thing that raged across the Channel, but as the brutal hand that would tear him from her and thrust him into a danger she could only imagine.

He broke away, letting out a long, steadying breath. "I want you to take this."

He held out his hand, his compass balanced in the middle of it.

"Oh, Paul, I can't. It's your talisman."

"It's more than that," he said. "It was my uncle's when he was in the Royal Flying Corps. It's one of the few things of his we have left, and it's my most precious possession."

"No, I won't have you flying without it." She closed his hand around it and brushed her lips against his cheek. "If you really want me to have it, give it to me the next time we meet."

He shuddered, as though he was trying to hold back a wave of emotion too powerful to name, but he nodded nonetheless. "I should leave. I just might stand a chance of making it back to base before anyone notices I'm gone."

She nodded, no longer trusting herself to speak.

He pocketed the compass and then pressed a piece of paper into her hand. "This is my service number. Write to me, Louise. Promise me you will."

"You'll write to me too?"

"Every day I'm able," he said.

They stood together, looping their arms around each other's waists as they crossed the ivory carpet that was her mother's pride and joy. At the door, he kissed her again, with a soft brush of his lips, and then smoothed her hair out of her face.

"Be happy, Louise Keene," he said. And then he was gone.

In the hall, she swept away her tears and swallowed hard. She placed one hand on the banister, ready to climb the stairs to her room when the dining room door swung open so hard it hit the wall.

"You irresponsible, uncaring girl," her mother hissed. "What were you thinking?"

"I don't know what you mean, Mum," she said, her voice unnaturally calm despite her shaking hands.

"Carrying on with that pilot when Gary is actually fighting."

Enough. What had started as dropped hints and sighing wishes had become a strange, twisted idea of her future. She'd indulged her mother too much, knowing it was easier to simply nod and smile than to risk a spiraling rant.

"There is nothing between Gary and me except for your hopes," she said.

Her mother crossed her arms. "He's the only boy in Haybourne suitable for you."

"And what if I don't want to stay in Haybourne?" she snapped. "What if I don't want to spend my days keeping Gary's house and arranging flowers for the altar at All Souls and seeing the same people I've seen every day of my life?"

"You ungrateful child. Gary will give you a good life, which is more than you deserve."

"I don't care about any of that!"

Her mother rushed forward, grabbing her by the back of her neck. Louise yelped, new tears springing to her eyes at the tug of the hair caught between her mother's pulling fingers.

Drawing Louise's face close, her mother dropped her voice to a dangerous whisper. "I've done everything for you, and I will not see you give it all up for a pilot who will forget you as soon as he leaves Cornwall."

"Mum!"

"Nineteen years. Nineteen years of cooking and cleaning and laundering for a child I hardly wanted, and this is how you repay me? You were supposed to be worth all of this."

"You're hurting me," Louise whimpered, her hands clasped around her mother's wrist as tears flowed freely down her face.

"What is this?" Her father's voice boomed through the entryway. In an instant, her mother's grip loosened, and Louise stumbled back. She pressed a hand to her scalp, trying to dull the throb of pain at her roots.

Her mother threw out a hand in Louise's direction. "She's going to ruin everything, Arthur."

Her father's gaze sliced over to Louise. "Go upstairs to your room."

It had been years since her father had sent her to her room as punishment for some childhood transgression, but she didn't protest. Instead, she lunged for the banister and scrambled, half falling, up the stairs. But at the top, she stopped when she heard her mother say, "You coddle that girl."

"And that's worse than what you do to her?" her father shot back.

"I am trying to give her a better life."

"The life you wanted to have? You've made it clear from the day we married that you weren't happy with me, but these airs, Rose? They stop now."

"It's not putting on airs to want to not be the postmaster's wife and have a house barely big enough to entertain."

"This is our home," her father said. "This is our *life*."

"I was supposed to have more than this," her mother hissed. "That was the plan, but if you'd taken more precautions—"

"Then you wouldn't have fallen pregnant and had to marry me and stay in Haybourne? It's been nineteen years. Just say it."

Louise squeezed her eyes shut, her breath coming fast and ragged. She had to leave. This house. This village. In her mother she saw what her life would be if she stayed.

Creeping down the carpeted hall, Louise let herself into her room. She'd been silent and still for her whole life. Paul had been the first real risk she'd ever taken. The first time she'd ever dared step out from within the tight confines of the box her mother had kept her in for all these years. And what was worse, she could see now that she'd *let* her mother do it. But her mother would not be the one to blame if Louise allowed this to go on.

She pulled out her old school bag, a battered leather satchel with the soft brown patina, and set it on her bed. Moving methodically, she began to pack. In went underthings, stockings, a sweater, two shirts, her green tweed skirt, and a brown dress with fluted sleeves. Her mac was hanging on a hook downstairs by the door, but her good wool coat was still in her wardrobe. She grabbed it and the soft cherry-red muffler she'd knitted for herself last Christmas out of wool unwound from an old sweater.

From out of her nightstand drawer, she pulled her diary. Carefully, she tucked the scrap of paper Paul had pressed into her palm between the pages marked by a red ribbon. She'd memorize his service number later, because she didn't trust herself not to forget it now, as adrenaline pumped through her body. She slipped the diary into her bulging satchel and swung the long strap over her head.

She stopped, giving one last glance around her room. It had been her sanctuary for so long, but she could see now that if she stayed, it would feel like a prison.

Her eye landed on the postcard. Its cheeriness was incongruous with her life, but she crossed the room, wiggled the card free, and tucked it into her bag before buckling the flap closed.

She took a deep breath. "You want more." Then she unlocked the window, slid it up, and hooked her leg over the sill.

The satchel bumped against her back as her feet caught hold of the trellis nailed to the side of the house. Fortunately, it was March, and the broad beans her father had trained up it had all died back that winter. A few scraggly, dead vines clung to the wood frame, but nothing impeded her progress.

This was the first time she'd climbed out of her window, and her hands shook a little as she inched her way down. The trellis would hold—she knew that much from the number of times Kate had stolen up it on her way home from some date or another—but knowing that and putting it to the test were two entirely different things.

One foot, one hand, she chanted in her head, forcing herself to make slow progress. The trellis moaned once, and she froze, fearful her parents might hear her. But no one came.

When her feet touched the ground, Louise sagged against the wall to catch her breath. Even through the glass of the kitchen window she could hear her parents' raised voices. They might still be in the entryway, but it was more likely that her mother had marched into the dining room, drawing the curtains so that none of the neighbors would see the fight. Even though the room faced the sea, Rose Keene would take no chances that a passing neighbor might catch a glimpse of anything but the perfect picture of domesticity she worked so hard to craft.

Moving carefully, Louise made her way through the garden. Once on the street and out of sight of the house, she broke into a run. It was only ten minutes to Uncle Jack's house. Louise made it in five, gasping for breath as she skidded to a stop. There was no fence, so it was nothing to skirt around the box hedge that separated the cottage from its neighbor and tap on Kate's window.

Her cousin glanced up from her bed, throwing the book she was reading down when she spotted her.

"Louise!" Kate looked astonished as she opened the window.

"Help me in," Louise said, handing her cousin her bag.

Kate gave her a look but took the satchel without question. Then she helped haul her into the room.

Louise slumped on the floor under the windowsill, sucking in air to try to catch her breath.

"Is everything okay?" Kate asked, bustling over with a half-drunk cup of tea that was rapidly cooling in a cheap chipped mug.

Louise took a sip and shook her head. "No, it's not." She told her cousin of coming home to find Paul sitting in the front room. Of his departure and his making her promise to write. Of her mother's rage and her father's anger. Of climbing out the window and racing here.

"So you've run off?" Kate asked. "This will be the first place they'll look tomorrow when they realize you aren't at home."

"I know that," she said, "but by then it won't matter."

"What do you mean?"

"How do you feel about doing your part for the war effort?"

Kate scrunched her nose. "You mean knitting more socks? I don't know that my wrists can take it."

"No." Louise lifted her chin. "I mean, how do you feel about joining up?"

8

CARA

Cara wiped her hands on her apron. The worry that she'd forgotten something nagged at her even though she'd nearly memorized the checklist she'd written out two days ago. The wine was chilling, and the chicken was in the roasting tin with leeks, carrots, and parsnips. The cottage was clean, and she hadn't splattered anything on her clothes as she cooked. Whether or not she felt it, she was ready to host her first dinner in years.

She'd spent the better part of the week convincing herself that tonight was a good idea, but twice as she'd been cooking she'd picked up the phone to cancel. Just as often, she'd made herself set down the phone and think like a rational person, because turning all the lights off and hiding in her bedroom was not an option. It was a Thursday night—low pressure—and he had a good reason to be showing up on her doorstep—the diary. This was friendly, neighborly. Tonight was the chance to recapture a bit of the person she used to be—one who enjoyed cooking and entertaining and opening herself up to new friends. It had been so long, she'd almost forgotten who that woman was.

"And who on earth dates their neighbor?" she murmured to herself, banishing the last of the teasing texts Nicole had been sending her all week to the back of her mind.

When a sharp triple knock announced Liam's arrival, she hurried to open the front door. He grinned at her from the bottom step. He'd worn a blue sweater, white collared shirt, and gray slacks, and the tips of his hair were just a little dark with damp, as though he'd just showered.

"Hi," she said.

"Hi. I like your apron."

She looked down, realizing, to her horror, that she was still wearing it. A splash of wine marred the heavy cream fabric, and a couple of bright orange carrot peelings poked out of one of the pockets.

"Oh, I meant to take this off." She tugged at the ties frantically, but one end slipped through her hand, tightening the knot. Her cheeks burning, she tried to stick her thumbnail into it while stepping back, "I'm being rude and leaving you standing on the front step. Come in. I'll just—"

Liam mounted the steps, set the bottle of wine he'd been holding down, and placed one gentle hand on either of her forearms. She stilled immediately, her eyes wide and blinking as she gazed up at his soft smile. "Let me help."

Carefully, he turned her around. She held her breath as he leaned down, his fingers light on the ties, barely brushing her back. The fabric tugged this way and then that.

"It's pretty tight," he said.

Her head dropped back as she sent up a silent prayer that the god watching over awkward divorced women would take pity on her and either imbue her with a shot of confidence or make the the earth open up to swallow her. She wasn't sure which would be better.

"One sec. I think I've got it . . ."

The fabric gave and she sagged forward, lifting the neck strap of the apron over her head.

"Thanks," she said, balling the fabric up in her hands.

"Is everything okay?" he asked.

"Yes. I just—" She laughed. "I'm nervous. It's been a long time since I had anyone over for dinner."

Since I had a man over for dinner.

He leaned in a little, a conspiratorial glint in his eye. "I have a confession to make."

"What's that?" she asked.

"This is the first time in a long time I've been to dinner at someone's house, but I remembered to bring wine." He held up the bottle to show it off. "And it's chilled."

She smiled at the sight of the bottle, sweating condensation so that the spray of festive, curling silver ribbon stuck on with a bit of tape threatened to slip off at any moment. "And it has a bow."

"Mum would never speak to me again if she found out I showed up empty-handed," he said. "Leah either."

She thanked him and took the bottle, keeping a finger discreetly on the bow to make sure it didn't fall off.

He looked openly around the entryway as he crossed the threshold. "Your cottage is different from mine."

"How so?" she asked, leading him past the sitting room and down the narrow corridor. Her hands, she was pleased to discover, no longer shook despite the nerves that had been sitting in her stomach all afternoon.

"I think someone gutted my place a few years ago and fitted it with all modern fixtures. The only real period details left are a couple beams. But this," he said as they passed into the kitchen, "this is almost like stepping back in time."

Her shoulders relaxed a little as she watched him take in the space. It was a pretty room—her favorite in the house—with a small, black iron wood-burning stove on the wall opposite the oven, her reclaimed farmhouse table she'd set for two, and the gray and white–painted Welsh dresser Gran had given her because it was too big for her Widcote Manor flat. "I wouldn't have the heart to gut a place like this. I love the feel of the old cottages. Cozy, comfortable, lived-in. It was one of the reasons I took this house."

"What were the others?" he asked.

"Just the garden, really," she said, nodding out the kitchen window to where two large bushes of bold pink Skylark roses bloomed, casting their apple pie scent into the air, and white-and-gold Japanese anemones swayed in the border along the fence separating their two yards. "I've had a few good afternoons sitting out there."

"I wondered about that," he said.

"You have?"

"There's a gap in the top of the hedge by my kitchen and I can see your back patio." Then, all at once, he looked horrified. "Not that I've been watching you. That would be creepy. I just meant—"

She burst out laughing and, inexplicably, relaxed.

He ran his hand over the back of his neck and shot her a rueful smile. "We're making a hash of this, aren't we?"

"We really are."

"What are we going to do about it?" he asked.

Watching him leaning against her kitchen counter, long arms crossed over his chest, she could think of several things, but that was for a future Cara. One who hadn't just finalized her divorce and uprooted her life. Right here, right now, what she found herself wanting most was a friend's company.

"I should finish dinner," she said.

He nodded. "I would offer to help, but I don't trust myself not to ruin everything. Why don't I open the wine?"

"The corkscrew is in the drawer to your left. Glasses are above your head."

He set about cutting the foil while Cara slipped on a pair of mitts. She stood a little back as she opened the oven door, heat bursting forth in an angry cloud. Focusing on not burning herself while pulling out the heavy iron pot gave her something to concentrate on other than the tall man standing in her kitchen opening a bottle as though it was the most normal thing in the world.

Grabbing a little cream from the fridge, she removed the cast-iron lid and poured in a dash, stirring the broth that had formed in the bottom of the pot. Then she tested the flavor, added a touch of salt, and stirred again.

She looked up. Liam was watching her, the corners of his lips tilted slightly, glass of wine in his hand.

"You love cooking, don't you?" he asked.

"Why do you say that?"

"You look peaceful."

Those three words startled her in their accuracy. She did feel at peace when she cooked, all of her worries falling away. She tucked his observation away, wanting to unpack it later, when he'd gone.

"For a long time I didn't cook much. My career back in London was too busy, with too many late nights. But I realized about a year and a half ago that I missed it."

"You cook just for yourself?" he asked.

She nodded. "I cook exactly what I want, every night. There's no one to tell me that they'd rather have takeaway or a dish is too spicy for them."

"It's one of the best parts of being single," he said. "Along with not having to fight about whose family to visit at Christmas."

"Or waking up freezing because your partner's stolen the entire duvet. Dinner's ready. Shall we eat?" she asked.

She maneuvered the chicken out of the pot and carved the meat. Then, into shallow pasta bowls, she spooned vegetables before layering the chicken on top, followed by a healthy ladleful of creamy broth. Her hand hesitated over her kitchen scissors to cut sprigs of thyme from the pot she'd carried inside earlier, wondering if Liam would think she was showing off. So what if she was? It was what she'd do for herself. She cut the herb and popped two sprigs each on top of the dishes as garnish.

Liam placed a glass of wine by her right hand as she sat down. When he picked up his knife and fork, she dropped her gaze to her own bowl, but she couldn't help sneaking a peek out of the corner of her eye.

"This is incredible," he said after chewing for a long, thoughtful moment.

"Thank you," she said with a sigh of relief. "It's probably a bit too rustic for a dinner party, but I enjoy it. How are you finding Barlow?"

"It's a beautiful town. Reminds me of Oxford a little bit."

He'd read history at Oxford. She knew because Nicole had done some light stalking and sent her a dossier via text. It had saved Cara fighting with herself about whether she should Google him or not.

"We don't have a river to punt on, which is a shame," she said.

"At least that way you get fewer drunk students falling in the water."

"Don't be so sure of that," she said, remembering Nicole's end-of-exams stunt in the pond.

"How did you end up in Barlow?" he asked.

She laughed. "There's a long and short story."

He tore off a chunk of bread to soak up the creamy, thyme-flavored broth. "Tell me the long one. We have a whole dinner ahead of us."

"Well, I was a student here from 2004 to 2007."

"What did you read?"

"Art history," she said.

"Too bad. I was hoping you could give me all the gossip about my colleagues in the history department."

"Sorry," she said. "I briefly flirted with the idea of academia after graduation, but my ex talked me out of it."

"That's a shame."

"Yes, well, there are a lot of things that were a shame in that marriage."

"What happened, if you don't mind my asking?"

She paused, her fork halfway to her mouth. That was a personal question—deeply personal. One she might've expected on a date.

"Simon turned out not to be the person I thought he was," she said.

"I'm sorry," he said. Simple. Unembellished.

"Thank you."

She waited as he tore off another chunk of bread, swirling it in the broth. Finally he said, "I had a fiancée before I moved to the U.S."

"You did?"

He chuckled. "You sound shocked."

"I just—"

"I'm teasing," he said. "Vivian was also a lecturer at Exeter."

"What happened? If you don't mind me asking, of course."

A sadness settled into the crease between his brows. "All of the worst clichés."

"Cheating?" she asked, a little ashamed at how much she wanted to know. There was comfort sitting in front of a person who knew what it was like to have their hopes raised up, up, up and then dashed indiscriminately by a partner they thought they knew.

"With my best friend. I even walked in on them. It was the whole Hollywood movie trifecta."

"Oh, Liam," she said.

"It was the first time I'd been in a fight since I was in school. I nearly broke my hand when I punched Tom. Nearly broke his jaw too."

"He deserved it," she said, more fiercely than she would've expected.

He grinned. "He bloody well did. And thank you."

She tilted her head. "What did you do?"

"I'd been offered the position at Reed in Oregon for the following academic year but was in negotiations, trying to figure out whether Vivian would be able to come with me. I emailed the head of the department immediately and told her I would gladly accept. Without a partner."

"How did you cope?" she asked.

He shrugged. "I didn't at first. But the distance was helpful. It meant I couldn't see Viv whenever I was feeling sorry for myself, and having to dial a country code to call stopped me more times that I want to admit."

"I only moved an hour and a half's drive away. Sometimes it doesn't feel like enough," she said, thinking back to Simon's call the previous week.

"It will make a difference," he said. "I promise."

They hardly knew one another, and yet something about his words settled her.

"Well, now that we've eaten, I suppose this is as good a time as any to talk about the diary. Shall we clear the table?"

He helped her carry the dishes to the sink, not commenting when she turned on the tap rather than loading up a dishwasher. Instead, he picked up a towel and began drying, stacking things away in the cabinets she pointed out as he went. He kept up a steady stream of conversation, wanting to know more about Jock and the shop and her work at the Old Vicarage. He laughed at her story of finding a mouse snoozing in a shoebox filled with magazine clippings tucked away in a broom cupboard, and listened carefully when she described how to estimate the age of a piece by looking at the tiny cracks, called "crazing," in the finish.

When the dishes were all done, she poured him another glass of wine and went to the second bedroom she was using as a study to retrieve the biscuit tin, the diary, and her notes.

"Here we are," she said, setting them down on the table. "A good thick diary. It's about half full, and I thought it would be a breeze, but her writing is tiny. She filled up pages and pages, and there's only so much I can read at a time while I'm supposed to be studying for work. Here's the photograph I think is her."

He held it up to the kitchen light. "She looks happy."

"She does, doesn't she? I recognized the uniform because Gran was in the ATS, but that's the closest I've come to identifying her."

"Let's see this diary," he said.

"In the part I'm reading right now, she writes about the drills, physical training, and classes to prepare her for the exams that were supposed to help place her in a unit. Her biggest fear seems to be that she'll be assigned to work in the kitchens. Here."

She opened up the diary, flipped back a few pages from where she had stopped last night, and began to read out loud:

31 March 1941

The start of my second week in Leicester, and again I woke up to rain. Still, nothing stops the ATS. We drilled in the yard as usual, stumbling when our boots stuck in the mud, and when we finally were released to the canteen we were all soaked through.

I sent a letter to Paul today, and I hope for one back in a couple days. These waits between letters seem longer and longer, and sometimes I think I can hardly stand it.

If I have one regret from that last evening with him, it is that I didn't tell him I loved him. Now it feels impossible to say—it's too big to write with just ink and paper. I worry every day that something might happen to him, flying his missions over the Channel and hunting for German submarines. I know it's selfish of me to wish that he'd never been sent away when he's protecting us, but I do.

I saw Kate in the NAAFI today with a soldier at each elbow. When she spotted me, she shooed them away as though she couldn't have cared less whether they ever came back. I should like, I think, to be a little bit more like her. It would be easier if it didn't matter to me whether Paul came back.

Kate told me I was looking tired and worn. I told her it was all of the studying for the exams we're to be given to test our aptitude and that I'd hardly had a chance to come to the NAAFI for a cup of tea or a sing-along around the rickety piano in the corner. She told me she thought it was Paul causing the bags under my eyes.

"He's ruining your complexion, darling. He'd better come out in one of his letters and make you some promises or you'll wake up at the end of this war and realize you've missed out on all the fun for nothing."

"Are there any letters tucked in there from Paul?" Liam asked. "Their service numbers would be on the envelopes."

She shook her head. "It looks like the best she did was transcribe the important ones into her diary. Look."

He took the diary from her and began to read out.

My darling, you can't imagine my shock at receiving your letter. I never would've thought that you would want to do something as rash as join the services. Of course I'm proud you want to do your bit, but now I'll be worrying about you while I'm flying missions. At least when you were tucked away in Cornwall, you were safe. I know you hate it, but it's a luxury for nothing to happen to a place during a war. I wish you'd written to me before deciding to do something quite so impulsive. I'd never have let you waste your time and your pretty face on army work.

Liam snorted. "He's proud but he thinks her decision to join up is foolish? He's not the most supportive boyfriend, is he?"

"Later in that entry, she says she told him that if she'd stayed in the house with her mother any longer she would've exploded. It sounds like the situation had become toxic."

Cara fished the locket out of the tin and opened it. "I think this is Paul."

Liam peered at the two halves of the heart. "Handsome, isn't he?"

"Her friend Kate told her he looked like Clark Gable."

"More like Errol Flynn," he said. "Did you find anything in that tin that looked like it could've had a service number on it?"

Cara shoved her long dark hair out of her face and sighed. "No."

"Well, there are a few things we could try," Liam said, leaning back in his chair. "We know she was doing her basic training at Leicester at the end of March in 1941. We could try to track her down that way, although a lot of women would've passed through there. Then there's her uniform." He pointed to a badge on the woman in the photograph's cap and a white lanyard hanging from her shoulder. "Those should give us some indication of what battalion she was assigned to, but I'm not an expert in twentieth-century military history."

"I'm sorry," she said quickly. "I shouldn't be asking you to do this. I know the term starts soon and—"

He placed a hand on her forearm. "I'm happy to, Cara. It'll be fun to research something a little more recent than the reclamation and clearance of monastic lands in the fourteenth century."

His hand slid away, leaving a prickling heat along her skin.

"If you don't mind, I'll photograph the diary so I can read through it too. And I have a colleague who might be able to help us. This *is* his area of study, so I'm sure he'll be able to get more from the uniform faster. The Leicester barracks too."

He stayed long enough to do just that, snapping photos on his iPhone. He chatted easily as he moved methodically, telling her more about his new position and what he was teaching that year. When he was finished, he straightened from the table.

"Thank you for dinner," he said. "I should go let Rufus out."

"How is he?"

"More trouble than he's worth. I'll tell him you said hello."

"Bring him next time." She hesitated, waiting for awkwardness to freeze her. After all, she'd just invited him again, as though it was no big deal, and this time she had no Nicole to blame. But the more she thought about it, the more the invitation felt right.

If Liam read anything into her moment's hesitation, however, he hid it well, only tilting his head to one side a bit and saying, "I'd like that."

At the door, she watched him walk down the garden path. Reaching the gate, he turned and called out a goodbye. She smiled—maybe a little too wide—and shut the door as soon as he was on the sidewalk.

Inside, she swept up her phone from the hallway table. Nicole had texted two hours ago.

How did it go?

She stared at the screen for a moment before slipping it back into her bag and going off to change for bed.

3 April 1941

A letter from Paul today and a gift. He sent me a locket with a photograph of him, tall and handsome in his pilot's garb. I almost cried when I put it on.

And the letter! It's so sweet I'll copy it out because I want to be sure that nothing happens to it. A girl from the D barracks next door told me that one of Judith Doughtery's bunkmates stole all her fiancé's letters off the shelf above Judith's bunk and read the racier bits aloud to the other girls. I hope no one in C barracks would be so cruel.

30 March 1941

My darling,

I hope that this letter will arrive before your examination. I have no doubt that you will pass, especially if it is, as you say, mainly a test of maths and intelligence. Haven't you told me before how easily the subject came to you in school and how you wish that you might've studied at university if your parents had agreed?

I, for one, am happy that they didn't, otherwise I might not have met you. I remember so clearly thinking what a bore that night was, the same sort of dance I'd been to a thousand times, until you walked up on Taylor's arm. You were the prettiest girl I'd seen in Cornwall, with your curling hair and your red dress, looking so innocent and fresh. I knew I had to dance with you even if I was nowhere near a good enough man for you.

I hope to dance with you again soon, darling. Maybe in London, where the bands seem to play on in the underground nightclubs even as the Luftwaffe bombs the city. I will do everything I can to secure leave when you finally find out where you're stationed so I can see you, but I will warn you that my group captain is a tough man. He's not sentimental about things like sweethearts, and he flouts all the RAF's rules about required leave. All I want is twenty-four more hours with you. Just promise me you won't volunteer for a posting on the army's switchboards in Cairo or some other far-flung place. I don't know that I could stand knowing you were so far away.

I'm sending with this letter a locket. Inside is a photograph of my ugly mug. The other side is blank. I thought you might fill it with a photograph of your parents, or the next time I see you, we'll take a picture together and you can wear that too. It isn't much, but it will give me hope knowing that I'm close to your heart always.

Yours ever faithfully,
Paul

Every time the post comes and there's a letter from him, I feel a little more sure of myself. Paul helped me find the strength to finally break away from home. I know he worries about me, but I really do feel that he's proud. If only I can pass the examination and find out where I'll be stationed, we can plan to see one another again.

9

LOUISE

Louise was lying on her bed listening to Doreen read out from one of the cheap novels her sister had sent, when Margaret, one of her bunkmates, came racing into the dormitory.

"What is it?" Louise asked, bolting up.

Margaret braced herself against the door frame, her round cheeks bright pink and her breath puffing. "The examination results are in. We have five minutes to assemble."

All at once, the five girls of C barracks who had been relaxing scrambled down from their bunks. Louise jammed on the stiff leather ATS-issued shoes that had torn her feet so badly in the first week until calluses had hardened on the backs of her heels. Sarah, a shy Welsh girl who had the bunk underneath her, hopped on one foot as she struggled to pull her stockings on. Louise put a hand out to steady her, and Sarah smiled softly up at her as she hooked a stocking onto her suspender belt.

"I'm so nervous. I can't be a cook. That's just the same as what I did at home in Aberystwyth," said Sarah.

"I'm sure you'll be fine," said Louise, also sending up a little prayer that she wasn't assigned to a canteen, doomed to peel hundreds of pounds of potatoes or scrub pots day after day. Paul had warned her that noncommissioned men in the forces didn't get a say in their assignments, and that she shouldn't expect to either. Still, she hoped her job would be more glamorous than helping the army win battles through its stomach.

The girls hurried into the yard where they drilled every morning. Their excitement made the air crackle with energy, propelling them forward with equal parts eagerness and trepidation. From across the hard-packed dirt, she spotted a flash of blond hair and saw her cousin turn to speak to another girl.

"Excuse me." Louise put her shoulder between the two women in front of her and pushed through the crowd.

"Kate," she said, catching her cousin's sleeve.

"Louise!" Kate cried, throwing her arms around her. "Darling, aren't you just a bundle of nerves? I'm so worried, although I'm certain you're bound to get something good like accounts. I've heard you can rise up the ranks fast there."

"What assignment do you want?" Louise asked, linking arms with her cousin, knowing the likelihood they would be separated was great. Even though Kate was housed in H barracks, it was a comfort to know she was near. But now they could be sent anywhere the army was stationed, keeping in touch only by letter.

"I'll be on the telephones, I should think," said Kate. "My typing isn't nearly good enough for me to be a clerk, and I don't have any experience driving, although I think it would be heavenly to learn."

Louise didn't think driving a heavy truck down cratered roads or through the debris of a London air raid sounded heavenly at all, but she wasn't going to argue. Besides, all life was dangerous in Britain now. Haybourne hadn't seen bombing as heavy as that in the East London docks or the single night of devastation that had set Coventry ablaze last autumn, but air raids happened everywhere. German bombs killed civilians and service members alike without prejudice. Chance and fate were coconspirators in this war.

As they shuffled into the hall where they'd taken their examinations, the women began to fall in line by their barracks, just as they'd been taught. Louise hugged Kate's arm to her. "Good luck, and stay safe."

Kate dipped her head, their caps just touching. "You too. You can't let anything happen to you, because you're going to be the bridesmaid in my wedding."

Louise pulled back. "To whom?"

Kate grinned. "Oh, some handsome officer or another, I suspect. I'll write and let you know when I've decided which one."

With a laugh, Louise kissed her cousin on the cheek and hurried to join C barracks.

Corporal Clovis, who, with her commanding voice, ran them through their drills every day, stood on a small stage at the front of the room, a clipboard in her hand. She slid a pair of spectacles on and peered up over them at the assembled women.

"As you all know, you took your examinations last week. The results have been considered, and you've been assigned your units accordingly. I will remind you that although you might have volunteered to join the ATS, these assignments themselves are not voluntary. You will not be able to argue or persuade me to change them. If you're lucky, after some months, you may be able to apply for a transfer if you can show reason why your skills would be more valuable in another unit."

Two women ahead of her, Sarah shifted from foot to foot.

"I'll start with the A barracks," said Corporal Clovis in her dry tone. "Calvi, accounts. Dardenne, cook."

There was an audible groan, and Corporal Clovis stopped. "Do you have something to say Private Dardenne?"

The woman straightened. "No, ma'am."

Corporal Clovis's eyes narrowed. "That's what I thought. Harrow, telephonist."

There were no more outbursts as the corporal made her way through A and B barracks, but the sinking shoulders or broad smiles broadcast how each woman felt about her assignment.

"Now for C barracks," droned Corporal Clovis.

Louise wiped the palms of her hands on her tunic.

"Arden, ammunition inspection," Corporal Clovis called. "Egerton, postal services. Hughes . . ."

Sarah's shoulders were nearly around her ears.

"Cook." Corporal Clovis stopped and adjusted her spectacles. "No, sorry. Hughes, driver. James, cook."

A little smile touched Louise's lips. So shy little Sarah would be the one careening around behind the wheel of an army vehicle. It was the furthest from cookery that her friend could've gotten.

"Kane, ammunition inspection. Keene . . ."

Louise squeezed her eyes shut. All she wanted was something that would make her feel as though all of the cold mornings spent shivering in the yard and hours studying had been worth it.

Corporal Clovis's mouth tipped up. "Ladies, congratulate Volunteer Keene. She, along with a few others, has received a special assignment. Report to me after this assembly to receive more information about your duties, Keene."

Louise's eyes snapped open as a murmur went through the crowd. No one had said anything about a special assignment.

"Quiet," barked Corporal Clovis. Silence fell over the women immediately, and the corporal began calling out names again.

Louise could feel everyone looking at her and, although she'd done nothing wrong, shame rushed up in her. Why had she been singled out? What had she done?

She barely heard when Kate was assigned telephonist, just as her cousin had predicted.

By the end of the assembly, five other women had been called for special assignment. Louise tried to sneak glances at her fellow singled-out sisters, but she couldn't make them out through the rows of women.

"You can expect to receive your orders soon. Some of you will even be leaving today. I advise you to keep your kit in good order, as you never know how long you'll have to pack. " Corporal Clovis paused. "Those of you who received special assignment, stay here. The rest of you are dismissed to your duties."

Pauline Norman, who stood behind Louise, tapped her on the shoulder. "Good luck."

Louise offered her a little smile as lines of women began to march out in orderly fashion.

"I'm sure it will be fine," said Harriet Kane. "You're probably going to do something terribly daring and that's why they can't tell the rest of us. Maybe you'll be trained to be a spy!"

"C barracks!" Corporal Clovis barked.

Louise's friends fell into line, their lips clamping shut, and filed out. Louise looked around the nearly empty assembly room, and the five other women were all standing where their barracks had left them. One she recognized as a Geordie girl named Lizzie who sometimes would sing war songs in the canteen if the soldiers on base asked her enough times, but the rest she didn't know. Most of them looked perturbed and a little nervous, except for one woman with fiery red hair who openly wore her excitement.

A metal door at the back of the hall was pulled open, and a tall man in a stiff peaked cap marched to join Corporal Clovis.

"Are these them?" he asked.

Corporal Clovis nodded and handed him the clipboard. "All six of them, sir."

"Ladies, I'm Brigadier Melchen and I have the privilege of overseeing one of the Royal Artillery's great experiments during this war." The way he said "privilege" made Louise suspicious of just how much of an honor he really considered it. "General Sir Frederick Pile has gotten his way, and moving forward we are to have mixed anti-aircraft batteries trained and in operation by the end of the summer. Naturally, women won't be permitted to fire. That will be done by a male gunner. But you will be trained in every other aspect of operating the sophisticated machinery of an anti-aircraft gun. Do you have any questions?"

The redhead stuck her hand up.

"Of course you do," Brigadier Melchen muttered to himself. "You there. What's your name?"

"Volunteer Charlotte Wilkes, sir," said the woman with a crisp salute.

Melchen huffed. "Given that you'll be in a mixed battery, you will assume the ranks of the RA. Your rank going forward will be private."

"Then I'm Private Charlotte Wilkes, sir."

"Yes, yes. Go on," he said.

"What exactly do you mean when you say 'mixed anti-aircraft batteries'?"

Melchen sighed. "A battery of six women and one corporal will operate various instruments that will allow a gunner—a man—to shoot Nazis out of the sky. You will also have two men to load the ammunition and maintain the gun. Is that clear enough for you?"

"Crystal, sir," said Private Charlotte Wilkes with a smile.

Louise and other girls all looked around. Anti-aircraft? That hadn't been one of the assignments they'd been told about.

"Any more questions?" Melchen asked.

"Yes, sir, if I might?" asked a beautiful brunette who'd been with E barracks.

"Name?"

"Private Vera Garson."

He squinted at her. "Any relation to Major General Garson?"

"Yes, sir. He's my uncle."

Melchen straightened his shoulders noticeably. "Go on, Private Garson."

"Why us?"

"Your examination results identified you as some of the brightest in the ATS. You'll go to Oswestry for additional training to hone your natural aptitude.

"*Don't* think that this will be easy. You'll be asked to do more than any other woman in the ATS. The work will be hard and the hours will be long. It's a dangerous job because you'll be trying to shoot down the very planes that are shooting at you. Anyone who isn't willing to take that risk should say so now, and Corporal Clovis will see to it that you're reassigned."

The room fell silent, each of the women refusing to flinch. It would be dangerous, yes, but what they would do would *matter*. They wouldn't just be support staff, confined to the administrative side of bases. They would be helping shoot down Luftwaffe planes and keeping the people of Britain safe. They would be helping keep pilots like Paul safe.

"Then, ladies, I suggest you look around," Melchen barked. "These are the women who you'll be living with and training with. There are some people who think women will faint away the moment the first gun is shot. I would advise you to do your very best to prove them wrong. Corporal Clovis, I'll leave them in your hands."

The corporal nodded and the brigadier marched back out, the metallic clang of the door echoing around the nearly empty hall.

"Fall in line here," Colonel Clovis ordered, pointing to a spot in front of the stage.

Louise and the rest of the women lined up shoulder to shoulder.

"At ease, privates," the colonel said, joining them on the floor and propping the clipboard against her hip. "I'm going to speak to you frankly now. As some of you know, I was in the service for many years, and I volunteered again when war was declared. I can tell you from personal experience that I've met some of the bravest people I know in the ATS— all women. Germans bullets don't care about your sex, and bombs don't know the difference either.

"Anti-aircraft is a dangerous assignment, but it's also a desperately needed one. If it wasn't, the Royal Artillery wouldn't be opening up these batteries. There are men who will do everything they can to see you fail, and I want you to remember that when your training feels impossible, because it will. But the RA doesn't just need your service. It needs your intelligence. You've all scored in the top of your aptitude tests. You're smarter than most of the men you'll meet in life, and I suspect you're tougher too."

The corporal looked at each of them and nodded. "Don't let me or your fellow soldiers down. Now, I suggest you say your goodbyes. You leave at seventeen hundred hours for Oswestry. Dismissed."

The collective group let out a sigh of relief, hurrying for the doors out to the drill yard.

"Well, that was something else. I'm Charlie," said the redheaded woman who had introduced herself as Private Charlotte Wilkes, sticking her hand out to Louise.

"We should all introduce ourselves, I suppose," said Vera in a clipped, proper tone.

"I'm Nigella Onslow," said a pretty, petite blond who looked like she might be blown over at the first strong gust.

"Mary Rogers," said a girl to Louise's right who had light brown hair and lips that turned down in what seemed like a perpetual frown.

"Lizzie Masterson," said the canteen singer with a little wave.

"Louise Keene," Louise said.

"Are you Kate Keene's sister?" Nigella asked in a breathy voice.

"Cousin," she said.

"We were in H barracks together. She's ever so nice and glamorous, like a movie star."

"That's Kate for you," Louise said.

"Well, I suppose we'd better get on with packing," said Charlie. "Plenty of time to get to know each other better on the train."

They all split off to go to their respective barracks and collect their things. Louise hardly had anything to pack. They'd shipped her satchel back to her parents' home when she'd arrived in Leicester, explaining that she had no need for civilian clothes in the ATS. She was a soldier now. All she had left that was her own was a bundle of letters from Paul and one from her father, her diary, and her postcard of sunny California that she'd displayed on the shelf above her bed.

Finding the barracks empty, she shoved her things into her kit bag and pulled out her writing paper and pen.

She would write to her parents first. Her mother hadn't sent a letter since Louise left home, instead conveying any news she wished Louise to know in the final paragraph of her father's dutiful, weekly letter. Paul had been too great a betrayal, and leaving the familiarity of Haybourne to join the service—and not even the navy's prestigious women's branch, the Women's Royal Navy Service, or WRNS, with their fashionable, tailored uniforms and their ranks full of debs—ensured that Rose Keene would never forgive her daughter. And now Louise would be serving with men and shooting planes down from the sky? It would be too much.

Dear Mum and Da,

I don't know how much I can say, but I'm writing to let you know that I've received a special assignment to work on the anti-aircraft guns. I don't yet know what that means, but it's exciting nonetheless. Several other girls who are here with me have been selected as well, and we'll go on to a base near the Welsh border for further training. When I find out what I can tell you and what I can't, I'll write more, but know that I'm doing everything I can to stay safe.

Kate has been made a telephonist, which means she could stay here in England or be sent anywhere the army has need of her. I'm sure Uncle Jack and Aunt Claire will receive their own letter, but I thought you would want to know.

All of my love,
Louise

Folding her letter into an envelope and marking the address, she pulled another sheet of paper free.

Dearest Paul,

After all of the examinations and waiting, I have finally received an assignment. I have no doubt there will be a great controversy over it, because you'll never believe what it is. I'll be working on the anti-aircraft guns! I can't tell you how excited I am. It'll be something real and concrete that I know will help win this war.

I miss you dearly, and I hate not knowing where you are or what it is you're doing. I suppose, however, that you must be feeling a bit like that right now too, because soon I'll be on a train to my new camp for more training. Just know that your girl is going to do everything she can to make you proud.

Yours always,
Louise

10

LOUISE

Almost four months later, Louise had to admit that Brigadier Melchen had been right. Life at Oswestry was *hard*.

After tumbling off the train at Oswestry at nearly four o'clock in the morning, the women had been given one day to settle in before their training started. Since then, they'd woken up at seven to drill and then spent hours attending classes, learning to identify every known German aircraft. Although it was important that all of them have a basic working knowledge of the Luftwaffe's craft, this would the responsibility of the predictor, a woman assigned to peer through the powerful binoculars and call out approaching aircraft. Two more women would operate the height and range finder by pinpointing the aircraft through their eyepieces. Finally, the two predictors would turn the dials to calculate with exacting precision how far the gun would have to fire, and the Sperry would set the fuse so the shell would explode at the precise moment to enact maximum damage. Then the Sperry operator would yell when there was a read, and the information would be relayed automatically from the predictor to the guns, and the gunner—always a man—would fire.

The entire operation was supposed to take a matter of seconds. The first time Louise and the women of B Section, 488 Battery, had tried to put all of the theory and learning they'd absorbed into practice it had taken them two minutes and thirty-eight seconds.

"Congratulations, ladies. The Luftwaffe just dropped a high-explosive bomb on an East London tube station entrance and killed the forty-one people sheltering there because you didn't stop them," Colonel Barker, a hard woman who lived up to her name, shouted at them. Louise had seen Charlie pinch Nigella to keep her from crying. The gunner, a hang-dog-faced man named Sergeant Cartruse, had lit up a cigarette and watched with a shake of his head while the two men who loaded the gun, Williams and Hatfield, snickered.

But, under the unrelenting drilling of Colonel Barker and the RA colonels, the women of B Section had grown faster and more certain in their actions. It quickly became clear that Mary had something of a photographic memory for German planes and proved herself to be an excellent spotter. Nigella and Charlie worked quickly on the height and range finder, and Louise, who could sometimes calculate sums faster than she could turn the dials, worked the predictor with Vera as Lizzie used the Sperry to set the shell's fuse. Slowly but surely, Cartruse had stopped sighing and asking, "You sure?" every time Lizzie called, "Fuse!"

Over their four months together, the six women had grown close, thanks to a mix of genuine affection and long shifts into the night that were part of their training in preparation for air raids. They would be alert and working when the rest of Britain tried to sleep in their beds and bomb shelters. Louise, Vera, Charlie, Lizzie, Mary, and Nigella lived to-gether, ate in the canteen together, and moved around the base in a pack. They were the ack-ack girls, the gunner girls, and, still a novelty among the RA, they were watched wherever they went. All of the stares might have bothered her once, but as part of this tight-knit troop of women, Louise hardly noticed.

One Thursday afternoon in late July, after a training session that had seen B Section hit eight out of their ten targets, all of them except Lizzie sat in the canteen, sipping cups of strong tea. Nigella had a bit of knitting on her lap and was clicking away with her needles, while Mary read out tidbits from a film magazine someone had left lying around on one of the tables. Charlie was sketching Vera's patrician profile with quick, efficient strokes of a stub of pencil in a plain paper notebook she kept in one of her uniform pockets. Louise, however, was absorbed in her own world, a letter from Paul dated five days earlier. Although she wrote to him every day, he wrote less frequently because he was in active combat. When his letters came, however, she always treasured the tenderness in them.

You must understand why I worry. Being part of an anti-aircraft battery means being closer to the action than any man would wish for the woman who holds his heart. I wish you would consider a transfer, for my sake as much as your own.

She chewed her bottom lip, stuck somewhere in the difficult space between happiness and disappointment. They'd had this argument too many times. Ever since she'd told him she'd been assigned to Ack-Ack Command, he'd started to fret. The work was too dangerous. She would be shot at. She didn't really know what she was getting herself into.

Each time she'd written him back. Yes, her work was dangerous, but so was his. Yes, she would be shot at, and so would he, when he was flying his missions. Yes, she knew what she was doing, and arguing was pointless. The ATS had selected *her*. The RA needed *her*. She was a gunner girl, and there was nothing Paul could do about it.

All of that logic laid out for him would calm him for a letter or two, but then he'd start again, pushing and pushing. This talk of a transfer, however, was new.

She read the paragraph again, her heart catching in her throat to see the words "holds his heart" in his bold handwriting. It had been so long since they'd met—nearly six months!—and all she had were passionate letters with no true declarations. He still hadn't said he loved her, although sometimes he came close.

She knew she couldn't place the blame entirely at his feet. She'd been holding back too. Paul was life lived at double pace, from meeting him at the dance to the day at the beach. He'd asked her to be his in a matter of hours and then, just a few weeks later, he'd been in her mother's sitting room asking her to remember him because the next day he would be gone. They'd hardly known each other a month, yet the force of her own emotions frightened her.

At the barracks in Leicester, too many girls had had stories of soldiers, sailors, and airmen who'd broken their hearts. Love came fast during these times, the danger of war thrusting couples into each other's arms with the irresistible pull of two magnets. Yet Paul was different from those men. It was in the worry of his words and the frequency of his letters.

I almost wish that you'd been shipped off to some foreign pocket of the war where you would always be on base and the most I would have to worry about is the baking sun burning you crisp. It would be easier knowing that my Louise was safe. Still, I suppose I must reconcile myself to it.

The one comfort is that it won't be long until I see you again. I think I've finally secured leave. It took every bit of persuading my commanding officer, but I was able to wrangle a week away. A week! Think of all we'll be able to do in that time if you too can secure leave. Dancing in London, dinners in restaurants with white tablecloths, introducing you to my parents. They'll adore you almost as much as I do.

I miss you, darling. I can't wait until we see each other again

Yours,
Paul

Louise sank back into her chair, over the moon with happiness. She'd be seeing Paul again soon. He hadn't mentioned the exact dates—she

knew he wouldn't do that until he'd secured his transportation passes—
but he was coming back to England. She'd have to figure out how to convince Colonel Barker to sign off on her leave, but she was determined. It had been too long since she'd seen him.

"Good news from your pilot?" Vera asked as Louise folded up the letter and stuffed it in its envelope.

"Don't move," Charlie ordered. "You'll ruin my angle for the sketch."

Vera scowled. "I'm not moving. And anyway, Louise has had a letter from Paul."

"He's managed to get leave," Louise said.

"That's wonderful news," said Vera.

"But he's still worried about me being on Ack-Ack," Louise added.

"If he wasn't, I'd be worried about him," said Charlie.

"He wants me to transfer," said Louise. "But of course I'd never do that."

"Hmmm . . ." Vera's lips thinned. Vera, unlike Paul, actually had the familial clout to put in a word and make such a transfer happen. Except she hadn't offered one to Louise. They were a unit, and it hadn't taken much for them to realize that they were better together. If one of them was falling down in her duties, the rest read up with her, reviewing the materials or procedures until they joked they could recite schematics for their respective instruments by heart. None of them had forgotten what Colonel Clovis had told them.

You're smarter than most of the men you'll meet, and I suspect you're tougher too. The Royal Artillery needs you.

"What I wouldn't give for a bath hot enough to boil myself in and a glass of sherry," said Mary, stretching in her seat.

"I still say we should take our next make-and-mend and find the nearest village pub," said Charlie. It was a favorite pastime of their unit, making plans for what they would do with their weekly afternoon off, only to fail to use that time for anything but sleep.

"What about the rules?" Nigella asked, her eyes wide.

The day they'd arrived on base, they'd been told to kiss alcohol and cigarettes goodbye. Shaky hands were a sure way to make errors on the precise instruments controlling the guns. Despite never having been a smoker herself, Louise thought it was unjust that Cartruse, Williams, and Hatfield were allowed to smoke and certainly drank when they were off duty.

"Rules be damned," said Charlie.

"A half-pint or two isn't going to send any of us down the garden path," agreed Vera. "I'd be willing to wager we could get to and from the Pig's Ear in an afternoon, no problems. It would be even faster if we could find some bicycles to borrow."

"I've never ridden a bicycle," said Mary.

"What?" Charlie dropped her pencil in horror. "How can you call yourself an Englishwoman?"

"Girls!" Lizzie called from across the mostly empty canteen. Behind her, she dragged Hatfield, who was blushing hard, by the arm. Cartruse and Williams followed close behind, laughing all the way. "Girls!"

"Why does Hatfield look like he wants the earth to swallow him up? Has Barker finally shouted so loud her passion killers split and he was there to see it?" Charlie muttered.

Louise and Vera stifled laughs, the image of their stern colonel exploding out of the notoriously voluminous ATS-issued bloomers too ridiculous.

Lizzie only let Hatfield go when he was standing right in front of the empty chair at the head of their table. "Hatfield has news," she announced.

"What is it, Sergeant Hatfield?" Nigella asked, her cheeks a pretty pink. They all knew that Nigella, who was the youngest of them and delicate as a doll, had developed a crush on the broad-chested Hatfield the moment she set eyes on him. It made her at once painfully shy but also eager to speak to him at any chance she could get.

"I'm really not supposed to tell, Lizzie," Hatfield said, taking off his cap and twisting it between his hands.

Lizzie stuck a finger in his face. "Don't you back down on me now, Hatfield. It's not fair to the rest of us."

Each of the girls leaned in.

"Go on, Hatfield. It's just us," said Vera, her soft, posh voice pitched perfectly for persuasion.

Hatfield glanced to the other men. Williams puffed on his cigarette so furiously one might've thought he would fall down dead if he stopped, but Cartruse just shrugged.

"I want to know too," Cartruse said.

Hatfield looked around and then sighed. Leaning in, he said in a low voice, "I'm not supposed to know this, but I think we're being shipped out."

"We've got our assignment?" Mary hissed.

"Where?" Louise asked.

"I really can't—"

"Hatfield . . ."

Hatfield shot her a pained look. "London. We're going to London. South of the Thames."

They all sat back at that, stunned. If they'd wanted action, now they had it. Although not as frequent as they'd been in the Blitz last autumn, when the Luftwaffe had struck London on fifty-seven consecutive nights, the raids were still very real. After weeks of shooting at target balloons and markers and wondering when they would finally be allowed to use their skills on actual German planes, B Section was going to be sent right into the belly of the beast.

"Are you sure?" Charlie asked.

"Yes, how can you be certain?" Vera asked.

Cartruse laughed. "Hatfield has himself a bird, doesn't he?"

"I don't understand," said Louise.

"He's been necking with one of the girls in the base's command office. Bet she saw our paperwork come through late yesterday," said Williams around his cigarette.

Louise cast a quick glance at Nigella. Her friend was staring hard at her knitting.

"Why are we only finding out about this now?" Mary asked.

"Because he meets her around the back of the garage at her tea break every afternoon," said Cartruse.

"Her commanding officer likes to take a snooze in his office, and no one notices if she's gone for twenty minutes," said Hatfield.

"Hatfield, you sly dog," said Charlie with a laugh.

"Wait, that means you waited all this time to tell us?" asked Louise.

"And I had to drag him here to do it," said Lizzie.

"No secrets in B Section," said Cartruse, clapping Hatfield on the back.

London. They were going to be sent to London. Yes, it was dangerous, but as Paul had pointed out in all of his recent letters, her entire job was dangerous. And she would be in London. Wonderful, centralized London, where he was planning to start his leave. She wouldn't have to travel to him. It would be so *easy*.

"You look happy, Louise," said Charlie, as the others chattered excitedly amongst themselves.

"I was just thinking that I won't even need to worry about train schedules now when Paul comes," she said.

"It looks as though the ATS is determined to play cupid for you." Vera glanced at Nigella and dropped her voice. "It's a shame I can't say the same for all of us."

"Do you think she'll be okay?" Louise asked. Nigella had started knitting again, but the needles trembled in her hands.

"She'll be right as rain soon enough. A shame her falling for one of her own section though," said Charlie.

"I don't think she's had much experience with men," said Vera, in a way that told Louise that Vera had had more than she might care for.

"She wouldn't, would she, what with her parents shutting her up in Catholic school," said Charlie.

"Well, she has to learn. We all have our hearts broken at some point. It might as well be now," said Vera.

∽

Hatfield's lady friend in the clerk's office proved to be a reliable source of information. In just seventy-two hours, the men and women of B Section, 488 Battery, were on a train from Oswestry to London, headed for the Woolwich Depot, where they would be stationed for the foreseeable future. It was a long, slow journey, with several changes to be made, and rolling into Birmingham as dusk fell, they got their first real look at the devastation the air raids had left behind.

"There are whole houses gone," Mary muttered, her hands braced against the train window.

"What did you expect?" Charlie asked, but the way she shivered when they passed the skeletal remains of buildings told Louise that, for all her bluster, the most outspoken one of their little band was just as affected as the rest of them.

"That's what we're going to London to stop," said Vera with a firm nod. "That's our job."

"My mum wrote when I was in basic training," said Williams, as he rolled a cigarette, then clamped it between his lips. "Said whatever we think we know about the Blitz, it was worse. People buried under buildings. Whole neighborhoods bombed off the face of the earth."

"Oh . . ." Nigella whispered softly, the pain in her voice easy to hear.

"And then even when people think they're safe in a shelter, you never know," Williams continued. "Look at Columbia Road in Shoreditch. Bomb went straight down an air shaft of a shelter. Killed entire families."

"Lay off, Williams," said Hatfield, as Lizzie shot Williams a hard look and looped an arm around Nigella's shoulders. It only made the girl tuck her chin further into her chest.

"Sorry, Nigella," said Williams with a small, crooked smile. "I read too many papers."

"I know Colonel Barker said we need to be tough, but all of those children," said Nigella.

"I know, pet," cooed Lizzie. "I know."

None of them spoke again until the train shuddered to a stop at the platform and the car doors were thrust open, the sound like a gasp of relief. Louise checked the letter from Paul that had come along with one from Kate and another from Da just before they'd loaded up to head to the station. She hadn't had a private moment to read any of them yet, but there was comfort knowing Paul's was tucked securely in her jacket pocket, a piece of him protecting her.

As Louise stepped off the train, her kit bag slid on her back, sending her off-balance. She grabbed for one of the long metal handles on the side, but another force swept her back on her feet. She looked down and found a man's hand around her waist. Glancing back, she saw Cartruse shoot her a rueful grin.

"Can't have one of our predictors out of this war with a broken arm before she even gets to London."

She nodded, and he set her down. Straightening her cap, she readjusted the straps on her shoulders and marched into the station with the others to wait for their train to London.

∽

In basic training, Louise had been deeply jealous of the women who could drop off to sleep at a moment's notice. The most she'd ever been able to manage was to doze in a strange limbo, not entirely awake and yet not sleeping. It was in one of these states, lulled yet kept awake by the methodical rocking of the London train, that she felt the first rays of dawn come through the windows as they approached the city. She rubbed the sleep from her eyes, patted her hair into place, and craned her neck to look out the window.

A tall plume of angry gray smoke billowed to the east, scenting the air like a campfire, except a campfire would've offered comfort. Mixed in this smoke was the acrid, harsh smell of wood, metal, chemicals, and other things she'd rather not think of.

As the train rolled on, she saw not just buildings with partially collapsed walls or missing roofs. What had once been entire blocks were now nothing more than smashed bricks and wood lying in a tangled heap in the middle of the streets. Between gaps in the buildings, she saw an ambulance swerve hard to the right to avoid a crater left by a bomb, and women in tin hats with long brown coats would appear in the hazy light. They were the air raid wardens she'd read so much about. Armed with nothing more than their helmets and a healthy dose of courage, they patrolled the streets, ensuring the blackout was done so no light shone through windows and helped the Germans.

From the seat across from her, with his hat still pulled down over his eyes, Cartruse said, "Won't be easy being here."

"No, it won't," she agreed, wondering for the first time since they'd been told they were coming to London if they were ready. They'd improved so much in training that they'd all arrogantly thought their one little unit could make a huge difference, but faced with the extremity of the destruction to the city, it was hard not to wonder if there was anything left to save.

"Williams was right, even if he goes about it in the wrong way," said Cartruse.

"I know, but does it really do anyone any good—"

"Doesn't it, though? Hearing about why we're all in the middle of this bloody war." He paused. "I'm sorry for cursing."

She laughed softly, mindful of not waking the others. "We shoot planes down together. You can say 'bloody,' Cartruse. And it *is* a bloody war."

"I'm from London, you know," he said, turning his head to look out the window she'd been gazing out of.

"No, I didn't."

In truth, she hardly knew anything about him, because he hadn't exactly been forthright with details. Instead, he'd stood aloof, smoking away and shaking his head at their mistakes until finally they'd made fewer of them. Now, every once in a while, they would all get a "Good job" from him, but little else.

"Where did you grow up?" she asked.

"Over the river in Putney. It's seen its share of bombing, just like everywhere," said Cartruse. "We've been lucky so far. No damage except a few broken windows, but my mum was a wreck the last time I came home on leave. A house four streets over took a direct hit."

"We saw some air raids around Haybourne, but they were hardly anything like this," said Louise.

"It's going to be worse than any of us expected. We'll need to be ready," he said with a shake of his head.

They were going to be stationed in an area of London that had seen some of the worst bombing. Even though the newspapers never showed bodies and the message from the government was one of pulling together and soldiering on, it was impossible to avoid the murmurs. East London had been devastated and although the bombing wasn't as fearsome now that the Blitz was over, the Luftwaffe still flew, trying to hit strategic locations throughout the city. Like the Woolwich Depot they would be defending, with its rota of trains coming in to pick up carriage loads of munitions.

"Well then," she said, pulling her shoulders back, "we will."

He grunted, touched the brim of his cap, and crossed his arms to try to sleep just a little more before they made it to the depot.

11

CARA

It had been three weeks since the trip to dispose of Lenora Robinson's estate, and Cara had been run off her feet sorting, listing, and shipping the contents of the house. And it looked as though it was only going to become busier.

Just that day, the phone on Jock's massive mahogany desk had trilled, and after a few minutes he'd walked out of his office and said, "I hope you enjoy the Cotswolds, Miss Hargraves. We've an appointment at Summerson House in Fairford next Monday morning."

"Another estate?"

His eyes twinkled. "That of a Mr. Nigel Egerton. His father, Bernard Egerton, was a popular Edwardian landscape painter, but his work fell out of fashion in the thirties. Mr. Nigel Egerton's son tells me that his father left him the bulk of the contents of his grandfather's studio. Sharpen your skills, Ms. Hargraves, and remember: F-S-P."

Then Jock had marched out, announcing that he was going out for a celebratory pastry and cappuccino. When he'd returned, he'd placed a steaming cup of Earl Grey on her desk.

It had been a good day.

At five, she slung her purse over her shoulder and called out, "I'm visiting my gran today so I'm off."

"Give Mrs. Warren my regards," said Jock.

On the street, Cara checked her phone. She had more email notifications than she wanted to think about, as well as a handful of texts from Nicole, her old colleague Monica from the events and marketing firm, and a couple London friends. She was just about to answer Nicole when a notification flashed up. It was from Liam. She'd given him her number after they'd run into each other at the pub just in case he needed to reschedule their diary investigation dinner. That he'd actually used it warmed her.

Making progress on our mystery. Think I can connect some dots for you.

Her pulse kicked up as she fired back a quick response:

What did you find?

Almost immediately he started typing:

Best to tell you in person. Fancy stopping by my office?

She stared at the phone. Going to his office felt intimate, like crossing a barrier she'd spent so much time erecting. It had been necessary after Simon. She'd pulled in on herself, walling herself off from any more hurt as she processed what he'd done and accepted the fact that—even without his betrayal—she'd fallen out of love with him long ago.

She shook her head. She was being ridiculous. Liam wasn't her ex-husband. He was just her neighbor, offering to help her with a project because he was kind and as curious as she was. That she liked him . . . Well, she didn't really know what to think about that. Their dinner together could've been an unmitigated disaster, awkward and stilted, because *she'd* felt awkward and uncertain. Instead, he'd made her laugh and she'd relaxed—even enjoyed their dinner-but-not-a-date.

Taking a deep breath, she messaged back:

Tell me where to go.

∽

Cara climbed the creaking, carpeted stairs to the second floor of Salisbury House, where Liam had his office on campus. The receptionist downstairs, a young woman with spiky pink hair and doe eyes, had told her that he might still be with a student. Sure enough, when Cara approached the office with a brass doorplate that read "L. McGown," she could see a young woman scribbling furiously in a notebook as she sat across from Liam.

"It's an issue of trying to do too much with such a limited amount of space," he said. "What you have is a topic for a graduate thesis. What you need is a *focused* topic for a research paper."

"There's so much to be written about the role of women in the church during this time," said the girl, pushing up her cat-eye glasses.

Cara heard Liam's chair creak, and although she couldn't see him, it was easy to imagine him leaning back, hands laced behind his head as he eyed this ambitious student.

"Then, Miss Okafor, I think you've hit on something. Refine your ideas a bit further and hone your argument, and you've got a head start on a chapter for your final thesis. Not bad for your first week back at Barlow."

The student began gathering up her things, so Cara rapped on the door frame. Liam looked up, a smile spreading over his lips when he spotted her.

"You're here already," he said.

"The shop is just in the center of town. Is now a good time?" She glanced from him to Miss Okafor.

"Yes, yes. Let me know if you have any further questions," he said to his student.

Cara stepped back to let the young woman out and then slipped inside the warm, comfortable office. There were already little personal touches: a photograph of him with three other men on top of a snow-covered mountain, a black baseball cap with an orange bill and a stylized "SF" embroidered in the same shocking color, a stack of Moleskine notebooks teetering on the edge of the desk. Every inch of wall space was taken up by already-filled bookcases, and his desk was a study in controlled clutter. Liam looked happy here, she decided. At home.

"Close the door, would you?" he asked as he flicked on the plug for an electric teakettle set up on a bookshelf. "If it's open, students tend to come crashing in. Tea?"

"Yes, please. I'm surprised you're already seeing students. I thought lectures only just started."

"They did," he said, dropping a tea bag into a blue stoneware pot with a chipped spout. "My predecessor left me some notes on some of his stars, and Miss Okafor was among them. She has ambitions to get her doctorate one day.

"Now . . ." He let his hands hover over the stacks of paper before snatching up a manila folder. "Here we are. I still haven't identified who our mystery diarist was, but we're closer. How far are you in your reading?"

She laughed. "When you ask it like that, I feel like I'm back in school."

The tips of his ears turned pink. "Sorry, force of habit."

"It's okay. I liked it," she said, before blushing herself, because the way she said it made it sound as though she liked him as well. Quickly she added, "When I fell asleep reading yesterday, her section had just arrived in London."

He nodded. "Then you'll already know that the white lanyard in our girl's photo means that she was attached to the Royal Artillery as part of the Ack-Ack Command. Those mixed batteries were sent all over Britain and the Continent at various stages in the war, and the ones sent to London would've been in place to try to defend key depots, artilleries, and factories, as well as the East London docks."

"She said she was stationed at the Woolwich Depot," said Cara.

He nodded. "South of the Thames. It was one of the key distribution points for munitions to and from the factories operating in that area of London, not to mention for ferrying troops to and from the capitol. It sustained serious damage during the first stages of the Blitz in September 1940 and was hit several times afterward. As you can imagine, it was a valuable asset for the British, so the Luftwaffe did its best to blow it up."

"She names some of the other women in her unit. If we can find them in the ATS or RA records, we should be able to find her through process of elimination, right?"

"You read my mind," said Liam, spinning in his chair to pour boiling water into the teapot as soon the kettle clicked off. "If there's one thing the military is good at, it's keeping personnel records. My colleague Felix is on sabbatical doing some research for a book at the Imperial War Museums' archives. He drove a hard bargain, but he said he'll look for us."

"What did you offer in return?" she asked.

"I'm picking up one of his Western Civ rotations next year," said Liam cheerfully. "Now, about Paul, our flier. Finding him may prove a little more straightforward. Costal Command had four Pauls on base at Saint Trebelzue in February 1941. Sergeant Paul Stephen Jackson. Flight Lieutenant Paul Edward Bolton. Flight Lieutenant Paul Charles Letchley, and Flight Captain Paul Harrow Yarlow."

Cara frowned. "She said he was an officer, so the sergeant is out."

"So either Bolton, Letchley, or Yarlow is our mysterious romantic pilot. I'll see about pulling their service records. Do you take milk?" Liam asked.

She nodded. "Enough to make the tea the color of a ginger biscuit."

She watched him fix her a cup of tea. When he handed it to her, his fingers brushed hers, and a little frisson of interest fluttered in her stomach. Their eyes locked for a second, but then Liam looked away, leaving her to wonder if there'd been anything there at all.

"There's something else," he said, pulling a laptop across the desk and typing in a password. "I wasn't able to find any online record of a shop called Bakeford's in Cornwall, so I reached out to a local historian." He clicked the the track pad a few times. "No email back yet, but we'll keep our fingers crossed."

She looked down at her perfect cup of tea with just the right amount of milk, suddenly a little overwhelmed at his enthusiasm and all he'd done. "This is so much more than I'd have been able to do on my own."

"You would've figured out how to go about it. I'm just used to mucking about in archives and shamelessly calling in favors." He paused to take a sip of tea and then set his cup down carefully. "Can I ask why?"

"Why what?"

"Why do you want to figure out who wrote the diary?" he asked.

"I want to return it to its owner or her family if she's no longer alive."

He raised his brows. "If that's all you want, you could hand it over to an archive and let them do the work."

"No," she said quickly. "No, I couldn't do that."

"Then what?"

"It's not enough that it's a mystery?" she asked.

"In my experience, people with busy lives don't spend their time chasing down questions like this. They might be interested. They might even have good intentions, but it's too much work."

"Why do you say I'm busy?" she asked.

"You said yourself that you fell asleep while reading. Plus, your lights are hardly off before midnight, and you're out the door before most people wake up." Sheepishly he added, "Rufus means I have to be out at all hours. I notice things."

"Maybe I'm just trying to distract myself," she said.

"Or maybe there's something about the diary that you're drawn to," he suggested.

She worried her lip, considering this, wondering what to tell him. All of it, she realized as he sat there, patient and open to whatever part of herself she was willing to give him. He was helping her. She owed it to him to try to explain why.

"I told you my gran was in the ATS. She never talks about it. We're so close, and she's a wonderful storyteller, but this one part of her life is closed off to me. When I first realized what I'd found, I'd hoped that the diary would bridge this gap that's always been between us—even more so since my mum died," she added, thinking about the fight she'd overheard.

"It didn't work," he said.

She shook her head. "Gran still won't talk about it. All I know is the year she joined and that she was demobbed two months after VE Day."

"I could pull her service records too," he offered. "It would be as simple as searching the right databases, since you know her vital details."

She considered the idea but swiftly rejected it. It would feel like a betrayal of Gran's confidence for Cara to go snooping around in her past without consent. Besides, she knew that without Gran's own account, a service record would just be a series of dates and unit assignments. The picture would be incomplete.

"You might need to prepare yourself for the possibility that she may never tell you," said Liam gently. "It might be too painful. She could've lost someone."

"But that's part of what I don't understand. She's talked about the boys and girls she used to play with in the schoolyard who didn't come back from from the fighting. I've heard those stories."

"She might be protecting you," he said.

Her laugh was sharper than she'd meant it to be. "Yes, well, that's what everyone I'm close to has done for the last two years, and I'm tired of it."

She *was* tired of it. She'd fallen apart after her parents' death in her own quiet way, swept away by her grief. But then she'd woken up. She'd come out on the other side stronger.

"What's your gran like?" he asked, as though sensing the brittleness of her nerves in that moment.

"Fabulous beyond words."

He laughed. "Really?"

"She's ninety-two and her life is exactly how she wants it to be. When she finally decided to sell her home, she didn't do it because of her health or because it was too much for her. She did it so that I wouldn't be hit with death duties, because I'll be the one to inherit it. She picked her flat in the retirement village she lives in. She has a regular driver pick her up for standing dinners in and around Barlow three times a week, and she's recently rediscovered ballroom dancing, although she admits the Latin dances are too difficult on her hips these days."

"I'd love to meet her," he said.

She looked up quickly. "You would?"

"She sounds extraordinary."

Touched, she looked at her watch. "If we go now I expect she'll make us a cocktail."

Liam barked a laugh. "Well, how I could say no to that?"

"Good, but first, we have a stop to make."

~

With Liam following in his car, Cara drove first to the market to pick up a packet of Tunnock's Teacakes and then on to Gran's place, mulling over all the different lines of inquiry Liam had set into motion. There were still so many questions to answer about the diarist, and Gran's unwillingness to share her own story only made her more motivated to make sure it ended up in the right hands. There was a family out there who deserved to know about the bravery of the unnamed woman who'd defied her family to join up and become a gunner girl.

She and Liam parked side by side and headed to the front entrance of Widcote Manor. The four-story redbrick mansion had once belonged to a family that had made its fortune in soap, but it had been converted to flats about ten years ago. They paused only long enough at the reception desk tucked into a corner of the elegant entryway for the concierge to call Gran before they headed up.

The lift doors had just opened when the door to Gran's flat flew open.

"Hello, my dear!" Gran trilled. "I was thrilled when Randall phoned to say you were downstairs. You caught me just as I was about to make myself a sidecar. Cocktails are always better with company, and I see you've brought a gentleman with you."

Cara exchanged a look with Liam before kissing Gran on the cheek. "This is Liam McGown. He's my neighbor."

"Delighted to meet you, Liam," said Gran, stretching out her hand.

Liam took it, his eyes twinkling. "Mrs. Warren, your granddaughter told me you were extraordinary, but she clearly undersold you."

"What excellent taste in neighbors you have, Cara," said Gran, and Cara knew that as soon as she was home she could expect a call demanding to know more about the admittedly handsome man.

"You're rather turned out for a random Wednesday evening," she said.

"Do you like my outfit?" Gran asked, modeling her wide-legged ivory trousers. They were the same color as the silk flower tucked behind her ear, and she had paired them with a muted gold ruffled blouse and slim, pointed-toe flats, topped off by a stack of gold bangles on her slim arm. Gran looked ready to sip Negronis on a sun-drenched balcony in the French Riviera. "I have a date with Peter from flat twelve at seven. He's seventy-seven and a widower."

"You're robbing the cradle," said Cara, pretending to be scandalized as she handed over the box of tea cakes.

"I know. Isn't it wonderful?" Gran's eyes flicked over to Liam. "You know, this one is better looking than Simon."

Cara choked a horrified laugh but Liam dipped his head in a game little bow. "I'm glad I meet with your approval."

"It would be difficult for you to do worse than that lout. Do you drink?" Gran asked as she glided into the flat's generous sitting room, depositing the confections on a cherry sideboard as she went.

"I do," said Liam.

Gran turned, her hand poised over a glass-and-metal cocktail shaker. "Spirits?"

"I'm an academic. I'll drink almost anything you put in front of me," he said.

"Better and better," said Gran.

Liam wandered over to the photo-covered sideboard while Cara sank down onto the sofa that faced the wide bay windows and Gran made the drinks.

"You were stunning," Liam said, picking up the photo of Gran and her fellow ATS girls.

"I *am* stunning." Gran tossed the correction over her shoulder.

"Who are the others in the photo with you?" he asked.

"Melanie Lovell and Janet Whittacre. They were the stationed with me."

"Where was that?" Liam asked.

Gran raised a snow-white brow at Cara as she passed around drinks. "As I told my granddaughter before, it hardly bears mentioning."

"Gran," said Cara, "you know I found a diary."

"Of another ATS girl, yes."

"I told you I want to figure out who its owner was. Do you know why?" she asked.

Gran took a long sip of her drink but said nothing.

"It's because somewhere there's a woman like you who has been separated from this diary for years," Cara continued.

"Maybe that's how she wants it," said Gran.

"But what if it isn't?"

Gran's lips thinned. "She's most likely dead. Even if she was lucky enough to make it out of the war, there aren't many people who live to be my age."

"What about her family?" Cara asked. "Don't you think they deserve to have this? It's a part of their history. I'd want to know. I—" She cleared her throat. "I *do* want to know."

Gran's expression softened a touch, but she still stood with her arms crossed protectively over her chest.

Not knowing when she would build up the courage again to ask, Cara forced out the uncomfortable words. "I want to know why you won't talk about the war . . . and I want to know why you argued with Mum about it just before she died."

All of the blood drained out of Gran's face, and for a moment Cara thought she might faint. Liam must've as well, because he put his glass down and took a step forward, but Gran put her hand up. "I'm fine."

"I overheard Mum on the phone," she pushed, despite Gran's discomfort. "She said that you'd kept something from her. Something that was her right to know. And she mentioned the war. Why?"

"We all did things we aren't proud of," said Gran, her voice almost a whisper.

"What do you mean?"

"I made a choice," said Gran.

Cara couldn't explain why, but unease pricked along the back of her neck. "What kind of choice?"

Gran shook her head, almost as though she was coming out of a fog. "Do you know, I think I made that sidecar a little too strong. I'm suddenly feeling rather light-headed."

"Gran . . ."

Gran tried to put on her best innocent look, but Cara didn't believe it for a moment. They'd come this far. She wasn't going away without at least something.

"Tell me what happened," she said. "I hate that there's a secret lying between the two of us." *I feel like you're hiding something from me, just like he hid things from me.*

Gran threw up her hands. "This is ridiculous. Your mother and I argued—mothers and daughters do sometimes. She found some photographs when we were sorting through the things in my house before my move, and she wanted to know more about the war. I wouldn't tell her, and she spun the whole thing into some dastardly secret, when all I want is to not have to think about some very painful experiences I went through more than seventy years ago. Is that so difficult to understand?"

Yes, because none of this explained why Mum had said it was her right to know, but Cara could tell that Gran was stretched to the breaking point.

Still, she said, "I just want to know something. Anything. It's important to me because you're important to me."

Gran closed her eyes and let out a defeated huff. "Do you still have the safe from your parents' house?"

Cara nodded. "It's in storage in London. Why?"

"Inside there's a box. You might not have thought anything of it when you were going through their things, but it's the most important thing in my life. I gave it to your parents to keep safe during the move, and since they died I haven't had the heart to ask for it."

Cara could certainly understand that.

"The box contains the photographs your mother found. Bring that, and I can show them to you, although I'm sure you'll find them as unextraordinary as they actually are." Gran looked up all of a sudden, as though remembering that Liam was there with them. "And you go with her. I don't want her doing this alone."

"Gran, Liam has things to do and—"

"I'd be honored to accompany your granddaughter," he said.

Gran tilted her head back a little as though she was trying to hold back the tears that shimmered in her eyes. "You should be."

Cara leaned over to kiss Gran on the cheek, trying not to regret her pushiness. "We'll leave you to your date. Love you to the moon . . ."

"And back, dearest," said Gran. "Thank you again for the tea cakes."

"It was a pleasure to meet you, Mrs. Warren," said Liam, setting his drink down on a coaster.

"Call me Iris."

"I will," he said.

"And be smart and ask my granddaughter out before she gets it into her head to start dating again. Then she'll be beating men off with a stick."

Cara practically shoved Liam into the hall and stuck her head back in through the open door. "You do realize you're becoming one of those embarrassing grannies people whine about, don't you?"

Gran's laughter echoed down the hallway all the way to the lift. When they were safely inside, Cara snuck a glance at Liam and said, "Well, now you've met Gran."

He gave a single laugh. And then another. And then, all at once, he was doubled over at the waist, laughing so hard that he had to take his glasses off and swipe at his eyes. "I like her. Very, very much."

Cara sighed. "Everyone does. When we were at uni, Nicole used to go round to Gran's for tea when I was working. The two of them together are a public menace." She paused. "You really don't have to come to the storage locker with me."

"I don't think Iris would ever forgive me if I didn't go."

The doors dinged. He offered her his arm, and she took it.

"It's just that she worries. After the divorce, it seemed only logical to store my things there because I was already renting the space," she said.

And there her things had stayed, an archive of her parents' deaths and her failure of a marriage. Every piece of furniture that had stood in her home in Chiswick carried the weight of memories. She could recall sweetly tender moments and painful fights had on the sitting room sofa. The kitchen table had a gouge mark in the finish where Simon had slammed down a bottle after she told him she'd been to see her solicitor. To go back and see all of those things again . . . Well, she wasn't entirely sure how it would make her feel, and she'd worked so hard to put him behind her.

Liam tugged at his arm so that she was drawn in a little closer as they walked. "I want to help. What are you doing on Saturday?"

"Working," she said, pulling a face, thinking of the stack of invoices and backlogged shipping she was still slogging through since the Old Vicarage clear-out had taken so much longer than expected.

"Sunday?" he asked.

"I'm free Sunday."

"Then it's a diary-inspection field trip," he said, as they finally reached their cars. "It seems silly that we brought two cars here. I'll drive on Sunday if you like."

"Okay."

"Well, I should to take my maniac of a dog out for a walk," he said, taking a step back.

"Then I'll see you around soon."

He nodded and stuffed his hands into his pockets as she climbed into her car. She stuck her key in the ignition but sat and watched as he drove away. It wasn't until his car disappeared from sight that she realized they'd walked all the way from her Gran's flat to their cars, arm in arm, and it hadn't bothered her one bit.

4 August 1941

Three letters, and one of them is so exciting I'm almost shaking! But I'll start with Kate first because it's been an age since I've heard from her.

28 July 1941

Darling Louise,

I've made it to Cairo. (That should make it through the censors because it's no great secret that the army is here.) Do you remember how I'd thought Greece would be all Mediterannian glamour and was so disappointed when it was nothing but army camps and hours of work? My predictions about Cairo were more accurate. I've never been hotter in my entire life. The sun rises and just sits there in the sky, baking all of us. If I stay out for even a moment, my nose goes bright red. It's horrible.

There's no NAAFI here, but in the evenings the boys transform the canteen. Some nights it's a cinema. Others it's a dance hall. One sergeant spent some time visiting family in Kansas City before enlisting last year, and he's mad to teach us all how to jitterbug. It's great fun, and I'm not half bad at it.

I have some friends here, but I miss you desperately. I sometimes wonder what would've happened if we'd been assigned to the same unit, but then you're doing ack-ack. I don't think I'd ever have the nerve for that.

Yours always,
Kate

2 August 1941

Lou Lou,

I woke up in the middle of the night and couldn't fall back asleep, so I've come downstairs to write you. I had a dream that something happened to you on the battlefield. Your unit was hit by machine-gun fire from a plane flying low over you. Instead of sheltering behind a concrete barrier like the men of your unit, you ran out try to drag one of your friends to safety and were hit yourself.

I know you've done your best in your letters to reassure me that nothing like this will happen, but I know that the Luftwaffe doesn't just have bombers. There are fighters, too, that try to take out the spotlights and the anti-aircraft guns. You're never going to be entirely safe. No one is.

No father wants to let his daughter think that he's scared when he's *the one who is supposed to pick you up when you fall and kiss scraped knees, but I'm afraid for you. I'm also incredibly proud of you. Your mother thinks you joined the ATS because you were angry about your pilot, but I want to believe that some part of your decision was because you knew you had to do something to help end this war. That's why, even though I wake up in a cold sweat when I have dreams like the one tonight, I know what you're doing is more important than anything I could have asked of you if you'd stayed in Haybourne.*

Your ever-loving
Da

Da is wrong, but so is Mum. When I ran away from home, I wasn't angry about Paul. I was scared that if I didn't leave Haybourne then, I would never get out. But now it's more. Now I'm a part of something important, something that matters, and Vera, Charlie, Mary, Nigella, and Lizzie all rely on me. No one's ever needed me to be anything other than a shopgirl before. Now I'm a gunner girl.

I've saved the best for last. Paul has written me—my first letter in almost a week.

30 July 1941

My darling,

It's taken moving heaven and earth and perhaps the moon too, but I've finally done it. My leave is scheduled, my transit passes are in order, and I'll finally be able to kiss you again on the first of September.

It was a struggle to set down the date. My commanding officer seems hell-bent on ruining every lovers' reunion, but even he couldn't argue with RAF regulations. He had to grant me leave, so I'll be making my way to Dover and then onto the fastest train I can find to London.

*Nothing will make me happier than seeing your beautiful face—
even if it'll be a shock to see you in drab ATS khaki instead of that
bright red dress of yours. There are so many things I want to tell you.
Things I've left unsaid for too long.*

I'm counting down the days.

Yours always,
Paul

*I cannot wait until the first of September, because I also have things
to say to him. I started to fall for him in Haybourne, but it was our letters
that made me realize how deep my love had grown. We hope, we quarrel,
we dream, we despair. And soon we'll see each other again.*

12

LOUISE

The sun was setting when Louise let her pack slide off and hit the bare wood floor of the room that would be her home for the foreseeable future. They'd bumped along cratered and debris-strewn streets in a canvas-sided truck, stopping first at the Charlton Barracks, where Hatfield, Cartruse, and Williams had climbed out. They would be billeted there, but the girls were two blocks away from the Woolwich Depot, in a five-story redbrick building that before the war had been a shuttered hospital. Nigella, Lizzie, and Mary had the first room off the stairs, and Vera, Charlie, and Louise had been assigned the one right next door. Now, taking in the Spartan look of the place, Louise could see that it had been hurriedly fitted out to cram three ATS women into two bunks and a cot that blocked the door unless it was angled just so.

"At least it's warm," said Charlie, laying out the three cushions that would form her ATS-issued mattress. Louise had learned to call the cushions "biscuits" during her first week of basic training, which was also when she had learned that the only way to keep the bloody things from slipping apart in her sleep was to lash them together with a spare blanket. If there was one.

"I hope it's warm," said Vera with a laugh, while she tugged at the heavy blackout curtains that covered every window in London to deter the Luftwaffe. "It's August."

Charlie smiled. "You never know in London, right, Louise?"

She shrugged. "I wouldn't know—I've never been."

Vera dropped her hairbrush on the floor with a clatter. "You've never— We've been training together for four months. How did you never mention it?"

"I thought your fellow was from London," said Charlie.

"He is, but we met in Cornwall, remember?"

"Well, that settles it," said Vera. "The first free afternoon we have, we'll take you for a grand tour of the city. Buckingham Palace, Westminster Abbey."

"Saint Paul's and the Embankment," Charlie chipped in. "There's so much to see, even if half of it's been bombed."

Louise's smile suddenly became a little watery at her friends' enthusiasm. The months of hard work, huddling around an electric fire in a little hut on the edge of a training field before the air raid siren sounded for their training drills, had bonded her to these women in a way she never would've expected. She missed Kate, but in Vera, Charlie, Lizzie, Nigella, and Mary, she'd found a different kind of kinship. Her father had been right in his last letter: they were all in danger, but at least they were in it together.

"I would love that," she said.

"Of course, the moment your flier comes to town you'll forget all about us," Charlie teased.

"Have you had any word from Paul?" asked Vera.

The smile she'd been holding in since Cartruse had fallen asleep and she'd finally caved to the desire to read Paul's letter broke free. "He's coming on the first of September."

"That's wonderful!" cried Vera.

"Finally," said Charlie with a laugh.

Louise fell back on her bunk, resting her head on one of the biscuits.

"His letter came just before we left base. If our train had been any earlier I'd have missed it."

"It would've been forwarded," said Charlie.

Louise smiled to herself, knowing that Charlie wouldn't have understood why the letter was important *now*. That night they would go on duty for the first time. They'd no longer be doing exercises on a training field.

"I wanted to read it when we arrived, but you were all asleep and it was so horrible seeing all of the destruction here. I opened it just before we pulled into the station, and I'm so glad I did. I can't tell you how relieved I am that he's finally coming," said Louise. "Sometimes I wondered if we'd ever see each other again."

"I suppose letters are a poor substitute," said Vera.

"They are," Louise said. "I want all of you to meet him. I think you'll adore him."

"I suspect he'll be much more interested in spending time alone with you than in meeting us," said Charlie with a laugh.

"Private Charlotte Wilkes, I don't know what you're implying," said Louise primly. She caught Vera's eyes and grinned, and they all burst out laughing.

A loud wail pierced the air, drowning their merriment. An air raid siren. Immediately, they flew into action.

"Those bloody Nazis can't even wait for us to get settled?" Charlie grouched as she dove for her kit.

Louise tore at the tunic skirt she'd worn for the journey from Oswestry and yanked on the trousers that were her battle dress. "What time is it?"

"Late enough," said Vera. "It was almost dark when I did the blackout."

Moving with the practiced skill of women who'd dressed under pressure countless times before, they yanked on their clothes and were in the hall in a minute flat. Nigella, Mary, and Lizzie were just leaving their room, their tin helmets jammed under their arms as they tightened jacket belts and tugged on sleeves.

Colonel Barker, who had traveled down on the same train but had been invited into a separate compartment, strode through the doors that led to the stairs. "Look alive, ladies. We need to be to those guns in less than five minutes!"

The girls fell into an automatic, side-by-side stride and marched their way to the stairs. When Colonel Barker threw open the doors, chaos greeted them. The slap of leather soles on the steps mixed with the excited chatter of women's voices in a deafening cacophony. Uniformed women pushed and shoved their way down, heading for the reinforced concrete shelter in the basement they'd been told of upon arrival.

"Hey!" shouted a blond woman next to Louise. When Louise turned, the blonde's eyes landed on the red and black bow and arrow of the Ack-Ack Command badge each girl had sewn to her sleeve and her expression changed.

"You're one of those gunner girls?" the blond woman asked. When Louise nodded, the woman gripped her arm. "You go shoot those bastards down."

Louise's mouth went dry. This was no training exercise. It was war.

Her nerves jumped in her stomach as Colonel Barker marched them through the streets to their post, a stout, sturdy-looking building just outside the north wall of the Woolwich Depot. Up five flights of stairs they went in the blackout-enforced darkness. When finally they pushed through a reinforced metal door to the rooftop, the silhouette of the massive gun was just visible in the waning light of the moon.

"Where are the men?" asked Lizzie, looking around as she moved to check the Sperry.

"The Charlton Barracks are half a mile away," squeaked Nigella, her hands trembling as she prepped her station at the height and range finder across from Charlie.

"All safe and sound away from Woolwich while we're stuck next to a veritable powder keg?" said Mary with a laugh. "Sounds like those three."

Charlie grinned. "The RA might have to finally let a woman fire one of these guns."

"Private Wilkes," Barker snapped.

"Apologies, Colonel Barker. I'm just excited to finally be shooting at something other than a flag pulled behind a plane," said Charlie cheerfully.

"Women do not *shoot*," said Colonel Barker. "That is an order from Parliament."

"But we do everything else," Vera muttered under her breath.

The metal door crashed against the wall. Cartruse, Williams, Hatfield, and Captain Jones, the RA officer who oversaw B Section, poured out of the dark stairwell. They were accompanied by a man none of them had ever seen before, in a perfectly pressed uniform, and Colonel Barker sharpened her posture and saluted the newcomer. "Sir."

"So these are the gunner girls," said the man, as though not entirely sure what to make of six women in trousers. "I'm Colonel Nealson. You were supposed to be briefed tomorrow, but there's no time for that. You were also supposed to have a radio operator in the building. No time for that either. We've reports of a formation of fighters and bombers approaching from the Thames Estuary. They were just spotted over Dartford."

Colonel Nealson's eyes narrowed. "I have three other sections protecting this depot. Some of the best men in the RA are on those guns, and they've sweated blood during the Blitz and after. Now they're sending mixed batteries with *women*. It's General Sir Pile's decision, not mine, and I hope it isn't the wrong one."

Afraid we'll faint at the first sight of an airplane? Louise's anger smothered her nerves, and she clamped her teeth tight to keep the words from slipping out. Back in Haybourne, it never would've occurred to her to talk back, but now she had the confidence of months of ATS and Royal Artillery training under her belt. She and her unit were sharp, shrewd, and well trained, and they weren't going to let anyone tell them they weren't ready.

"Any questions?" Colonel Nealson asked, turning for the door before he'd even finished speaking.

"Yes, sir," said Charlie.

Reluctantly he turned back. "Private . . . ?"

"Wilkes, sir."

"Yes, Private Wilkes."

"If we've no radio operator, when will we know to stand down, sir?" asked Charlie.

"Start shooting when you see an enemy plane. Stop shooting when you hear the siren to stand down. It usually comes at dawn. Do you think you can manage that, ladies?" Colonel Nealson asked.

Colonel Barker stepped forward. "Yes, sir."

Louise's eyes narrowed as the man and his polished boots retreated—he was Melchen from Leicester all over again.

"Get to your places," Colonel Barker snapped, as Captain Jones ordered Cartruse to go through his checks.

"Did you hear that?" Cartruse asked Louise, while she went over her predictor's controls one more time, determined not to botch anything on her first real engagement.

"What?" she asked, straining her ears against the sounds of her section preparing. Was that the drone of a bomber engine? From somewhere along the banks of the Thames, spotlights snapped on, flooding the London sky with harsh white light.

"He thinks you gunner girls aren't up to snuff," said Cartruse.

She steeled herself for the moment he took the connection they'd shared on the train and ground it under his heel.

"Too bad you lot are going to make him look like a damn fool," he said in a low voice.

Louise blinked, then a grin spread across her face. "That's insubordination, Gunner."

"That's the truth, that is," he said.

"Dornier Do 217 two points due east," Mary shouted, and the last of Louise's trepidation fell away, well-trained instinct taking over.

"Engage!" Captain Jones shouted.

Nigella and Charlie rotated the height and range finder until they spotted the plane through their viewfinders and began to turn the complicated series of dials on the instrument.

"Read," Charlie shouted.

"Read," Nigella shouted a half second later.

Louise plugged the data into the predictor, the dials bouncing as the gun rotated to track the progress of the plane.

"Fuse one-nine," Lizzie called out.

"Fire!" Captain Jones ordered.

The gun roared as it fired off the heavy shell that, if their aim was true, would blow a hole in the siding of the German bomber. They all held their breaths, eyes trained on the plane, and two seconds later a flash of orange blazed through the sky.

"Just left of the wing!" Mary yelled out from behind her high-powered binoculars.

Section B cheered. It wasn't a direct hit, but it was enough to force the bomber to bank and throw it off course.

"No celebrating yet," Captain Jones ordered. "I want a direct hit."

"Arado Ar 240," Mary said. "Three of them."

The sound of machine-gun fire ricocheted off buildings, and Louise's pulse began to pound in her throat.

"Which one are we going for, Rogers?" Williams asked Mary, grunting as he and Hatfield reloaded the gun.

"I've got a read on the front Arado!"

"Captain?" Charlie prompted.

"Focus on the bomber," Captain Jones ordered. "Those bombs will do a lot more damage than that machine-gun fire."

"Only if they don't fire at us," muttered Vera.

"Read on the Dornier," Nigella called out.

"Read," Charlie echoed.

Louise went to work setting the predictor. The gun swung around, tracking just in front of the bomber.

"Fuse one-seven!" Lizzie shouted.

"Fire," ordered Captain Jones.

They all held their breath as the shell roared toward the plane. But their aim was off. It exploded feet from the nose of the bomber, doing nothing more than sending a wash of heat over the glass-covered cockpit.

"Damn," Cartruse muttered.

"Engage! Don't let him drop those bombs," Jones shouted as the men reloaded the gun.

"Read!" Nigella shouted.

Machine-gun fire rang out closer this time, and the windows of the building across the street exploded as bullets smashed through the glass. B Section dropped to the ground, their hands over their tin helmets, even though they knew that nothing would stop a German bullet fired from a fighter at this range.

"Up, girls," Colonel Barker ordered, her voice wavering as though she didn't quite believe her own command. "If I see you hit the ground one more time—"

A tower of water exploded into the air as the first of the Dornier's bombs fell into the Thames. Four more explosions followed in quick succession, rattling the roof they were standing on and stealing Louise's breath. A flash of fire and a plume of smoke bloomed through the night air, and where a building had once stood on a corner less than a quarter mile away, there was a void. Smoke billowed through the empty shell of a building as fire licked at the neighboring structures. Even from the rooftop, Louise could hear the whine of a fire engine.

Louise's eyes met Vera's across the predictor box, the two women frozen for a moment with the reality of being in the middle of a real bombing. They could be killed at any moment, cut down by machine-gun fire or blown up by a falling bomb or crushed as the building collapsed. Then her eyes snapped to her commanding officer. Colonel Barker, the loud, brash woman who'd given them no ground during training, was slumped against a wall, pale in the faint moonlight.

"My God. My God," Colonel Barker muttered over and over as Captain Jones went to deal with Williams and Hatfield, who were arguing in heated whispers over something.

"Colonel?" Louise prompted, trying to snap the woman back to attention.

The woman's eyes were unfocused, terrified. "An entire building . . ."

"Colonel Barker," Louise hissed.

Her commanding officer lifted her eyes and met Louise's. "That was a block of flats. We passed it on the way in."

"I know," said Louise, forcing down the bile rising in her throat.

"There were children playing outside."

"I know."

Colonel Barker shuddered. "I can't—I can't—"

Gritting her teeth and breathing the acrid smell of smoke through her nose, Louise swung around. "Mary, what's the read?"

Mary ripped her eyes away from Colonel Barker. "Still in sights."

"Nigella, Charlie. What do we have?" she shouted.

The two women sprang into action.

"Read!"

"Read!"

"Fuse one-six!"

"Waiting on your call, Captain," said Catruse.

"Engage, Gunner," Jones ordered.

The sound of the gun firing ricocheted off the surrounding buildings, and they all held their breath. This time, the shell exploded right on the tail of the plane. Black smoke streamed off of it, a white ghost in the spotlight.

"Come on, come on," Louise muttered, her eyes fixed on the hobbled plane.

Slowly, the pilot rounded and pointed the nose back out to the east.

"Yes!" Hatfield and Williams shouted as Lizzie jumped up and down.

A hand fell heavy on Louise's shoulder. "Good instincts, Keene," said Jones over the clang of the gun being loaded again.

She glanced at Vera who, with raised brows, tilted her head to indicate over Louise's shoulder. Colonel Barker was slumped, legs splayed out on the ground, a pool of vomit to her side.

~

The Luftwaffe kept them at work until a rosy dawn broke out over the capitol just a few minutes after five o'clock. Captain Jones, who had ordered Colonel Barker off the roof in disgust, had deputized Louise to march the girls back to their billet. In truth, it was more scramble for sanctuary than march. The wind had picked up around three, chilling them all through despite the summer season, and by the time they poured into the canteen Louise was grateful for the mug of tea one of the orderlies shoved into her hand.

"What a night," Mary said, stretching her neck this way and that.

"Ten hours straight," said Vera. "And all of that machine-gun fire."

Charlie glanced around before leaning in. "Did you see Colonel Barker?"

"What happened to her?" Nigella asked.

"She's never seen combat," said Charlie with a shrug. "Cartruse told me he overheard Captain Jones talking to another officer about it. He was worried back in Oswestry."

"They should promote Louise," said Lizzie. "You jumped right in."

Louise blushed, pleased to hear the compliment. "I just got us back on track. You all know what you're doing."

"Bet we showed that Colonel Nealson," said Charlie, with a grin. "B Section with two direct hits and five planes turned around."

As they sat drinking their tea and nibbling on biscuits, the adrenaline of the night started to leave them. Louise could see the moment each of them hit a wall of exhaustion.

"Time for bed, I think," she said as the canteen began to fill up with ATS girls readying themselves for their day's work.

"I feel like Dracula," Mary moaned.

"You'll start looking like him too if you're not careful," Lizzie teased.

Louise hung back for a moment, smiling as the girls bickered and made their way out of the canteen. Finally it was only her and Vera.

"You know, Lizzie's right. You should put in for a promotion as soon as you can," said her friend.

Louise scoffed. "I'm hardly colonel material."

Vera raised her brows. "They made Colonel Barker a colonel, and look what happened. You need to be able to do more than shout during training exercises. You need steel."

Louise shook her head. "I'm just a girl from Haybourne."

"And I'm just a girl who grew up in a military family who knows what that sort of leadership looks like." Vera yawned. "Come on, let's get to bed before Charlie starts snoring."

"I should write to Paul first," Louise said, hauling herself up from the table.

But by the time she made it to their room, she was half asleep and fell into bed, promising herself that she'd write him when she woke up.

13

CARA

The coffee in Cara's mug trembled a little until she clamped her free hand around it and raised it to her lips to ward off the chill that radiated from her parlor windows. That Sunday morning, sleepy Elm Road was quiet except for a runner clad in black tights and a shocking-pink jacket, her thin black braids swinging across her back.

I should start exercising again.

Cara dismissed the thought with a snort. These days she was more likely to collapse into bed with sore muscles from hauling inventory around Jock's shop than she was to pull out a yoga mat or lace up her running shoes.

Out of the corner of her eye, she saw the door to Liam's cottage swing open. It was time. He was driving her to London, back to the storage facility that held all the artifacts of her past life. There would be no more delays. She'd already set too many things in motion.

She took a final sip of coffee before walking back to the kitchen and depositing the mug in the sink to rinse later. Then she gathered up her black leather jacket and slid on a pair of gray canvas flats.

Hitching her purse over her shoulder, she locked the front door and took a breath. Then she mustered the most convincing smile she could and waved to Liam.

"Good morning!" he called, catching sight of her as he rounded the short hedge between their drives. "Still up for our adventure?"

Not quite. On one hand, she was eager to retrieve Gran's box, desperate as she was for any scrap of information about her family's past and the secret that hung between them. At the same time, the thought of opening up the locker containing what was left of her parents' life and her marriage was daunting.

Still, she forced herself to smile. "I'm ready."

Liam's brow knit. He already knew her well enough to know that she was lying. "If you don't want to go—"

"No." She lifted her chin. "We should. I need to do this, and . . . I'd rather have company."

"Okay then."

He sprinted over to his car and opened the passenger door for her. Touched by the gesture, she climbed in and promised herself that everything would be fine.

∼

Everything was *not* fine.

The closer they got to London, the tighter Cara gripped the side of Liam's passenger seat. All through the hour-and-a-half drive, she'd fought to keep her nerves from boiling over, but as they drove past the sign for her old neighborhood, her anxiety rose. Now, in front of the building she'd never wanted to visit again, her blood pounded in her ears and her palms were clammy.

Liam pulled into a parking spot at the massive storage building's parking lot and turned off the ignition. Then he turned to her, his expression one of open kindness. "How are you doing?"

Unclenching her fingers from the seat, she said, "I've been putting this day off for too long."

Liam reached over the center console, hesitating a moment before picking up her hand and giving it a squeeze. "We don't have to do this. We can find a pub and sit down for a Sunday roast and drive back."

She looked down at their joined hands, shocked at how comfortable it felt sitting here with Liam. They'd only known each other for a few weeks, but he'd already shown he could offer comfort and understanding without treating her as though she might break.

"No," she said with a sigh. "This is the closest Gran has ever come to talking about the war. If I go back empty-handed, it'll only give her a reason to shut down again."

His thumb stroked the top of her hand once, sending her heart fluttering before he pulled away to unbuckle his seat belt. "Okay then. Let's find your locker."

The attendant at the front desk directed them to the right elevator bank. As they rode up to the tenth floor, Cara took the two padlock keys, one stainless steel and one brass, out of her pocket.

The doors slid open and they took a left down a hallway. Everything was quiet, save for the sound of their footsteps and the buzz of the fluorescent lights droning above them.

"Do you remember what you stored?" Liam asked.

"Too many things." *All of my things.* "I went from a five-bedroom house with a drawing room, sitting room, and dining room to a two-bedroom cottage with a parlor and eat-in kitchen, so there's a lot of furniture. But there's also my parents' things."

She knew she was talking too much, but the words kept spilling from her. "An antiques dealer like the man I work for came to help clear out the more valuable pieces I didn't want to keep. I was supposed to have time to sort through the rest of it, but the house sold faster than anyone expected. I had the movers bring everything here to sort out later."

As they approached locker 2027, her hands started to shake.

She fumbled a little, sending Granddad's dog tags jingling on the key ring as she stuck the brass key in the bottom padlock. It unlocked it with a gentle click. The stainless steel one gave just as easily.

Unthreading the locks from their hooks, she reached down and gave the heavy metal gate a tug upward. It moved about four inches, but then stuck.

"Here, let me," Liam said, bending down to grip the handle on the opposite bottom corner. Together they pulled, and the rolling gate revealed a lifetime of memories.

Cara flicked the light on in the wide locker, and the overhead fluorescent bulbs flashed once and then filled the space with harsh light. The movers had left sheets covering most of the larger pieces, which now rose up like ghosts. Plastic bins packed with dishes, utensils, and bric-a-brac lined one wall, while rolled-up rugs wrapped in sheet plastic leaned opposite them.

"Where do we start?" asked Liam, shoving a hand through his hair as he tried to take in the huge task of finding one safe in the mess of another family's possessions.

"My parents' things are all in the back. We might have to move items around a bit to get to them."

"How big is the safe?" he asked. She held up a hand to her waist. "You're kidding."

She shook her head. "Dad's great-uncle was a banker, and the safe came down through the family to him. No one wanted to inherit it because it meant having to move it. It became a sort of family joke. Dad made a snug on the ground floor of our house his study because he didn't want to make the movers bring the safe upstairs."

"All right then," said Liam. "Shall we?"

She pulled the first sheet off and winced.

"What's wrong?" he asked.

She pointed to the quilted headboard she'd picked out with Simon. "My old bed. I have no idea why I still have it." Neither of them had wanted to keep it after the divorce. It was too painful a reminder of what their lives had once been, but still, she'd wound up with it.

The next sheet revealed a pair of bookcases; the third, a pair of round side tables that had once flanked the drawing room sofa Gran had given her for her twenty-eighth birthday.

"Can you help me shift these a little?" she asked, resting a hand on one of the twin tables.

"I can do one better," said Liam. "I can stack them."

It took them a half hour of lifting, moving, stacking, nudging, and occasionally cursing as they made a pathway to the back of the storage unit. Midway through, she shrugged off her puffy vest and Liam pulled his fleece quarter zip over his head. The sweat on the back of her neck was a good sign. The physicality of today kept her mind occupied, didn't give her time to think.

"This is good," said Liam, sitting down in one of the straight-backed chairs that had made up her parents' dining room set.

Regency chestnut dining chairs, set of eight. Paired with chestnut table with two leaves and brass fixtures. British. 1821.

"We're to the back. Now we just have to decide whether to go right or left," he said, casting a weary gaze around.

"Regretting this?" she asked, more to distract herself than anything else. Her thoughts had begun to creep in the moment they'd stopped, and she felt her past pressing down on her.

He shook his head. "Not even a bit. How else would I have learned you used to pretend the dining table was a cave when your parents had dinner parties?"

She smiled weakly. "You could be doing other things with your Sunday."

He shrugged. "So could you. And remember, I promised Iris I would come with you. I have a feeling it would be best not to cross your gran."

"You're probably right," she said.

"Sit down and have a rest," he said, moving one of the dining tables.

But she couldn't stop. Instead, she tugged on a sheet next to her. It slid to the floor and revealed her great-great-uncle's heavy black iron safe.

"Is that it?" Liam asked.

She laid a hand on the cool metal, her memory flashing to all the times she'd seen it behind her father's desk when she'd brought him a cup of tea or nagged him for permission to visit a friend Mum didn't quite approve of. "This is it."

"Do you have the combination?" he asked, eyeing the pair of tumblers and the large steel handle on the door.

She opened the notes app on her phone and scrolled until she found the combination she'd stored there on her father's instructions years ago. It took her two tries—the top tumbler was stiff—and when she went to open the safe, the handle hardly budged. She pushed down hard, but all the metal did was bite into her skin.

"Would you mind?" she asked, gesturing to the handle.

As Liam's arm brushed hers, she shivered and hugged her waist as she watched him struggle to open the safe. It was a strangely old-fashioned thing, asking a man to use his brute strength to help her open something. She'd been on her own for so long—longer than she'd been divorced, really, if she thought of how little she and Simon had seen each other in the last year of their marriage. She didn't mind being her own savior from time to time if it meant independence, but she found that she also didn't mind accepting Liam's help.

He grunted and threw his body weight onto the handle. There was a click, and he shuffled to the side between a bookcase and a tower of cardboard boxes.

"Would you like to do the honors?" he asked.

When she eased the door open, it all came back to her at once. The horrible journey home from Cumbria, furious with Simon for so many reasons and devastated knowing that she would never see her parents again. It had been a blessing, really, when they'd arrived home and

Simon had packed himself off to the guest room. They'd never slept together again.

"It's okay," Liam said softly. "I'm right here."

She looked up and found Liam kneeling in front of her, his hands clasping hers. "It's just a safe."

"But it was your dad's."

"Yes," she breathed. "It was where Dad kept sensitive files on cases and where they kept my mother's jewelry. I had to go into it after their deaths, and it felt so wrong."

"You did what they would've wanted you to do. The wills were important."

She drew in a shaky breath and nodded.

"And now we have the mystery of Iris's box to contend with." He nudged her gently. "You seem to be collecting mysteries, Cara."

The safe was fuller than she'd remembered. One of her father's colleagues had cleared out his case files, but plenty had been left behind. There was a small velvet box on the top shelf, and when she opened it, she saw a single lock of her baby hair. A file held birth and marriage certificates and photographs of her parents on their wedding day—Mum in an A-line ivory dress she'd sewn herself because she'd hated '70s fashion so much and Dad in a plain black suit with lapels that gave away its era. And pressed up against the back of the safe on the second shelf was a scuffed wooden box.

"I think I've found it," she said, but when she went to pull the box free, it dislodged a file and sent papers scattering.

"Damn," she cursed softly. They both bent to scoop the papers up, but she stopped, lifting a yellowed document up to the light. It was an old medical record with "Iris Warren" typewritten neatly at the top, followed by her address, national insurance number, occupation ("housewife"), blood type ("B"), and allergies ("none").

"Why would Mum and Dad have Gran's medical records?" she asked.

"Did Iris have major surgery at some point?" he asked.

She shook her head.

"Then maybe they came across the records when they were cleaning out her house." He held up a piece of paper. "Looks like your mother's birth certificate."

"That's odd." She reached into the safe, pulled out the file of vital records her father had kept there, and shuffled until she found Mum's birth certificate. "Why would she have two copies?"

Liam glanced at the paper in her hand. "That explains it. The one you've got is the short-form certificate. This one is the long-form with all of the parental information on it. Maybe she was applying for a government document that required the long-form."

With a frown, she closed the records and slid everything back onto the safe shelf. Then she turned her attention to Gran's box, which was sitting, temporarily forgotten, on a nightstand they'd uncovered. She ran her fingers over the wooden top. A few scratches marred the finish, but otherwise it was unremarkable—so much so she hardly remembered having seen it when she was looking for the wills.

"Are you going to open it?" Liam asked.

She stared at the box. "I don't want to give her any reason not to tell us everything."

I don't want to give her any reason not to explain her reluctance.

"I was dreading coming here, you know. I barely slept last night," she said.

"And now that you're here?" he asked.

"Everything is so sad. When Jock first told me I'd be coming with him on site visits, I was excited. I wanted to learn more about the people who owned the things we were selling. I guess I glossed over how emotional it must be for the people who are selling off their loved one's things."

She could feel the solidness of him next to her, surveying all of her things with an outsider's eye.

"Do you know what I see when I look around this storage locker?" he asked.

"What?"

"A woman who's torn. Part of her wants to believe that these are all just things, but part of her knows they're much more than that."

"You think I need to make a decision about what to do," she said.

"I'm saying it's complicated, and that's okay. The answers to these questions aren't always neat. Now"—he glanced at his watch—"if you want to go see Iris, we can probably make it in time for cocktails."

Taking up the box, she went to close the safe. She paused, hand on the handle, staring at the records they'd found. On impulse, she grabbed them, stuffing them under her arm, and closed the door. She wasn't certain why, but she wanted to have them with her.

Cara picked her way out of the storage unit while Liam grabbed the layers they'd shed. He was just about to pull down the door when she stopped him with a hand on his arm.

"I think," she said slowly, "that it may be time to close this chapter. It's time to start selling off the things I don't want."

"You're sure?"

She nodded, glancing up at him through her lashes. "Would you mind coming back with me one day and sorting through all of this? I could use the help."

He dipped his head, but not so fast that she missed the little smile that played over his lips. "I'd be happy to help, Cara. That's what friends do."

As he pulled down the gate and secured the locks, she wondered if friends was what she really wanted to be.

19 August 1941

Another long night at the top of the Ack-Ack Shack, as all of us have taken to calling our little patch of roof. The sirens went just after nine tonight, but there were no planes spotted over our part of the Thames, even though we could see orange glow of the fires to the south near Croydon.

It seems strange, but those nights are worse than the ones when we see bombers flying right into range. We spend all our time on alert, knowing that at any moment Mary could yell out the name of a German plane and we'll have to jump into action. There's no time for hesitation when seconds mean the difference between a direct hit and a far-off miss. Still, it can make for long nights and frayed nerves. It's those times Charlie says she wishes we were allowed to smoke, "damn the RA and ATS regulations."

We could've all done with a drink by the time the sun came up this morning. Mary was exhausted and Williams and Hatfield's teasing of everyone had become a little too pointed. When Charlie snapped at them, they set about sulking, and then Lizzie tried to sing and Cartruse told her off. As for me—well, I was in my own foul mood.

It was yesterday's letter from Paul that set me off. I still can't believe the gall of him.

16 August 1941

My darling,

I must say, I'm surprised and disappointed that it's been nearly a week since I've had a letter from you. I know you've made your journey from your training camp to your new post, but surely you could've found time to write to me if you'd really tried. It's enough to make a man resent this war because it's turning his girl's head.

I depend on your letters, darling. Knowing that you're waiting for me gives me the comfort I need to climb into the cockpit day after day. It's what all of us fliers rely on, but maybe I misjudged the depths of your feeling for me.

Perhaps it's best then that I can't come to London. I can't say much other than we're being sent on a mission and all leave has been revoked. No exceptions.

He wrote more but I can hardly hold my pen straight because I'm shaking from anger. How could he question that I care for him when I pour myself into every one of my letters? I've been writing him every day for months, while he's the one who writes in fits and spurts. For two weeks I'll receive long, loving letters that tell me how much he adores me and wants to see me again, and then for a week nothing. I accepted this because I knew he was flying and I was training, yet now that I'm on active assignment I'm not allowed to lapse for a week while I'm changing bases and shooting down bombers? Sometimes I wonder if, for all his fretting about how dangerous this job is, he thinks of Ack-Ack Command as nothing more than a sewing circle. If only he knew that yesterday a fighter's bullet hit so close that I found brick dust in my hair back in the canteen.

I'm so furious I could scream!

20 August 1941

I wrote Paul back and told him that if he has so little faith in me, perhaps he should find another girl to write to. One who isn't a gunner girl and can stay at home, doing nothing but pine for him. I told him that he was acting like a man who wants to infuriate his sweetheart so much that she breaks things off.

It felt good to write the words, my half of a delayed argument. But just like in an argument, I'm now having doubts about what I said, wishing I could take it back. I feel ill wondering what he'll write back. If he writes back.

21 August 1941

No sirens tonight. We spent our shift in the makeshift mess we've created in an old office just off the stairs of the Ack-Ack Shack. There's an electric fire and a gas ring so we can heat water for tea. Williams, who is quite the card shark, has taught us poker to go along with the game of gin some of us girls were already playing. We play for the biscuits we're issued at the end of every shift, saving them up for the next night's game. Nigella is turning out to be a brilliant student and ends every night with a pile of biscuits in front of her, although Cartruse steals them as soon as her back is turned, claiming he's always hungry.

Our radio operator still hasn't appeared. And we've had no replacement for Colonel Barker yet either. The RA and the ATS seem to be content to leave us in the hands of Captain Jones. He's not a bad sort.

No letter from Paul. I know it would be too soon, but I still jumped when Mary came around with our post.

24 August 1941

No letter from Paul today.

25 August 1941

What have I done?

26 August 1941

He wrote to me. Toward the bottom there are spots where the ink is smeared, as though he was writing so fast he didn't stop to let it dry before folding it up into its envelope.

23 August 1941

My darling,

I received your letter and I realized what a brute and a fool I've been.
How could I doubt your devotion? I've neglected you horribly, and
I was feeling the sting of that, wondering if you'd forgotten me for
another man. There are the officers stationed in London and the ones
on leave. And I can't help wondering if the men you work with are in
love with you. Of course they are. How could they not be?

I know it's no excuse, but I behaved badly because I miss you so
much. Learning that I would be unable to take leave was a blow, and I
lashed out. It's easier sometimes to convince myself that you don't truly
care for me—that your letters are because you pity a pilot who is in too
deep to understand that our time together in Cornwall was just your
way of offering a bit of comfort during this war. Nothing more.

You see, without you, darling, it feels as though a part of me is
missing. I think about our afternoon drinking champagne at that
little hotel on the cliffs above the beach and the many times we sat
in the cinema together, so happy just to be holding hands. But those
memories alone aren't enough to keep me warm when I'm flying.
Knowing what your lips taste like is no longer enough. I need to feel
them against mine again and so much more.

It's a cruel trick of fate to find the woman you want in a little
village hall in Cornwall, only to be sent away again. If I had my way,
I'd wrap you in cotton wool and send you off to safety in the country
with my parents.

All I can do is pray that soon I'll be able to take my leave so that I
can travel to London and kiss you again. If you'll forgive me.

With all my love,
Paul

I teared up reading his letter, and I had to stop and compose myself twice. He's never once told me his worries that I'll meet another man or that this has all just been a fling I don't have the courage to let go of. If he had, I could have reassured him by telling him the truth. I love him—I truly do—and it hurts to think that he doubts that.

I'll write to him and let him know he's forgiven. I only wish I could say the words to him.

14

LOUISE

It wasn't just nights in the Ack-Ack Shack that kept B Section busy. Afternoons were occupied with debriefs and lectures and constant retraining to keep them sharp. Therefore, three weeks had passed before the ATS and the RA granted B Section twenty-four hours' leave, and when it came there was no question that Charlie, Vera, and Louise would go into town.

They giggled all the way on the bus from Woolwich to Shoreditch and then to the tube station, sobering up only when they saw the long lines of people already milling around waiting for the gates to open so they could spread out over the platforms.

They disembarked at Monument and walked until they reached St. Paul's. No matter where Louise looked, London was in a state of destruction and repair. Some bomb sites lay fallow, stubborn buddleias blooming as their roots clung to what little soil was scattered over the remnants of houses. On other lots just a few houses away, men climbed up and down ladders to fix roofs, board up windows, and try their best to make the structures sound again before the biting chill of autumn swept through the city.

Still, despite the constant reminders of war, Charlie and Vera did their level best to show Louise the sights and sounds of the capital.

"If we weren't in war and rationing wasn't on, I'd insist we get ice creams," said Vera who walked on Louise's right as the three girls, arms linked, strolled down the Embankment toward the Houses of Parliament, Big Ben looming in the distance.

"We'll just have to dream of all that," said Charlie, sighing.

They walked by a couple of soldiers who craned their necks to stare.

"It's like they can see right through the uniforms," said Vera with a tug at her tunic.

"All they'd get is an eyeful of passion killers," said Charlie.

"I wish the uniform was a little more . . . flattering," said Louise.

"I'll never understand how those stuck-up Wrens wound up with better uniforms than we did," said Charlie with a laugh tinged with equal parts jest and jealousy over the streamlined, flattering cut that the women in the navy's auxiliary branch wore.

"Vera should've been a Wren," Louise teased.

"You know I couldn't go into the WRNS. I'm from an army family," said Vera.

"But they're so posh, Miss Finishing School," said Charlie.

Vera's snort was decidedly unladylike. "You mean the school that taught me nothing more than how to instruct servants and climb into and out of a car without letting my slip show?"

"Destined to be a lady," said Charlie.

"Oh, what an ambition," said Vera.

"What would you rather do?" Louise asked.

"I don't know, if I'm being truthful," said Vera. "I just know that I don't want to sit on committees and hold teas for charities, like my mother."

"What about you, Charlie?" Louise asked.

All at once, Charlie seemed to have been hit by an uncharacteristic bashfulness, as she toyed with the box camera that hung around her neck, one of her few possessions she'd hauled from Leicester to Oswestry to Woolwich.

"You won't laugh?" Charlie asked quietly.

"It can't be more far-fetched than what I'd want to do if this war wasn't on," said Louise.

Charlie blinked up at her a couple times and then smiled. "All right then. I'd want to be a journalist."

"You should've tried for it when they asked us what we wanted to do in Leicester," said Vera.

Charlie shook her head. "They give those jobs to the men."

"Not all of them," said Louise.

"She's right. Things are changing," said Vera.

"You don't think my idea's silly then?" Charlie asked, and Louise's heart broke just a little knowing that at some point in her life someone had told her friend that it *was* silly. Just like she'd been told time after time that Haybourne would be her life.

"It's not sillier than my idea," Louise said firmly. "I thought that after this war I might go to California and see if there's a university that will enroll me. I want to study maths."

"California?" said Charlie, eyes wide. "It seems like a whole world away."

"It is," said Louise with a grin, "and wouldn't that be wonderful?"

"Stop," Charlie ordered and they all abruptly halted. She lifted her camera and pointed to a spot where the walkway jutted out in a little mock battlement. "Lou, go stand over there. I'm going to take your picture."

Louise rolled her eyes at Charlie's bossiness, but went to the spot anyway.

"Now turn to face the water," Charlie ordered. "Good. And look back at me. Tell me where it is in California you want to live?"

"Oh, I don't know," she said, the breeze lifting up her hair.

"Hollywood?" Vera asked.

Louise shook her head. "My cousin Kate's obsessed with Hollywood and I like the pictures enough, but I think I'd want to be somewhere close to the beach. I've lived by the water my entire life."

"I hope it's cleaner than the Thames," Vera said, peering over the edge.

"Anything's cleaner than the Thames," Charlie muttered, still lining up the shot. "Can you laugh?"

Louise did her best to titter while looking back over her shoulder.

Charlie looked up. "Can you not look like you're trying to make it through a painfully dull cocktail party?"

"What am I supposed to laugh about then?" she asked.

"Hatfield falling on his backside yesterday night," said Vera, that snort sounding again. "I can't believe he fell asleep standing up."

Louise's chuckle was genuine this time. "It serves him right when he spent half the morning trying to flirt with one of the orderlies in the canteen."

"Says who?" Vera asked.

"Says Cartruse," said Louise.

"Got it. You're free to move about again, Lou." Charlie wound the film to prepare it for the next shot that struck her fancy. "You and Cartruse are close, aren't you?"

Once she might've blushed, but she knew these women too well. They lived together, ate together, and fought together. There was little left to hide.

"I warmed to him after he stopped being so rude in training camp. He's a friend," she said.

"Just see to it that your flier doesn't get the wrong idea," said Charlie.

"For him to get the wrong idea, he'd have to actually come to London," Louise grumbled.

~

Despite weeks of teasing that they'd all take their first twenty-four-hour leave in London to scatter to the wind and finally get some time away from one another, B Section all met up by silent agreement at the NAAFI near the Charlton Barracks that evening.

Louise walked through the doors with Charlie and Vera on either of her arms, and the excited sound of service members letting loose rose up around her. A gangly man in an RAF uniform was playing "I've Got My Love to Keep Me Warm" on the piano, and a couple of Women's Auxiliary Air Force girls in distinctive blue WAAF uniforms were leaning down to flirt with him.

"There they are," said Vera, tugging on Lou's and Charlie's arms and guiding them around a pack of marines to the tables were Mary, Nigella, Lizzie, and Hatfield sat.

Dropping down into a chair, Charlie said, "I'm bushed. I think we walked half of London today."

"Cartruse and Williams are just fetching some tea," said Mary.

"I still don't know how we wound up here rather than the pub," Hatfield grouched.

Lizzie batted Hatfield on the arm, and Nigella ducked her chin with a smile. Louise had noticed in the last few weeks that Nigella seemed to have progressed from having a hopeless crush on Hatfield to being mildly amused by him. Hopefully the sweetest member of their unit had decided Hatfield's eye for every woman who crossed his path—except the gunner girls of B Section—was best left alone, but Nigella was timid enough that Louise didn't dare ask. Vera, who had assumed something of the mother hen role, would hear it from Nigella herself soon enough.

"The tourists are back." Williams laughed as he bobbled a tray laden with teacups and glasses of juice in his effort to set it down.

"Careful there!" Lizzie said, steadying his arm.

"Where's Cartruse?" Vera asked.

Williams shrugged. "Talking to some bloke he knows from Putney. How was your adventure?"

"It feels like we've seen all of London," said Louise, "but these two tell me I haven't even scratched the surface."

"It's too bad so much of the city's a wreck," said Mary.

"Even Buckingham Palace was hit," said Nigella.

"Do you think Princess Elizabeth will serve?" Lizzie asked.

"She's just fifteen. Let's hope this war doesn't last long enough to find out," said Vera.

"From your lips to God's ears," said Williams, tapping out a cigarette from a paper-wrapped pack.

"Oh, don't smoke that around me," said Mary, her eyes growing positively lustful. "It's torture watching you."

"All I have to do is load the shells," said Williams, the cigarette bouncing as he set a match to it and drew on it until the tip glowed orange. "No steady hands needed."

"I'm not even on the instruments," said Mary with a sigh and a longing gaze at the cigarette.

"It's the booze I miss," said Lizzie, inching her juice away from her. "Give me a good gin and tonic any day."

"Can we talk about something other than the vices we can't indulge in anymore?" Vera asked.

"Lou, how's the famous Flight Lieutenant Paul Bolton?" Williams asked, flicking the end of his cigarette into an ashtray.

"He's fine, thank you," she said primly.

"You know, if you were really loyal to Ack-Ack Command, you'd be with an RA man, or at least an army man. Not a pilot. You're really letting this side down," said Williams.

"Not this again," muttered Charlie.

"It's too bad then that I know you too well ever to dream of being with you, Williams," Louise said with a sweet smile.

The rest of the table laughed, but before Williams could respond, a low, painful keening cut through the din. The NAAFI froze as a WAAF struggled up from a table near the back. Tears streamed down her face, and her mouth opened to the unearthly sobs. In her hands she clutched a slip of paper.

"Oh my word," said Mary, crossing herself.

Two women at the WAAFs' table closed around her, holding her up as she began to sag to the floor. In a flash, Cartruse appeared out of nowhere, sweeping the woman into a chair before she collapsed. He dropped to her side, his hands on the woman's arms as she rocked back and forth, the sobs growing louder.

"She had a telegram," said Vera, her mouth a thin white line.

Louise looked up and saw a WAAF officer standing at awkward, if respectful attention, her eyes fixed on the grieving woman. She didn't have to ask to know that the officer had been the one to deliver the news. Missing or killed in action. Either way, the woman had lost someone that afternoon.

Her thoughts immediately flashed to Paul. If he died, she might not know until weeks later. She wasn't a wife. She wasn't family. As a sweetheart, she had no official claim on him. His mother would be the one to open that telegram. Louise would have to rely on the thoughtfulness of the other men in his unit who'd heard about her. One of them would have to fish out a letter from Paul's effects to find her service number.

Her stomach twisted at the thought. She could only pray that Paul would be kept safe.

Two RAF sergeants appeared next to the grieving woman, helping her friends lift her up and half carry her out of the NAAFI. Everyone watched the door shut behind them, plunging the place into an uncomfortable silence.

After a few moments, people began to shift about, but the man who'd been playing the piano closed the keyboard cover and slipped off the bench.

Louise watched Cartruse come to their table, his face even more solemn than usual. He dropped into the chair next to her and scrubbed a hand across his jaw.

"It was her husband," he said after a moment. "They were married in January before he shipped out." They all murmured in sympathy, but he went on. "Her parents were killed in the Blitz so she joined up. Said she doesn't have anyone left."

"It was good of you to comfort her," she said.

"What comfort can you offer a woman going through something like that? What do you say?" he asked.

Louise laid a hand on his arm, and he looked up at her. His eyes were so tired.

"You say whatever you can," she said.

His mouth twisted, but after a moment he patted her hand.

That night, Louise wrote to Paul fifteen words.

I love you. Tell me you love me too. Tonight I need to hear it.

15

CARA

They were twenty minutes out from Widcote Manor when Liam ended the silence that had hung about the car since London.

"Will you tell me what happened?" he asked.

He didn't need to elaborate. She knew what he wanted to hear, and for the first time in a long time she felt like she could start to tell the story to someone who hadn't seen the ugliness unfold.

"My ex wasn't the person I thought he was, or maybe he was and I just couldn't see it in the beginning. It started when Simon was made redundant in 2015, and all of his promises to find a new job never panned out."

"It's a tough market," said Liam.

"You're being much, much too kind. When it first happened, he seemed determined to get another job. A better one. But after a couple months of hunting he sort of gave up.

"At uni, he'd cultivated a group of friends who were all members of private clubs who would go to hunt balls at the weekends and play polo in the summer. We were comfortable with both of our salaries, but we couldn't keep up with them, though Simon tried.

"After he lost his job, it became worse. We'd bought the house and we were relying on my income to pay the mortgage and everything else. Yes, it was a tough market, but after a while I realized he wasn't looking for a job. I got suspicious that he always seemed to be meeting some uni friend or another and I'd cross-check our credit card bills. Turns out that when I was at work, he was eating at expensive restaurants or going to his club. Tennis matches, rounds of golf, days at Lord's, poker tournaments. He spent one afternoon racing vintage Morgans in the Malvern Hills. That set us back a couple thousand pounds, plus another thousand for bets he lost."

Liam winced. "Did you know?"

Cara sighed and pinched the bridge of her nose. "I knew about some of it, but not as much as I should've. I was working more than I've ever worked in my life to bill as many hours as possible because I told myself that was the only way we'd stay solvent. The truth is, I *wanted* to work. I knew we were drifting apart, and it was easier it was to stay away than to deal with that."

She crossed her arms over her stomach. Thinking about the whole mess never failed to make her feel like a fool. She'd known that Simon liked to keep up appearances, but she'd thought it was simple male competitiveness, never once believing he was capable of putting them on the path to a level of debt that would've meant bankruptcy if she hadn't stopped it. She'd been played, but she'd had all the evidence in front of her. She'd let it happen.

"One afternoon, I couldn't ignore it anymore," she said. "I'd come home from work early with a migraine. Simon was passed out on the sofa, a bottle of gin next to him, and his phone was dinging with messages from friends wondering where he was. He'd promised to show for a high-stakes poker game but had gotten too drunk.

"I don't know why that was what made me snap, but I went straight up to his office and began going through his records. I found seven credit cards in both of our names that I'd never seen before, all of them at or near their limit. Overdraft notices. Casino receipts and IOUs for private gambling debts. There were unpaid bills for the utilities and the mortgage. I opened up our joint account and realized that he'd been pulling money out in increasingly large increments every week. I hadn't noticed before, because he'd taken over paying the bills, since he wasn't working and had more time.

"When he was sober enough to talk later that evening, I told him I knew everything and wanted an explanation. He became defensive, and when I asked him if he had a problem with gambling and drinking, he denied it." She snuck a glance at Liam, who looked straight ahead, his hands tight on the wheel. "That night he snuck out of the house. When I woke up that morning, he still hadn't come back. I went into his email and found the receipt for a car-hire app in his email. He'd gone to the Park Tower Casino in Knightsbridge."

"Was that what did it?" Liam asked.

She laughed. "No, of course not. There were four more months of fighting and crying and him promising to get help, but I would come home and find him drunk and passed out. Then a drunk driver hit my parents. I got the call from the hospital that they were in critical condition. They died before I could get there.

"The day after the funeral, I went to my solicitor's office and filed for divorce." It wasn't the entire story, but it was as much as she was willing to tell him right now. Even this had wrung her out.

"As a condition of the divorce, I paid off Simon's debts and he walked away from everything else. The house, the cars, the furniture."

"The things we just saw in storage," Liam guessed.

"Yes. I just wanted to close the door on it all."

"I can understand that," he said.

"Is that what you did when you found out about Vivian and your best friend?" she asked softly.

It was his turn to laugh. "I didn't just walk away, remember? I moved my whole life out of the country. I arrived in Oregon in the early summer and locked myself in my office and in the archives, researching an article for an academic journal I'd been invited to submit to. I spent most of that time in a fog."

She nodded, the feeling so familiar. "I think I spent the six months after my parents died in a fugue state. There are so many things I can't remember doing, even though they're on my calendar."

"And you do everything you can to convince yourself that it's normal, you're normal, until one day you sort of crack. It was four months after I moved when I came home and found a package on my front doorstep. It was a bread machine from an old friend from uni and his wife that was meant as a wedding gift. Apparently Vivian had missed them when she was calling around to tell people the wedding was off, and they'd tracked me down in Reed thinking that we'd love the surprise. I opened it and the next thing I knew I was ugly-crying on the laminate floor of my rental kitchen."

"That's terrible," she said.

He shrugged. "I don't know. They were so mortified when they found out that they refused to let me return the bread machine. I had fresh bread whenever I wanted for two years until I moved back to Barlow and had to leave it behind."

She cocked her head to the side. "The wrong kind of plug?"

"Exactly," he said.

"That moment happened to me in a Waitrose. I picked up a bag of granola because I knew we were running low in the pantry, and I realized there was no more 'we' and that I hate granola and that I never had to buy it again."

"At least it happened in a posh grocery store," he said after a moment. "Did you ugly-cry?"

She laughed, her tension uncoiling a little bit more. "I was wearing mascara. I promise you that my ugly cry was uglier than yours."

"Do you know the one thing I've found that helps? Talking about it. I know it's cliché, but after the bread machine, I made myself start talking to my sister and my mother." He glanced over at her as the sign for Widcote Manor's off-ramp came into view. "And now I'm talking to you."

As the car glided onto the winding service road overrun with late-blooming buddleia, she realized he was right. She had talked to him and she did feel better—as though a weight that had been pressing down on her chest for so long had suddenly lifted. They hardly knew each other and it didn't make sense, but Liam somehow made her feel lighter, easier, more like herself. Just his company was beckoning her back into the world again.

"Thank you, Liam," she said as they parked outside of Gran's.

"For what?" he asked, turning his body fully to her for the first time since they'd left London.

She shook her head. "For agreeing to come with your divorced neighbor to her storage locker. For driving. For helping with the diary. For liking Gran."

"I want you to know that I'd like Iris whether she was your gran or not."

"Even when she's flirting with you?" she asked.

"Especially then."

She jerked her head toward the back seat. "Then I suppose we should go bring her this box."

"And hopefully you'll have the answer to another mystery by the end of the day."

Liam was out of the car and around to her side before she'd pulled her purse from the back seat. He held open the door for her, and it almost felt as though this was the beginning of something.

In the lift, Cara clutched the box, staring as the numbers ticked up one, two, three.

"Are you nervous?" Liam asked, as the doors slid open on Gran's floor.

The muscles of her jaw worked as she tried to articulate what she was feeling. "I don't know. Gran's held this part of her life back from me for so long. At first I didn't think too much about it but now . . ."

"You're wondering why," he finished for her. "I think it's time you asked her again."

She knocked, and almost immediately the door swung open, as though Gran had been waiting for her.

"Cara, you've brought your handsome professor back."

"Hello, Iris," said Liam, kissing Gran on the cheek.

Rather than flirt with him further, Gran's watercolor-blue eyes fell to the battered wooden box. "You found it."

Cara nodded.

"Tea first." Gran glanced down at her watch. "Or a drink. It's nearly five o'clock."

Anticipation shimmered in the room even as they made small talk about the drive to and from Barlow, the state of the storage container, and the strength of Gran's drinks. Finally, when everyone was settled with a gin and tonic, Cara gestured to the box.

"It was in the safe, just as you said. I can't believe I didn't remember it when I was looking for Mum and Dad's will."

Gran smoothed a hand over the unfinished grain. "I've often wondered if I was right to keep it."

Cara held her breath as Gran lifted the lid and smiled the sad little smile of a woman being forced to remember things she'd rather forget.

"Where do you want me to start?" Gran asked, peering down at the things in the box.

"At the beginning," Cara said.

"I joined up as soon as I turned eighteen," said Gran. "Conscription for young, unmarried women was in place then, but I would've gone no matter what. Barlow didn't see the kind of bombing the ports and industrial cities suffered, but the war was everywhere—in the films we watched, the newspapers we read, the radio programs we listened to. Everyone knew a boy who was fighting and a girl who was working in service as a medic or a driver or a clerk.

"But the war wasn't just dreary tragedy. It was adventure too. I was convinced that I was going to be sent to Malta or Italy or some exotic place. Instead, I was stationed in Buckinghamshire." Gran laughed when Cara sat back a bit. "I told you it isn't much of a story."

"What were you assigned to do?" Cara asked.

Gran waved her hand. "I was a clerk. At first I was nothing more than a glorified runner, zipping between army offices, but I had a knack for note taking and could type thanks to a secretarial course I'd taken when I was seventeen."

Gran picked up a piece of paper from the box and handed it to Cara. "There's a photograph of me on the day I left home."

Cara looked at the picture of a very young Gran standing in front of a white door, wearing civilian clothes and the same brilliant smile Cara knew so well. She passed the photo to Liam.

"My old ration book," said Gran, passing over the green book with thin, dry pages that crackled beneath Cara's fingers. "Iris Parsons" was written in looping blue ink on the front.

"I didn't use it until I was demobbed at the end of the war. Then we were given clothing coupons, cigarettes, and chocolate, and sent on our way.

"And here are Steve's letters to me. Do you remember much of Granddad, Cara?"

She shook her head. "Only a little."

Gran nodded. "You were so young when he died. He was a good man." Gran lifted a bundle tied up with pale pink ribbon. "These are why I asked your father to keep the box in his safe. These are more precious to me than the world."

"Can I read them?" Cara asked.

"You'd better let me have a look first. Ours was a whirlwind romance. We met and four months later we were married, although we hardly had any time together. Peace had been declared in Europe, and your granddad was sent to Germany to help with the stand-down. He wrote me love letters that would've made the censors blush."

Liam barked a laugh, and Cara flushed. "Gran."

Gran arched a brow. "I'll have you know, I was young once."

"I don't doubt it," muttered Cara.

Gran slid her glasses on and scanned the first letter in the bundle. "Here, this one is fine for your young eyes."

Cara took it gingerly and read out loud, "'Dearest Boudicca—' Why did he call you Boudicca?"

"Because he used to say I was Queen of the Britons and, when we fought, I would never surrender."

"'Dearest Boudicca,'" Cara started again, "'the nights are colder now and they say we may see snow tonight. I know I say this in all of my letters, but I wish I was dancing with you again.'"

"We met at a dance in London," Gran interrupted.

Cara resumed reading. "'Instead I'm in a sorry excuse for a tent with Miller and Harrison to keep me company. I'd rather be back outside your billet in Fenny Stratford. I miss you more—'"

"Did you say Fenny Stratford?" Liam asked.

"Yes. It was perhaps the most boring place in all of England during the war, but at least we were safe," said Gran.

"Where is that?" Cara asked.

"I told you. Buckinghamshire," said Gran.

"Who did you clerk for?" Cara asked.

Gran shrugged. "Whoever needed me. There were army offices there, just like all over England at the time."

"What was your home base?" Liam pushed.

"I believe this is my story to tell, young man. If you'll let me tell it," said Gran sharply.

The air snapped with tension, and Cara looked between Liam and Gran. Yes, he'd asked a few questions, but nothing out of the ordinary. He was curious, just like she was.

Gran, seeming to realize that she'd been rude, set a photograph she was holding down, and said, "I apologize, Liam. I didn't mean to be short with you—it's just that I have something of a headache."

But Cara knew better—Gran had done this to her too many times before. Cara wasn't going to allow her to shut things down now. Desperate to keep the conversation going, Cara dove back into the box and pulled out a photograph.

"Tell me about this one," she demanded.

She held up the photograph of Gran, young and pretty, standing next to a man. His arm was looped around her waist, as though someone had interrupted them while dancing and they'd looked back.

"That's Edwin Godfrey," said Gran, her voice thick.

"Who was he?" she asked.

"My superior officer."

"You danced together?" Cara asked.

"The rules could be loose sometimes," said Gran.

Cara pulled out another photo from the box. "And this?"

Gran sat between two men, Edwin Godfrey and another, her head tipped so that her hair brushed Edwin's shoulder.

"Oh, who knows?" Gran said, snatching up the photographs of her with Edwin Godfrey quickly.

Sensing they were now on precarious ground, Cara said, "There was something else in the safe."

"What's that's, dear?" Gran asked distractedly as she tucked the photographs underneath Granddad's bundle of letters.

"Why would Mum have your medical records?"

Gran stilled, her eyes fixed on her hands. "Your mother was keeping them safe for me. So many things were in disarray during the move."

"Gran," Cara said carefully. "I want to ask you again, what was the fight about? I could hear Mum's side, but I don't know yours."

All at once, her vibrant, irrepressible Gran went pale and waxy and she looked every day of her ninety-two years. "That was the last conversation I had with my daughter. A fight. A ridiculous, stupid fight."

"Did it have to do with why you refuse to talk about that period in your life? I won't judge you for the things you had to do. It was a different time," said Cara.

"Don't press me, Cara. Not about this."

"But, Gran—"

Gran rose to her feet, imperious as a queen. "It's time you remembered that you're my granddaughter and that I deserve the respect of being left alone when I tell you I don't wish to speak about something."

"Iris, she just wants answers," said Liam.

Gran rounded on him. "Really, young man, this is not any of your concern."

"Don't snap at him," said Cara. "He's done nothing wrong."

"I think you both should leave."

"Iris, if I said something to upset you, I apologize," said Liam, clearly trying to mend what had suddenly broken.

Gran nodded stiffly, and for the first time in her life, Cara was angry at Gran. Liam was only trying to help and didn't deserve to be a target of anyone's ire. But it wasn't just that. In that moment, she felt a loyalty to him and with it a protectiveness.

But this was not the place to parse that out. Instead, she walked to the door, Liam trailing behind.

"We'll leave you alone, Gran," Cara announced. "I'd like to like to take the box with me."

"I doubt there will be much of interest in there," said Gran reluctantly.

"That's what I've been trying to explain. *Everything* about you interests me. You're my only family left, and it hurts to know you're keeping secrets from me no matter how I ask."

Gran's eyes flashed to the letters, and she stooped to scoop them up and hold them to her breast. "Leave these with me."

Cara softened a bit at the sight of her Gran clutching the link to her past, as though holding them would connect her to her husband.

"Of course."

She and Liam were out the door and halfway down the hallway when Cara realized that she'd left without saying a proper goodbye. Turning, she said, "I love you to the moon . . ." But all she saw was the door to Gran's flat closing.

It was ridiculous, really—just a little silly thing they'd said since Cara was a girl—but it was the first time in her life that Gran wasn't waiting with her usual, "And back."

After she'd stared at the door for moment, a hand lit on the small of her back. Liam.

"Are you all right?" he asked.

"She's never been like that with me before," Cara said.

Moving carefully, he took the box from her. She had been gripping it so hard her knuckles were white.

"Sometimes opening up the past can be painful. For everyone," he said as they stepped into the waiting elevator.

"All I want is to know."

"Even if you find out things you'll regret later? I think you should prepare yourself for the fact that Iris doesn't want you to know because there's something she's afraid will change your relationship."

Just like the fight had marred Gran's relationship with Mum just before Mum died. Cara felt a stab of pity for Gran then, knowing that her last words with her daughter would always be an argument with no chance of apology.

When they reached the car, Liam propped the box on one hip so he could open her door. He handed it to her before he slid into the driver's seat.

"I'm sorry that Gran was snippy with you," she said, as he turned over the ignition.

He shook his head. "It's no bother."

"Why did you ask where she was based?" she asked.

Liam hesitated for a split second before shoving his glasses higher on his nose and letting off the parking brake. "I just become fixated on things sometimes."

"Are you sure? Because if you need to look some things up you could bring your laptop over. I could cook dinner and—"

"No."

The flat-out rejection knocked her back hard.

Liam shoved a hand through his hair. "I'm sorry, it's just that it's been a long day and I have a lecture tomorrow on Charlemagne. I'm trying to figure out a way to make sure seventy-five eighteen-year-olds don't use it as a chance to catch up on their sleep."

The urge to offer to help tugged at her. She could listen to him run through his notes and . . . what? Help with his lecture prep? She wasn't an expert or a trusted colleague or even his lover. She was only his neighbor, a once-broken woman who was just now piecing her life back together. What man would want to get mixed up in all of that mess?

"No, you're right," she said, forcing a false cheeriness into her voice. "I should get ready for the week."

"Maybe another time," he said.

She nodded and turned to gaze out the window. She spent the rest of the ride home willing them to get to Elm Road as quickly as possible and wishing they could drive forever because she feared there wouldn't be another time.

14 September 1941

I still haven't had word back from Paul. I want to pretend that this doesn't worry me, but in truth it's gnawing at me. I told him I loved him, and nothing.

I shouldn't have asked him to tell me the same. If he doesn't love me . . . I don't want to think about it, but I am. Constantly.

I thought I was hiding my worry well—not even Vera and Charlie have said anything—but this morning as we left the Ack-Ack Shack, Cartruse pulled me aside.

"Something's wrong, Lou. You going to tell me what it is?"

I was so startled, I stopped on the stairs leading down to the street. "What do you mean?"

He squinted up at me against the rising sun before shaking out a cigarette and lighting it, blowing the smoke out of one corner of his mouth so it didn't stream at me. "We've known each other long enough that it's obvious when something's bothering you."

"No one else has noticed."

He opened his mouth but then closed it just as fast, sticking his cigarette in the corner and shaking his head. "You don't have to talk about it if you don't want to. That's your prerogative. Just know someone noticed."

Maybe I should've told Cartruse my fears—that I'm losing Paul—but something held me back. It just didn't seem right, and so we walked back away from Woolwich Depot without another word.

16

LOUISE

"Anything, Private Rogers?" Captain Jones shouted from his post.

Louise craned her neck to search the slowly lightening sky as Mary took another look through the viewfinder. The lights over London were still sweeping, but the spotlight operators hadn't picked up anything for an hour. It seemed as though the last wave of German bombers had turned around and made for the coast just after four that morning.

"Nothing," Mary confirmed with a shake of her head.

"Once the all-clear sounds—" The splitting ring of the all-clear cut the captain off and he gave a gruff chuckle. "Stand down. Good work today."

It hadn't been, really. A handful of fighters and three bombers had come within their sights, but none of had been in range for B Section to get off an effective shot. The best they had done was create a bit of bother for the German fliers. But it was the last day on duty before seventy-two hours of leave, and all of them were relieved.

Now that it was mid-September and the nights had started to turn cold, these long, ineffectual shifts were becoming harder and harder to bear. Two nights ago even Captain Jones hadn't objected when Hatfield convinced Lizzie to sing ballads while Williams whistled along.

The members of B Section groaned and stretched sore necks as they clattered down the five flights of stairs to the street.

"Aircraft identification lectures at fourteen hundred hours on Thursday when you're back," Captain Jones reminded them.

They nodded wearily and began the trudge back to their respective billets. The men had taken to walking the women back since the ATS billet was on the way to the Charlton Barracks. Cartruse fell into step next to Louise as he'd been doing more and more in the last few weeks. Charlie liked to tease that he fancied her, but she brushed it off. She had Paul, even though it felt like a lifetime since she'd heard from him.

"How long do you think before everyone knows?" Cartruse asked.

"I'm sorry?" Louise asked.

He jerked his head behind him. "The lovebirds."

She glanced back and saw Lizzie and Williams walking a little apart from everyone else, their heads close together. "Lovebirds?"

"Don't you think?"

Glancing back again, she had to admit he was probably right. "A week, maybe less. We're a nosy bunch."

He pulled out a pack of cigarettes and lit one, his large hands cupped around the flame to buffer it from the morning wind. "You are a nosy lot of women."

She nudged him with her elbow. "No one is worse than you three men."

"That's not true," he protested.

"Do you think Jones will have something to say about it, with them working together and all?"

"That was some of the worry when these mixed batteries were announced," he said.

"And I thought it was just that we're the weaker sex."

"I think you've proven everyone wrong about that. You girls are made of sterner stuff than most of the men I grew up with. Then again, they're not in the RA," he said, tapping the Royal Artillery badge on his cap proudly.

"You RA men have a high opinion of yourselves, did anyone ever tell you that?" she asked as they rounded the last corner.

But however Cartruse answered was lost, because standing in front of the billet's door in his well-tailored uniform was Paul. A group of ATS girls, up early, were smoking on the steps of the building and openly eyeing him, but he wasn't looking at them. Instead, his eyes were fixed right on her, a smile blooming across his handsome face.

Her heart squeezed, stealing her breath until she almost burst with it. She broke out into a sprint and flung herself into his arms, her cheek pressed hard against his chest.

"You're here," she murmured. "You're really here."

A hand stroked down the back of her head—her cap must've fallen off.

"How could I not be, after your letter?" he asked.

Relief rushed through her. Her letter hadn't frightened him off. He was here.

"I wanted to write back to you, but then I remembered that you'd told me about your leave. I did everything I could to arrange to be in London at the same time. I wanted to surprise you," he said softly.

"You did."

He pulled back, his expression serious. "I'm so sorry. The things I wrote to you last month—"

She cut him off with a kiss that felt like coming home. The lips she'd thought of, worried over, dreamed about, molded to hers, and she let herself fall back into the simplest moments of their relationship, when it had all seemed like it would go on for years uninterrupted by war or family. Her hands clutched at the lapels of his uniform jacket and he cupped her face.

Behind her, whoops and hollers rose up and she broke away with a grin. "We have an audience."

He snuck another swift kiss. "I don't care, but perhaps you should introduce me."

Everyone crowded around except Cartruse, who stood a step away, assessing Paul with guarded curiosity. As she made the introductions, Paul pressed each of the women's hands and shook the men's with more vigor.

"We've heard an awful lot about you," said Charlie, with a sly look at Louise.

"Hopefully none of it awful. It's been a fight to get a week's leave, but as soon as I had it I was on a boat across the Channel. I couldn't wait to see my girl again. And"—he stepped back with a laugh—"when I get here, I find you in trousers!"

She blushed, suddenly aware of the fact that she was in battle dress, her hair windswept and wilted after a long night manning the predictor. "Trousers are better for long nights outdoors."

"The last time I saw her she was wearing schoolgirl sweaters and old-fashioned skirts six inches past her knees," he said.

His tone was light but there was the slight sting there. From the way Vera lifted her brows, Louise could tell her friend had caught it too, but she shook it off. Paul was here, and that was all that mattered.

"Well, I don't know that any man dreams of asking a woman this while she's wearing trousers but . . ." Paul got down on one knee, the long fingers of both his hands wrapped around hers. "Louise Keene, would you do me the very great honor of making me the happiest man in the world?"

The gasps of the women in her unit was lost in the sound of the blood roaring in Louise's ears. The weight of nine pairs of eyes was bearing down on her, and she didn't understand what was happening. How had they gone from kisses to months of letters to *this*? She loved him, but it felt as though he was skipping steps—important steps—and she didn't know how to catch up.

"Paul." She choked on his name and gave a slight tug on her hand, as though if she broke the connection of skin against skin she might some-how be able to think clearly again.

A brief flicker of doubt passed over his features. "Darling, I thought—"

"Paul, what exactly are you asking me?"

Then the brilliant, teasing smile that had dazzled her on the dance floor of St. Mawgan was back. "I'm asking you to marry me. Will you?"

A squeal burst out, and they all spun. Lizzie stood there, her hands clapped over her mouth and her eyes shining bright. "I'm so sorry," Lizzie said, lowering her hands from her lips. "I was excited."

Louise raked her gaze over all of her colleagues, each of them looking at her with barely contained anticipation except two: Cartruse stood, arms cross and lips twisted, and Vera's face was completely neutral as though she were waiting for the answer before calling up the right reaction to broadcast. Louise desperately wanted to pull the slightly older and slightly wiser Vera aside and ask her why. Why was she not thrilled like the other girls? Why was this all happening so fast? Did she really want to marry Paul?

"Darling," he prompted, shaking her hand a little.

She pressed her free hand to her forehead. "It's all just happened so fast. We were just fighting in our letters last month."

"And there's no woman I'd rather fight with than you," he said.

"Paul, be reasonable."

"I don't want to be reasonable. Maybe I should've waited, but I know I want you to be my wife. I want our lives to start now." He slipped a hand in his pocket and when he opened it, she saw the little brass compass he'd tried to give her when he left Cornwall. "I haven't had time to buy you a ring, but you know how precious this is to me. Nothing would make me happier than knowing it's protecting you now, my wife."

She swallowed. She loved this man—she'd told herself that enough times that it had to be true—and now he was standing here before her, asking her to leap with him. She was just nervous at the enormity of saying yes to such a simple question.

"You haven't told me you love me," she whispered.

His eyes crinkled. "Is that all, silly thing? Of course I love you, darling. I didn't realize I needed to shout it from the rooftops."

For some reason, his laughing words made her blush even harder. She should've known, he seemed to be saying. Maybe if she'd been a little more sophisticated she would've known how to handle a man's affection.

"Of course I will," she said, swallowing around the lump in her throat.

A cheer exploded as Paul swept her off her feet and kissed her. Buoyed by the others' elation, she set her head back and laughed, letting herself be carried away by the collective joy.

When he set her back down on her feet, Paul slung an arm around her waist and pulled her close to him before turning to the girls. "Which of you are staying in London?"

"I am," said Charlie.

"Then you'll play the part of witness," he said. "Make sure my girl doesn't get cold feet on Wednesday," said Paul.

"Wednesday?" Louise asked. That was just two days away.

"I've already written to a pastor who said he'd make all the arrangements and marry us. He has a soft spot for couples in service and knows how to make sure a quick wedding goes off without a hitch," said Paul.

A quick wedding. In Haybourne, the only women who had quick weddings were those who *had* to. Claris Glisi, for instance, who married a man in a fast ceremony and had a baby six months later at seventeen. Thea White, whose husband left her pregnant with a second child two years after their fast ceremony. Louise's own mother.

Louise tried to let the implications roll off her shoulders, knowing she was being horribly provincial about it all. Plenty of couples in the service married quickly, happy to grab whatever time they could while they were in the same place.

"All right," she said, pulling her shoulders back. "Wednesday it is."

Paul kissed her on the temple. "A wedding and then the wedding breakfast at the Dorchester, I think."

Charlie cackled at the mention of the posh hotel, and all of the other girls looked downcast, regretting that they had plans to see worrying family members that they couldn't break.

"Will your parents be there?" Louise asked, realizing with a pang that her own wouldn't be able to make the trip from Cornwall in time.

"They're off in the countryside, remember? Evacuated London as soon as it started raining bombs," he said. "Now, what do you think about changing into a proper skirt again and letting me show you the real London?"

"Yes, of course. I'd love to see where you grew up," she said.

"I'll meet you down here in twenty minutes. We'll get some breakfast into you and then set off."

The girls crowded forward, each offering some way for her to change her appearance or brighten up the uniform she would have to wear for her wedding. When she turned back, Paul was accepting congratulations from Hatfield and taking a cigarette. She caught Cartruse's eye. He nodded once before stuffing his hands in his pockets and continuing down the road back to his barracks.

∽

"But this isn't where you live?" Louise asked. It was more than twelve hours since Paul had appeared on the steps of her billet. Her flipped schedule of night shifts meant that her head felt as though it was full of cotton wool because she hadn't slept since midmorning the day before.

"No," said Paul, turning the large brass key in the lock of the a terrace house in Kensington where he'd told her his friend kept a flat on the ground floor.

"What happened to your bedsit?" she asked, remembering so clearly the way he'd described the little flat to her.

"My landlady wrote to tell me the building across the street was hit by a bomb. It broke all the windows in my flat, and she hasn't been able to find a glazer to fix them. The demand's too high with all of the bomb sites across the city." He pushed open the door and flicked on the hall light. "Just through here."

Louise pulled at the hem of her uniform's tunic and looked around.

It was a nice enough hallway with carved crown molding and a neat set of stairs up to the flat above, but it wasn't Paul's place, and that was disappointing.

She'd been hesitant at dinner about coming back with him. He'd told her she looked as though she was falling asleep in her soup, and suggested they turn in for the night.

She could've insisted that he take her back to her billet, and he would've, but instead she'd let him walk her to the Piccadilly line and board the train that took them to Earl's Court. They were going to be married in two days. Maintaining any modesty now seemed ridiculous. She'd decided, as their feet scraped against the pavement out of the station, that she was going to absolve herself of any guilt she might feel about exploring an intimacy with this man before they were married.

He unlocked at door with a brass "1" nailed to it and stepped back to let her inside. It was chillier in the sitting room than outside, if that was even possible, and Louise wrapped her arms around herself as she looked about. Despite the cold, it was a comfortable room with a pair of green tufted sofas facing one another in front of an elaborate iron fireplace and a few paintings covering the walls. She'd just moved toward one of a seaside that reminded her of home, when Paul's hand fell on her waist.

"Where are you going?" He drew his hand up her back, his fingers dancing over her uniform as though it were of the silkiest satin. "I've been waiting all day for us to be alone."

She turned to him, her hands resting softly on his chest. The scent of him, spiced bay rum, wrapped around her as she breathed in deep. But even as she lifted her chin, something held her back.

"Are you nervous?" he asked, resting his forehead against hers.

She toyed with one of the brass buttons on his uniform. "No. Yes. I don't know."

"You can trust me, darling."

Her eyes must have betrayed her, because when their gazes met he cradled her to him.

"I've done this all wrong, haven't I? You want a big wedding in your parish church with all of your nearest and dearest."

She knew he didn't mean it, but when he teased like this she couldn't help but feel entirely unsophisticated.

"No, it's not that," she said quickly. "We just haven't known each other for very long."

He tucked a knuckle under her chin and gently raised it. "I knew the moment I met you, Louise, that you would be mine."

"I did too," she said automatically.

"Then you know that this is right."

"I . . ."

"You're not sure," he said, sadness breaking his voice.

Guilt churned in her stomach as he made as though to walk away. She caught his hand as he'd done to her, and he stilled.

"I'm sorry, Paul. It's just that it's been difficult without you and now it's confusing with you standing right here where I can actually touch you. It almost seems unreal."

She could see the touch of a smile warm his profile. "I know, darling. I know that you sacrificed everything in Haybourne because of me. It's only natural to have moments of doubt."

She wanted to tell him that it hadn't just been for him that she'd joined the ATS. She'd done it for herself too, but the words felt impossibly thick on her tongue.

In the end, he saved her from having to explain, because he kissed her. Only this kiss wasn't like the ones before. This one was hard, as he crushed his lips against hers and raked his hands through her hair. He pulled at her hair, bending her back so that he could kiss the side of her neck, his other hand darting up to cup her breast. A frisson of heat shot through her, desire and surprise and hesitation all at once.

"I want you. You must know that," he said, breathing heavily as he kissed down to the top of her uniform's shirt.

Here in this perfectly respectable flat he had become something altogether less respectable. Gone was the polish of a well-heeled childhood spent in a mansion flat, a public school education, and reading at Cambridge. Now he was just a man overcome by a woman. She was that woman.

The seductive knowledge of her own power surged up in her. Sliding her hand up his shoulder to his neck, she guided him back up to meet her lips, slipping her tongue between his lips.

He groaned, "Louise . . . I can't wait any longer."

Careful not to break his gaze, she lifted her hands to the buckle of her tunic and undid the wide belt. His eyes fixed on her fingers as she swiftly unbuttoned the heavy garment and let it slide off her shoulders. Then she picked up his hand in hers and said with more surety than she felt, "I'm ready, Paul."

With one more swift kiss, he pulled her into the darkened bedroom.

17

CARA

Cara hit save on her work laptop, laced her fingers together, and stretched her arms high over her head. The last of the items from the Old Vicarage were catalogued in Wilson's inventory and up on the auction sites Jock favored.

Already a few pieces had sold, with others going to private clients Jock kept apprised of his stock. Just two days ago, an American woman on holiday had bought a Tiffany lamp they'd found in one of Lenora Robinson's guest bedrooms. The woman had been delighted with the maze-like shop, all enthusiasm and praise for the rambling rooms jammed full of furniture, paintings, pottery, and objets d'art. Cara had chatted with her as she took the woman's details to ship the lamp back to her home in Iowa, and when the woman left, Cara had the comforting feeling that another of Lenora Robinson's things had been placed into good hands for this next part of its life.

The experience had prompted her to pick up the phone and call one of Jock's associates working out of London. Her parents had had some good pieces that were in storage, but either because they clashed with her own style or because of the close quarters of her cottage, Cara didn't want to keep them. She and the dealer had arranged a time to meet in early November, and when she'd hung up, she'd felt somehow buoyed. There was still loads to do, but this would be a start.

Cara began to weave her way from the office off the storeroom to the kitchenette at the back of the shop to fill the electric kettle and celebrate with a little tea break, but before she could get there the door jangled. She stilled for a moment, waiting to see if Jock would intercept the person or whether she'd be needed. The low rumble of a male voice followed by another drifted back to her. She was off the hook.

She was just pulling down a Burleigh teapot with a cracked lid Jock had rescued from an estate sale years ago when her boss appeared in the door. "Miss Hargraves, you have a visitor."

He stepped back, revealing Liam.

"What are you doing here?" she asked, surprise and pleasure pinking her cheeks. She'd spent half of the past four days telling herself that Liam had just been tired when he'd turned down her invitation to dinner and the other half chiding herself for worrying that he was done with her. But now he was standing in her shop—well, Jock's shop, but still.

"I have news," he said. "About the diary."

Cara slanted a look at Jock, who stood back, his arms over his chest, observing them as though he were a spectator at a chess match.

"And you came here to tell me?" she asked.

"As soon as I found out. I tried you on your phone but I couldn't reach you and it didn't seem fair me knowing something before you. Do you remember that Cornish historian I told you I'd reached out to?" he asked.

"The one who was going to figure out where Bakeford's was."

He nodded. "It's in Haybourne. Or at least it was."

"Where?" she asked with a frown.

"Haybourne is a tiny village on the Cornish coastline," said Jock, earning stares from both of them. "I used to spend my summers in Newquay when I was a boy."

"I'd never heard of it before, so I looked it up on a map. It's just down the road from Saint Mawgan," said Liam.

"Where she had her first dance with Paul," Cara said.

"Exactly."

The kettle clicked off its boil, and she set about pouring the hot water over the leaves and pulling down three mugs. Liam was staying for tea.

"We've been trying to track down the author of that diary I found at the Old Vicarage," she said by way of explanation for Jock. "If we know where she's from, we can track her down."

"I see," said Jock.

"There are the initials on the back of the photograph. 'L.K.,'" she said, thinking through everything they knew. "Do any of the women in the mixed batteries come from Haybourne and have those initials?"

Liam pulled a paper out of the back pocket of his jeans. "One step ahead of you."

He handed the paper to her, and she opened it, fingers trembling. It was a printout of what looked like some kind of dossier. At the top was the name "Louise Keene" along with a date of birth, service number, battalion assignment, and date of demobilization.

After weeks of reading and wondering who their mysterious diarist was, it seemed almost surreal to finally have a name. To know what to call her.

"Louise Keene. You're sure?" she asked.

"I had my friend at the National Archives cross-check everything. There was only one ATS member assigned to Ack-Ack Command from Haybourne. A Louise Keene."

"It looks as though you've solved your mystery," said Jock.

Liam and Cara shared a look. "Far from it," she said. "I still want to know what happened to Louise Keene and Paul, the pilot."

"What else was with the diary?" asked Jock. "I know you found it in a tin."

"Here." Liam pulled his phone from his pocket. "I took photographs of everything."

Jock perched his reading glasses on his nose and bent a little to peer at the phone's screen.

"The ticket is from a cinema in Cornwall where Paul and Louise went on their first dates," said Cara.

"The monogrammed handkerchief must be his," said Liam.

"What about the compass?" Jock asked.

"He told her that it had belonged to his uncle who died in the Royal Flying Corps during World War One. It was one of the things recovered with his body," she said.

Jock squinted up at her and then looked down at the phone again. "No."

"No?" she asked.

"I'd need to see it in person to be positive, but I'm certain that's a British-made army-issue escape compass. From World War Two," said her boss.

"How can you be sure?" she asked, her pulse ticking up another notch. Why would Paul have lied about something like that?

"When I was first starting out, I had a client come in with dozens of these. His father had been a collector," said Jock.

"What exactly is an escape compass?" Liam asked.

"The RAF and the army issued them to pilots and soldiers who went on dangerous missions across enemy lines. They were often hidden in the backs of buttons so that a serviceman could use one to escape if he was captured, but this looks as though it's just one of the tiny compasses that could've been tucked away anywhere," said Jock.

"And you're certain it's not a World War One–era?" Liam asked.

Jock straightened and removed his glasses. "As Miss Hargraves will tell you, I never encourage guessing about the origins or provenance of an antique, but I'd be willing to bet my Montblanc on it."

Liam raised a brow, and Cara nodded. Jock carried that pen everywhere, taking it out and polishing it from time to time.

"Now, Miss Hargraves, am I given to understand that you are finished with the Robinson inventory?" Jock asked.

"I've only just finished it. How did you know?"

"I'm not so ancient that I cannot use a computer. I was looking at our inventory when Mr. McGown arrived. And given the completion of the inventory and your recent discovery, I should think you'd like the rest of the afternoon off."

"Really?" she asked in surprise.

"Do I ever jest?" Jock asked severely, but she could see the glint of amusement in her employer's eye.

"Never," she said gravely.

"Then I suggest you both decamp before I change my mind."

"Thank you," she said, grinning at Liam. They had a diary investigation to continue.

∼

"Fancy a cup of tea?" Cara called to Liam as they climbed out of their cars in their respective driveways, rain pelting them. The skies had opened the moment they'd both pulled away from Wilson's and showed no signs of letting up.

His grin widened. "Always. Is there any chance you have biscuits?"

"I'm English, aren't I?"

He laughed and the pair of them sprinted through the driving rain to her front door. In the entryway, she shucked off her jacket and shook out her hair from the braid she'd tied it in to keep off the worst of the wet. When he saw her unzip her boots, he did the same and padded behind her to the kitchen.

"Can I do anything to help?" he asked, as she started pulling the tea things down.

"You could light the fire in the front room. I'm trying not to turn on the central heating until it gets really cold, and I like an excuse for a fire."

He shuffled off while she put the water on and pulled out a package of biscuits. She was just arranging them on a plate when he called out, "Do you have matches?"

She opened the cabinet to her left and plucked the little Waitrose Essentials box off the shelf. He shuffled on his knees to meet her halfway across the kitchen, their fingers brushing when she handed the matches over. Her heart leaped in her throat, and Liam's gaze flew up to hers. For a moment, they remained frozen, the tips of their fingers touching.

"Thanks," he murmured.

"Of course."

A little dazed, she watched him retreat again before shaking her head and fixing tea.

She carried the plate of biscuits into the front room to drop them off while the tea steeped, stopping only to retrieve the biscuit tin from her nightstand.

She eased open the heavy oak door with her shoulder, balancing the tin in one hand and the biscuits in the other. Flames crackled, catching on dry paper, and the wood burner's vent squeaked as Liam adjusted it. She set the plate down, folded herself onto the sofa, and popped the top off the tin to pull out the photograph of the woman on the Embankment. No, not "the woman." *Louise.*

The sofa dipped a little as Liam took the other end, leaning over the gap between them. "That's our girl," he said with a nod to the photograph of Louise. "Someone must've taken it when she was stationed at Woolwich. Her service record says she was there from August 1941 to February 1942 when she and her unit were moved up to Glasgow to defend the shipyards. Then they were sent to Brighton and finally to Germany."

"When was she demobbed?" she asked.

"1945, after VE Day."

"Like Gran," Cara mused. "But the diary ends in 1942. There's almost three years of war that are unaccounted for. And what happened to her afterward. Is there a record of that?"

He shook his head. "That's where the military records end. A lot of women went home after the war."

"Paul proposes to her. She could've ended up with his family, although the last page of the diary makes it seem unlikely."

"Have you peeked at the ending?" he asked.

She shook her head. "Not since I first found it. You?"

"Just the last couple entries. They're pretty thin. Also, there are gaps in time." He paused. "There's something else."

"What?"

"Louise Keene doesn't come up in any local registers in Haybourne after the war, but there is another Keene. Katherine. She's registered as the mother to a child born in Haybourne in 1944 with the married name of Mathers."

"Katherine like Kate?" she asked with a frown.

"What if Kate wasn't Louise's friend but her cousin?" he asked.

Pieces began clicking into place like one big jigsaw puzzle. "And that was why Kate was so willing to help Louise sneak around with Paul. And why Louise went to her when she rowed with her mother."

"And also why Kate's mother would've insisted it was Louise who went with Kate to the Valentine's dance in Saint Mawgan in the first place," he said.

"Liam, this is amazing," she said.

He held up a hand. "I'm not finished yet." He unlocked his phone and flipped it over to show her a picture of an older woman with the words "Laurel Mathers, Executive Director" written in bold under it. "That's Katherine Mathers's daughter, who runs a small arts outreach organization in Cornwall. And her email address is listed on the site."

"Her email . . ."

"If you reach out, she may be able to fill in some of the gaps about what happened to her aunt."

"Do you think I should?" she asked.

"I think you have to. You need to see this story through to the end," said Liam. "Just like you want to with Iris."

"Liam, in the car on Sunday, I'm sorry if I overstepped."

He tilted his head to the right, studying her. "Overstepped?"

"When I offered to cook. You'd already done so much that day and I wasn't thinking—"

"Do you know what I did when I got home?" he asked, the corners of his lips tilting up.

"No."

"I kicked myself for turning you down. I must've been out of my mind."

"You turned down dinner," she said with a laugh, remembering all the times he'd disparaged his own cooking.

"I turned down dinner with *you*," he said.

He heart squeezed, and she dipped her head. "I thought my life became small after the divorce, but I realized that it already was before that. All I did was work and come home. I didn't see my friends, have hobbies, or explore. I wasn't living a full life. I'm trying to make sure that doesn't happen again, but it's been a long time since I've reached out to anyone."

He reached across the gap and tucked a strand of her dark hair behind her ear. "Then I'm honored you've made a little room for me."

For one mad moment, she wanted to lean into his hand. Instead, she stayed stone-still, hardly breathing for fear of breaking the moment while she relished being cared for just a little.

Slowly, he drew back. "Do you know what I think we should do right now? You should write to Laurel Mathers, and I'll go check on my dog." She was about to protest when he added, "Then I'll come back and pour the tea."

"Why don't you bring Rufus? I hate to think of him all alone while we're here," she said.

He grinned and leaned back against the sofa cushions and looking for all the world like he belonged.

"I'd like that very much, Cara. Very much."

∾

As soon as Rufus came through the door, Liam rubbed him down with a towel and the dog went to Cara's side. Rufus accepted a head scratch and then dropped to the floor by her feet with a content sigh.

"I think he likes you more than me," said Liam with a laugh.

A happy warmth spread through her, and she simply smiled.

"Did you email Laurel?" he asked.

She nodded. "Now I keep staring at my phone, waiting."

"Well then"—he snatched a biscuit off the tray and bit into it with a snap—"I'm glad we have provisions. I'll pour the tea."

"No, don't worry about that. I'll get it."

But as she began to set the diary down, Liam held his hand up. "Rufus looks like he's in heaven. I'll do it. Just tell me which cabinet the mugs are in."

"To the right of the sink," she said, secretly pleased at his offer. It had been ages since someone had offered to bring a steaming cup of comfort to her while she read. She was growing to like her independence, but there were little things about having a partner she missed.

Snuggling a little deeper into the burgundy throw pillows she'd ordered just a few weeks ago, she gave the dog's head another pat and went back to her reading. It was strange to think her once-anonymous diarist had a name now, but perhaps no stranger than that Cara had started to think of Louise as her own. Despite having no relation to her, she felt a deep connection with this woman that went beyond the desire to return the diary to its rightful family. She understood something of Louise's journey from shy and unassertive girl to gunner girl, as glamorous and brave as she was determined and hardworking.

Liam returned to hand her a cup of tea that had enough milk in it to turn it the color of a ginger buscuit—just the way she'd told him she liked it.

As he settled back onto his end of the sofa, she thanked him and asked, "Have you read to the part about Louise and Paul going off to his friend's flat together?"

"Yes. Very saucy, even if she doesn't give much detail."

She chuckled. "I don't know why I was so shocked at that. Of course people slept together before they were married."

"We think everyone before our generation was Victorian in their attitudes to sex, when it couldn't be further from the truth. People have been sneaking off together for millennia."

"I suppose you're right," she said.

"Plus, there was a war on. From what I've read, there were a lot of men and women falling into each other's arms because they didn't know what tomorrow would bring."

"You don't know if your air raid shelter will be destroyed by a bomb, so you might as well live it up," she said.

"Exactly."

Cara paged forward in the diary, but other than a few more entries in September, the dates began to spread out again as Liam had said.

"Not much more left," she said.

She watched Liam fish around in the biscuit tin until he pulled out the locket. The hinge moved easily, despite its age, as though it had been opened and closed countless times. He held up the picture of Paul, handsome and smiling, next to the photograph of Louise. They would've made a beautiful couple; he was glamorous and sophisticated, while she was sweet, her laugh full of genuine joy.

"What do you think?" he asked.

"It's a shame we don't have a photograph of them together," she said.

"Maybe Laurel Mathers has one," said Liam.

On the coffee table, her phone dinged and they both craned their necks. An email notification illuminated the screen.

"Is that from Laurel?" Liam asked.

Cara scooped up her phone and looked up sharply. "It is."

Quickly, she keyed in her pass code and pulled up the email from Laurel. She read it out.

Dear Ms. Hargraves,

I must admit, I was surprised to receive your email. I did have an aunt named Louise Keene who served in Ack-Ack Command in the war. Sadly, she passed away six years ago peacefully in her sleep.

My mother, Katherine Mathers, is nearing the end of her life but is blessedly lucid. I moved back to Haybourne after my divorce almost twenty years ago and have been taking care of her in her later years. She enjoys nothing more than reminiscing about her girlhood in Haybourne and her time in the ATS. She tells me that those were the best years of her life, serving in Belgium, Egypt, and Greece.

I was at my mother's care home when I received your email. She would like very much to meet you if you ever come down to Haybourne. I think it would bring her a great deal of joy to tell someone new all of the stories we've heard dozens of times, but I would encourage you to come soon. I don't know how much longer my mother's health will hold out, as she seems more frail by the day.

"And then she gives her phone number and a recommendation of a hotel to stay in. It's the Star Inn Louise wrote about. I guess it was renovated about ten years ago and a chef trained in a Michelin kitchen was brought on," Cara finished.

"You have to go. I don't think you'll get the answers you're looking for if you don't speak to Katherine," he said.

"Kate," Cara corrected him with a smile. She petted Rufus as she thought over the prospect of driving down to Cornwall to see an old woman in her last days. But then, she'd been invited, and Laurel didn't seem put out by the idea. Still . . .

"Come with me," she said.

Liam swallowed a large gulp of tea. "To Cornwall?"

"You're as much a part of this as I am," she said, growing more assured of the idea as she realized how *much* she wanted him there. It
was strange to think that at the beginning of September she'd shied
away from this warm, generous man when his sister had suggested
something as simple as dinner. Yet there was something here, small
and delicate, but growing, and she no longer wanted to hide from it. Instead, she'd rather nurture it with patience and trust, giving it a chance
to flourish.

"I'm happy to pay for our accommodation," she offered.

"I couldn't let you do that."

"Why not?" she asked.

"For one thing, I'd like to be there as much as you would." He paused.
"You really want me to come with?"

"Yes." And the more she thought about it, the more certain she was.

"When?"

"Laurel makes it sound as though her mother may not have much
longer."

"I'm free next weekend," he said.

Whatever was between them grew a little stronger. "So am I."

"If we leave on Friday and come back on Monday, we could find
where Bakeford's stood, and the Smuggler's Cave."

"I'd like that." She paused. "You're sure?"

He spread his hands wide. "I'm all yours, Cara."

As they settled back to continue reading the diary together, she lifted
her tea to her lips to hide her smile.

23 September 1941

*I spent last night with Paul, wrapped up in him in that borrowed flat off
of the Earl's Court tube stop. Maybe I should feel guilty about that, but I
don't. Not when I think about tomorrow. Not when it felt right.*

I came back to the billet this morning to pack my dress uniform and

bring it back to the flat, but I'm taking a few minutes to write to Da.
The one thing I regret is that he won't be there tomorrow. He and Mum,
because I do want her there too. If she'd made an effort to know Paul even
a little bit, I think she would've been impressed with him. Not just that
he's posh and from London, but that he's kind and he loves me.

18

LOUISE

Louise's wedding was nothing like she'd imagined. When she and Paul climbed out of a cab—an expense he'd insisted on, much to her delight, because she'd never been in a cab before—Charlie had been waiting outside a church that looked as though it had sustained at least one hit from a bomb. Paul had laughed at her horrified expression and patted her hand. Because the church had been damaged, they'd be married in the vicarage around back where Father Norwood was staying because his own parish had been even more horribly damaged in the Blitz.

Then Reggie, Paul's childhood friend, had rolled around the corner, weaving as though he was standing on the bow of a ship. He was spectacularly drunk, but Paul slapped him on the back and introduced him to Louise.

"Caught him, have you?" Reggie laughed, bringing Louise's hand to his lips and giving it a loud smack. "I hope you plan to keep him on a pretty tight lead."

Paul had laughed, but Louise and Charlie exchanged startled looks.

"Has he been drinking since he woke up?" whispered Charlie, watching Reggie try three times before he successfully lit his cigarette while Paul had a word with Father Norwood. "It's barely eleven in the morning."

Louise stared in shock. "I really don't know. Paul told me we were lucky Reggie was able to come at all. He's attached to the foreign office, and it was touch-and-go as to whether he'd be able to take a day's leave."

"Good lord, if that's who's working in the foreign office, we're all doomed," said Charlie.

When Paul jogged back to them, she pulled him aside and whispered, "What on earth is wrong with your friend?"

Paul glanced over as though realizing for the first time that Reggie was three sheets to the wind. "Oh, don't worry, darling. He's always like that."

"Will he be able to even witness the ceremony? Will it be legal?"

Paul kissed her on the cheek. "Everything'll be right as rain. Come on now."

The ceremony, such as it was, was swift. Father Norwood sped through the appropriate readings in the vicarage's front room while Louise clutched her bouquet hard enough that she surely bruised the stems. Everything about it was surreal, as though everyone else had been handed a script and she was the only one who was really present, until Paul produced a ring from his uniform pocket.

"Darling," he murmured. She let out a breath she hadn't realized she'd been holding and gave him her hand. Paul was all that mattered.

As he swore to love and protect her, a lump formed in her throat. She was so far from the path she'd thought her life would go down. This wasn't Gary, the local golden boy; it was Paul, a sophisticated man who told her he was crazy for her. Educated, erudite, brave, and handsome, he was everything a girl should want.

But still, it wasn't perfect. The groomsman was drunk, the priest seemed more intent on getting through the ceremony than on imbuing it with any weight, and she knew she and Paul would be separated less than a day after they were married and returned to their respective services. Still, she was determined to make the most of it until they could be reunited to start their lives together in earnest.

She repeated her vows, her eyes locked on his, and lifted her lips to his as Father Norwood pronounced them man and wife. Reggie shouted "Hip hip hooray!" A smile broke out over her face even as Paul kissed her. She was married to Paul Bolton.

They'd decamped to the Dorchester in Mayfair. Louise couldn't help but stare at the vast dining room with its mirrored walls and soaring gold chandelier as they were led to their table in the center of the room. The menu was limited, a concession to the war, but the consommé was excellent and Paul ordered champagne, sending her back to the day in the Star Inn where she'd tried it for the first time. Unlike on that day, however, today she felt as though she belonged in this glamorous world of champagne and three-course luncheons served on translucent bone china. Whether it was because of the man by her side or the uniform she wore, she couldn't be certain, but she held her shoulders back and lifted her chin with a confidence she couldn't have believed a year ago.

That boldness softened as the meal progressed. When the main course was cleared and a third bottle of champagne opened, Louise felt light as a feather, tipsy on bubbles. Everything seemed to shimmer around her. As Reggie boasted about another posting in another city, she smiled at Paul. He raised her hand to his lips as he'd done several times throughout the meal.

"And then I said, 'We should all just go to the pictures,'" said Reggie.

"And where was this?" Charlie asked, her head cradled in her hand, her tone bored but tolerant thanks to a liberal application of champagne.

"Edinburgh, I think," said Reggie. "This was when you were at RAF Dyce in Scotland, isn't that right, Bolton?"

"I have no idea."

"No, you remember, you were there," said Reggie. "You used one of your forty-eight-hour passes."

Through the fizzy haze of tipsiness, Louise's brain grasped onto that information.

"Forty-eight-hour pass?" she asked.

Reggie laughed. "Bolton's always up for a jaunt when the RAF lets him off his leash."

She pulled her hand back. "You've had leave? When was this?"

"It was nothing," Paul said, shooting a glare at his best friend. Reggie, oblivious, merrily snatched up his champagne glass and took another slug.

"Reggie, when did Paul see you in Edinburgh?" Louise asked.

Reggie blew out a loud breath. "I'm not very good with time, but it wasn't that long ago."

"Reggie," Paul barked, but Louise was already rounding on him.

"You said your commanding officer wasn't allowing you to have leave at all. That you had to stay on base and that's why you canceled your visit to see me. Why I couldn't come to you," she said.

"Reggie's wrong, darling. It was *last* July. When I was flying over the North Sea. Before I met you."

"But you never told me you were stationed at RAF Dyce," she pressed. "You mentioned being based in Devon for Costal Command and that you did your training at RAF Halton, but not Scotland."

"There are a lot of things I haven't told you about," said Paul. "But I promise I will. We're together now."

She sat back heavily in her chair, her eyes fixed on a little stain of sauce on the tablecloth. He was trying to placate her, and she didn't like it. Reggie might've been confused about the dates, but she didn't think so. Paul had been too sharp with his friend, as though he was desperate to shut the man up and control the damage.

"We need more champagne," said Paul loudly. "I'd like to make a toast."

"Hear! Hear!" Reggie nearly shouted, until Charlie smacked him on the arm to hush him.

"You can't agree with a toast until I say it," Paul said with an exaggerated scowl. "Now, I'd like to make a toast to my beautiful bride, Louise." He tipped his glass to her as she watched him with a thin smile. "You are the bravest woman I know."

Reggie laughed. "She's brave for taking him on, that's what I say."

"Brave in *all* ways," said Charlie. "You all forget that I'm the only one who's actually seen Louise in action."

"Do tell," said Reggie, leaning on the table and nearly putting his elbow in the butter.

"The first night we were stationed at Woolwich, we were shot at and our commanding officer went into a state of shock," said Charlie.

"You can hardly blame her though. It was terrifying," said Louise.

"I can blame her when she spent our entire time at Oswestry convincing us that she'd been through battle and back. It turned out she'd been an ATS clerk who'd hardly even heard a live round until she was promoted and transferred. What they were thinking putting her in charge of the women in one of the first mixed batteries, I'll never know.

"When Colonel Barker snapped, it was Louise who stepped up and got us all to focus again. A fighter was shooting at us and bombs were falling, but Louise kept a cool head and did exactly what needed to be done." Charlie smiled. "So you see, Paul, you may just have married one of the bravest women in the ATS."

Louise waited for embarrassment to rise up, but then she stopped herself. Charlie was right. She *had* done those things. She had every right to be proud, and she was. Since joining up, she'd done things she'd never dreamed of, and she was eager for more. It wasn't the destructive power of her job that drew her in but the knowledge that she was doing something that mattered. She wasn't tucked away in a corner of the country, whiling away her days in a shop and waiting for a life of village committees and gossip. Her work was important—just as important as Paul's.

She lifted her gaze to her new husband, but his expression was unexpectedly flinty. "I don't want her brave. This bloody war . . ."

"Really, Paul," she chastised him lightly.

He swore, snatching up his glass. "If you ask me, they should've never started women's auxiliary branches. It's too dangerous, not to mention the distraction."

"What?" She'd heard that argument more times than she could count, but she'd never thought she'd hear it from Paul. Of all the men in her life, he should be the most supportive.

"We're doing vital work," said Charlie. "Everywhere you go there are posters and newsreels and radio reports telling women to join up and free up posts for men to go fight."

Louise jumped in, saying, "We're protecting cities and helping fliers like you—"

"Now I'm supposed to be grateful that you might shoot down a pilot I miss in a dogfight because I can't hit him on my own?"

"That's not what I said."

He pounded his fist on the table. "That's what it sounded like, and I won't have it, Louise. I won't have it at all!"

Silence blanketed the table, and even Reggie stared. Louise sat frozen as her new husband lit his cigarette and threw the gold lighter down next to his plate. He took a draw and closed his eyes, and his shoulders seemed to drop an inch. When he opened his eyes again, his gaze slid from face to face.

Instantly, his demeanor changed. He sagged in his chair, placed two fingers to his right temple, and rubbed the spot as though a headache was to blame for his outburst.

"I'm being a brute, darling. An absolute brute. I'm sorry," he said.

He wanted her absolution, but she couldn't give it to him. Not when his words still hung in the air.

The worst part was, now that she thought of it, it wasn't just this outburst. How many times had he written to her in the past five months arguing that Ack-Ack Command was too dangerous?

"You don't understand what it's like knowing you're in the middle of bombed-out London, waiting for the Luftwaffe to take potshots at you," said Paul, his voice rough.

"I do know," she said quietly. "That's how I feel every time you write to tell me that you've flown a mission or shot down a plane or been shot at yourself."

"But you're a woman. You're better equipped to deal with these sorts of things. Fear. Emotion. Men go off to war, and women stay behind and tend the home fires, like Odysseus and Penelope."

She shook her head. "I would have gone crazy at home waiting for you. I had to come out and do something."

I wanted to be something more.

"Hear! Hear!" Charlie said softly, mimicking Reggie's earlier outburst.

Paul covered Louise's hand with his. "One day, this will all be over and we can go back to the way things were."

"The way things were?" She laughed. "That was me in a pokey little town with no hope of ever leaving." That would be her crammed back into a small life, her path planned out for her by other people determined that they knew what was best for her.

His lips thinned. "You know what I mean."

"I'm not sure I do. I like wearing this uniform. I like working. Why do you want me to give that up?"

"Come on now, darling. You can't blame me for not relishing the idea of my wife going up on a roof to play around at war."

Her chest constricted at the insult. *"Play?* You think I'm dressing up and playing like a child?"

His lower lip popped out in a sulk. "You know what I mean," he said again.

Never before had Paul shown this old-fashioned, stringent side of him. In his letters he'd expressed his worry for her, but she'd assumed he would appreciate and understand her situation. Now, for the first time since she'd joined up, she wondered if she'd had him all wrong.

"When I go up to that gun, I'm as much in danger of being hit as any man," she said as calmly as she could. "The Germans shoot at us because we're shooting at them. They don't think we're playing."

"Well, yes, but—"

"And I will *not* stand for anyone doubting the importance of that. Especially my husband."

The word seemed to snap Paul back to the charming man she knew. He took her hand, kissing the back of it. "Forgive me, Louise. I hate to be separated from you. You don't know what it did to me leaving you behind in Haybourne."

"And what of the things it did to me?" she asked.

"I know you left home and joined up because of me," he said.

That's not true sat heavy on her tongue. Paul had been the catalyst, but the desire to cast off the restrictive future her mother dreamed of for her had been building in her long before she met him. She'd just been waiting for the right moment to break free and find her own life. One with work and friends and purpose.

But she held back because they'd quarreled enough for one day— their wedding day. Delicately, she lifted her champagne to her lips but found that the bubbles had already started to go flat.

Paul squeezed her fingers gently. "Be patient with me, darling. I'm trying my hardest."

She gave the slightest of nods.

"I think it's time for another bottle," said Reggie, breaking through the mood.

Paul threw his head back and laughed a little too loud, trying to show that the fight was nothing more than a lovers' tiff. "Why not? How often does a man get married, anyway?"

Reggie snorted and waved for a waiter. "*Garçon!*"

Louise sat back as the waiter hurried over, watching her new husband's profile. They had their entire lives ahead of them, but she was no longer sure it was the life she'd imagined.

After the wedding breakfast, Louise and Paul retreated to the borrowed flat. She'd been prickly the entire way back, but when they crossed the threshold he'd kissed her slow and deep and her annoyance had diminished to a simmer. He'd made love to her, whispering all of the endearments she'd wanted to hear so badly from his lips over and over again.

But later that night, when they lay in bed, the blackout curtains drawn and his arm and leg thrown protectively over hers, the fight at their wedding breakfast came back to her.

"Paul," she said as she stared up at the ceiling.

He lifted his head from the pillow. "What is it, darling?"

"We haven't talked about what we'll do when the war ends."

He rolled over and scrubbed a hand over his eyes. "That's because this bloody war seems to be going on forever."

"I want to talk about it. It'll give me something to hope for when things seem particularly difficult."

He blew out a breath. "I won't be going back to Cambridge."

She turned to face him, propping her head on her elbow. "Why not?"

"Aviation is the future. No one is going to want to take trains and boats when planes are faster. You mark my words, there will be a boom, and I plan to be one of the commercial pilots at the forefront of it."

"That's exciting," she said.

He traced the line of her jaw. "And what's your heart's desire, darling? A big house, a big car, a mink?"

She nudged him with her foot. "Be serious."

"I am. I'll drape you in diamonds and pearls."

"And what would I do with them?" she asked.

"Wear them?"

"I've been thinking we could go to California. I could enroll at a university and get my degree. I'd like to study maths."

He frowned. "Maths? And what would you do with that?"

"I could teach, do any number of things."

The creases on his forehead deepened. "You want to work?"

"Well, yes," she said.

His gaze fixed on the ceiling. "Louise, I think it's time that you come to understand something. If I'm a pilot, I'm going to be traveling a great deal. You'll need to be home, taking care of our children here. In England. It's where my family is. It's where your place will be."

"But Paul—"

"No. This is not something that is up for argument. You're my wife. Your role is to support me."

A chill went through her. He was serious. Deadly serious. Had she walked from one person's idea of how she should live her life straight into another's?

"Now, we only have a few hours left before I have to report," he said, rolling on top of her. "It's time to make sure you remember me when I'm gone."

19

CARA

"We should establish ground rules," said Liam.

Cara turned over her keys in the ignition of her Vauxhall, the jangle of Granddad's dog tags a comforting reminder of her childhood, when Mum would get behind the wheel of the car and they'd go for a drive to a country pub, dog tags and keys clinking together merrily as they bumped along twisting single-lane roads.

"I'm sorry?" she asked.

"Passenger selects the music."

She laughed. "Driver has veto privileges. We're sharing six hours of driving. I'm not sure I can put up with it if I find out you have a secret love of ABBA."

"ABBA is the greatest Swedish export since the Volvo," Liam said.

"I should've known. Of all the professors in the world, this ABBA-loving one gets into my car."

"Now you're butchering lines from *Casablanca*. Don't think I'll stand for this for one moment."

A fizz of excitement rippled through her as she put her little car into reverse and backed out of the drive. Everything had come together so quickly. Liam had no lectures on Fridays or Mondays, so it had just been a matter of her asking for two days around the weekend. Jock had been surprisingly good-natured about it when he found out the trip was connected to the diary. The Star Inn was happy to give her two rooms next to one another as the season began to slow in October. Then it had just been a matter of packing and taking care of their individual tasks. Cara had gone to Gran's, armed with tea cakes, to explain that she would be away for a few days to meet Katherine Mathers, neé Keene. It had been tense at first, both of them on edge after her last visit, but Gran had perked up when she learned Liam would be traveling with Cara.

"But you've booked two rooms?" Gran had asked at least three times during Wednesday's visit.

"Yes. Liam will have his and I'll have mine," she explained. Again.

"Wouldn't it be more convenient for the two of you to just admit that you're attracted to one another and save the money on the second room?"

"Gran . . ."

"Oh well. Since you're being unreasonably puritanical about it, I'll just have to hope there's a freak snowstorm and you're snowed in."

"In Cornwall?" Cara had asked with a laugh.

"Or maybe the inn will have lost the booking and there will be only one room left when you arrive and you'll have to share it." Gran wiggled her eyebrows. "Wouldn't that be something?"

"One of these days, I'm going to come in here and take all of the romance novels off your shelves. You're already dangerous enough without them."

"I need them," said Gran with a sniff. "They're good reads, and I'm also waging a campaign of seduction on Charles Erskine on the first floor."

"Does Mr. Erskine know?" Cara asked with a sigh.

Gran's brows danced a wiggle. "Oh, he knows."

Liam had the additional task of arranging for a dog sitter for Rufus who, when Cara had seen him a few minutes ago, was delighting in having a new friend with the boundless energy of a nineteen-year-old.

Now their houses were locked up, and they were officially on the road, speeding—with any luck—toward answers.

"Do you know, I keep thinking about Louise's wedding," said Liam as they hit the main road.

"What about it?"

"It read like a disaster," he said.

"I can't imagine a wedding happening that quickly. How many days had they spent together?" Cara asked.

"That's wartime weddings for you."

"I wonder how many people were demobbed, came home, and realized they'd made a huge mistake."

The car fell silent until Cara merged on the motorway headed south. A thought rolled through her mind, nagging at her until finally she said, "I worry that Gran and Granddad were a mistake."

"Why do you say that?" he asked.

She shrugged. "I hardly remember him. Most of what I know is because of stories she or Mum told me. But they married fast too. They'd only known each other for four months. Seeing Louise and Paul marry quickly and all of her reservations right after the wedding makes me wonder."

"Are those his dog tags on your key ring?" Liam asked.

She nodded. "Mum started carrying them after he died. She once told me that having them with her kept him close." She paused. "Mum had them on her during the crash. A first responder found them in the wreckage when they pulled her out."

"Cara, I'm sorry," he said.

She glanced over and gave him a little smile. "Thank you. Anyway, they're a little dinged up after all they've gone through, but you can still read everything. Name, hometown, blood type, serial number, next of kin. It's all still there."

"Do you ever worry that the more you dig into Iris's past, the more likely it is that you'll find something you wish you didn't know?" he asked.

"Constantly, but I need to know," she said.

Out of the corner of her eye, she thought she saw him open his mouth to say something, but when she turned he was reaching for the radio and the latest auto-tuned pop hit began to groove out of the speakers.

∿

They traded spots midway through the drive, and at just five o'clock Liam turned into the Star Inn's car park.

"It's huge," Cara said, craning her neck to take in the entire stone building. It was shaped like a U, with wings flanking a central building. A sweeping lawn stretched up to a covered latticework porch that offered holidayers a shady place to sit along the front of the building, and three tall white flags on the roof flapped in the sea breeze.

"Calling it an inn feels a bit like false advertisement, doesn't it?" Liam asked.

They climbed out of the car, grabbing their weekend bags from the trunk, and trooped through the front door. The interior was no less grand, with marble floors, chandeliers dripping in crystal, and light blue walls that picked up the white lattice room dividers mirroring the front porch.

A woman with a prim bun and tailored green suit greeted them at the front desk.

"I believe you have a reservation under McGown," said Liam, sliding his ID across the desk.

Cara held her breath as the receptionist tapped away on her keyboard, wondering if Gran's wishes would be granted.

"Yes, we have two rooms next to each other for you," said the receptionist.

Cara blew out her breath.

The woman's hand paused over the stack of blank key cards. "Is that satisfactory?"

"Yes," Cara said.

After programming the keys and writing their numbers on the hold-ers, the receptionist slid them across the desk. "Here you are. The lifts are just behind you. And the restaurant has asked me to let you know that your table will be ready at seven thirty, Mr. McGown."

"Your table?" asked Cara with an arched brow as they made their way to the lifts.

Liam cleared his throat. "Yes. I thought we might have dinner here tonight since we've been driving all day. Too tired to get in the car again and all that."

There was something about this man, handsome yet bashful, con-siderate as he was enthusiastic. She liked him in more than a friendly, neighborly kind of way.

"I think that's a wonderful idea. I'm glad you thought of it." She was also glad, she thought as they stepped into the lift, that she'd thrown a black dress into her bag.

They stood in comfortable silence, the spark of energy that had been flowing between them all day quieter but still there. She was, for the first time in her life, on holiday with a man who wasn't Simon. It wasn't a romantic holiday, but she'd decided somewhere around Taunton that it counted. She *wanted* it to.

"This is me," she said, holding up her key slip to show him the 413 scribbled on it.

"And this is me," he said, pointing at 415.

"I think I'm going to take a bath," she said, realizing that even though they'd spent all day together she didn't want to leave him.

"I have some thesis proposals to read through," he said.

"This is taking you away from your work. I'm sorry."

He shook his head. "This is giving me some much-needed adventure. Shall I pick you up at your room just before half past seven?"

"I'd like that very much," she said.

Liam looked as though he was about to say something else when his phone rang. He smiled apologetically and glanced at the screen. "I'd better take this."

"I'll see you in a bit," she said.

The room was lovely—no great surprise, given what she'd seen downstairs. She dropped her purse and overnight bag in the center of the king-size bed and went to the window. The hotel had been built on top of a cliff, offering sweeping views out to the Celtic Sea. A sailboat heeled hard to one side in the wind, and if she shifted her gaze to the right she could see a sandy little cove, about which several people walked.

A glance at the clock told her she had about two hours until dinner. Plenty of time to wash away the grimy feeling of too many hours in a car. But first, she fished her phone out of her purse and called Nicole.

Her best friend picked up on the fourth ring. "If you're not snogging the professor by now, I'm hanging up."

"I'm not," she said.

"Hanging up," trilled Nicole.

Cara laughed. "Stop it."

"Fine, but the fact that we're even having this conversation tells me that it isn't out of the realm of possibility."

Cara sucked in a breath. "It's not."

"I'm so happy I could scream," said Nicole.

"I'm glad to hear that."

"What changed? Did he woo you on your cross-country drive with trivia?"

"No, but the conversation was good. He likes ABBA, by the way," she said, pulling a face.

"I will never understand your hatred of ABBA," said Nicole, not needing to see Cara to know her feelings on the subject. "'Waterloo' is a fantastic song. So is 'Fernando.'"

"You and Liam have no taste."

"You're just jealous," said Nicole. "Now, what's bothering you enough for you to pick up the phone and call me?"

"I don't know. I just had the unsettling realization that I feel more like myself around him than I do around anyone else," she said.

"Hey," said Nicole.

"Except you."

"Thank you."

"Is that crazy?" Cara asked. "I hardly know him."

"Of course it isn't crazy. You're a different person than you were before you met Simon. You're a different person than you were when you were married to Simon. What I'm most concerned about is that you're comfortable and happy, and it sounds like you are. And, for the record, you do know Liam. You two have spent more nerdy time together over this diary than I thought possible. And he's met Iris."

"Who likes him."

"And, as we know, Iris is never wrong," said Nicole.

"Don't tell her that. We'll never hear the end of it."

"Do you know what I think you should do?" asked Nicole.

"Tell me."

"Don't listen to what any of the rest of us have to say. Trust your instincts. They took a battering in the divorce, but you know yourself now in a way you never did before. These last couple years have been good for you, but it's time to move past all of this."

"Thanks, love," said Cara quietly.

"If you do decide to snog the professor, call me and give me all the details," said Nicole.

Cara rolled her eyes. "Now I'm the one hanging up."

Nicole started to shout something down the phone, but Cara was already ending the call. She threw her phone on the bed and peeled off her jumper, ready to sink into a bath and indulge in the anticipation of a dinner date with Liam.

25 September 1941

I said goodbye to Paul this morning. He tried to talk me into staying in bed, but I told him that would be desertion.

The truth is, I was still feeling unsettled after some of the things he said yesterday. But then, while I was bathing before we left the flat, he ran out and persuaded one of the cabmen's huts to give us a bit of weak tea and rolls. When I came out, he had it all set up on the table and sat me down to apologize.

"I woke up in the middle of the night, horrified that I'd embarrassed you yesterday, darling. Sometimes I think Reggie is a bad influence."

"You're blaming Reggie?" I asked.

He shoved his hand through his hair, mussing it up deliciously, even though he'd already combed it down with water once that morning. "He goads me, you know."

I took a sip of tea, refusing to let him out of a full apology. After a few seconds, it came.

"I'm sorry. It's just that I worry so much about you," he said, spreading his hands wide. "There's nothing I can do to protect you when I'm on base or flying missions."

"And there's nothing I can do to protect you either, Paul," said I, touching his cheek. "You aren't the only one who worries."

"I know that. Am I forgiven?"

I pulled away a little. "What about after the war, when we're together again? I won't be dictated to. I didn't leave my mother's home only to lose myself again."

"I would never do that to you, darling. You must trust me."

29 September 1941

Da has written back.

27 September 1941

My dearest Lou Lou,

I'm stunned but happy to hear your good news. I wish you every
congratulation, although I must confess a little sadness too. I had
hoped that one day I would be the man walking you down the aisle,
but you've shown us all that you don't need anyone leading you. You've
become quite the independent young woman.

    I'm sorry to say that your mother has not taken your news as well.
I suspect it won't be a surprise to you, but she'd hoped that you would
forget Paul and be content to wait for Gary. However, don't let this
diminish your happiness. You have made your own choices, and I
couldn't be more proud.

With all my love (and Mum's too),
Your father

15 October 1941

I've hardly had time to write a word here or, I'm sad to say, to Paul
except for a scribbled note here or there. B Section has been run
off our feet between lectures about new bombers, meteorology, and
further fine-tuning of our technique, and our shifts. The skies have
been unsettled with air raid sirens, but often the planes veer off,
heading northward. But it's no matter to us. We remain ever vigilant
on our rooftop perch, the lights guiding us as we search for our
enemy.

3 November 1941

Rumors abound that our battery may be sent north to Liverpool, Newcastle, or Glasgow. The Luftwaffe have been bombing those cities heavily, trying their best to dismantle whatever factories and depots they can.

Most of this kind of speculation around the canteen and the NAAFI never comes to pass, but this feels different. I shall write to Paul after I finish this and tell him. It'll make it harder for us to see one another because the train journey will be even farther than London, but perhaps I can come to him. He dismissed the idea in his last letter, but that was nearly two weeks ago.

Two weeks! I might be hurt at his negligence except I've been so exhausted that many days I can't see fit to raise my own pen. It's been five days since I wrote him myself.

It's no excuse. Not with what he means to me. I will have to do better.

7 November 1941

I wrote to Paul as I said I would, but I shouldn't have bothered. I could've written his response back because it's the same every time. It hardly bears transcribing.

He wants me to transfer out of Ack-Ack. It's too dangerous. He doesn't want me to be in Liverpool or Newcastle or Glasgow because they're too far north and harder for him to get to when he's on leave. If he ever manages to receive leave again.

Sometimes, when I'm at my angriest, I wonder if Reggie really did confuse the dates of his leave in Edinburgh or whether Paul has been gallivanting around, enjoying the idea of having me waiting for him without having to make the effort of coming to see me.

14 November 1941

No letter from Paul since I wrote to him on the seventh. We think
Glasgow is our most likely next assignment because the shipyards have
been battered with German bombs recently.

I won't transfer.

5 January 1942

Everything is over. I thought I loved him.

20

LOUISE

"Rumor is more rationing's coming," said Mary as she flipped the pages of the abandoned newspaper she'd scooped up from the table in the NAAFI.

"What is it this time?" Charlie asked, laying down the jack of spades on the discard pile.

Louise watched Nigella pluck it up and lay down three jacks, discarding her last card facedown on the pile. "Gin."

Charlie threw down her hand. "If I'd have known you'd develop into such a card shark, I never would've suggested starting this game."

Louise shook her head, tallying up Nigella's points and Charlie's losses and adding it to the score that was already in the tens of thousands. "You could just admit that she's better at this than any of us."

"No. I'm about to go on a hot streak here any moment. Just you wait," said Charlie.

"I don't know why I keep winning," said Nigella. "I swear I've never been particularly good."

"What's Nigella good at?" Cartruse asked, dropping into the chair next to Louise.

"Gin."

"Drinking it or playing it?" he asked.

Nigella gasped. "Cartruse, how could you even ask such a thing?"

Cartruse grinned. "Easily. I'm just trying to decide which answer I'd like better."

"Cards," said Louise. "Otherwise she'd be out of a job."

He grunted and reached for the scoring sheet. "So Nigella's winning."

"By about two thousand points," said Louise.

"Hot streak, any moment," said Charlie.

"What was it you said was going to be rationed, Mary?" Nigella asked again.

"Rice," said Mary, "although there's nothing official yet."

The women all groaned, knowing they'd be receiving letters from their mothers and sisters moaning about the scarcity of rice in just a couple weeks' time, even if they hardly ever cooked with it.

"Anyone up for the picture they're showing tonight?" asked Cartruse.

"I never go to the pictures," said Charlie. "What's the point, when we have to leave to go on duty halfway through?"

Cartruse shrugged. "You can see half of everything now and watch the rest when the war's over."

"So I watch Cary Grant or Humphrey Bogart try to win the girl, but leave before I get to see the kiss? I don't think so. That's the wrong half of the love story for me," said Charlie.

"What about you, Keene?" Cartruse asked, nudging her with her elbow.

She shook her head and shoved her hand in her pocket to draw out Paul's compass. All of the girls knew what Cartruse didn't. That she and Paul had quarreled about the rumors that B Section might be going north.

She'd thought it would be easier when they were married. The fight on the wedding day had been rooted in ignorance, she told herself. He, like so many other men around him, assumed what they always had: that women were weaker, more frightened, less suited to serve. But she would talk to him, reason with him. She would make him understand that what she was doing was important. But to do that, she needed to see him or at least hear from him.

They'd experienced these gaps in communication before. When he'd moved bases or when she'd jumped from Leicester to Oswestry to London, there had been a lapse of a few days when the post had to catch up with them. Yet this was stretching from days to weeks, and she was beginning to worry.

"Maybe I'll see the picture another day," she said, tipping Paul's compass to watch the needle quiver as it pointed north. Since Paul had given it to her, she'd taken to worrying it in her pocket, smoothing her thumb over the dinged corner.

Cartruse frowned, but the door of the NAAFI flew open and Vera walked in holding a clutch of letters before he could reply.

"Post's come, girls!" Vera called, waving the letters over her head.

The anticipation that today would be the day Paul's letter would come nearly felled her, but she forced herself to stay in her seat as Vera handed out letters. She was a married woman now, not a lovesick girl.

"Two for Mary. One for Nigella. Four for Charlie. How many soldiers have you got writing to you now, Charlie?" Vera asked.

"Wouldn't you like to know?" Charlie said with a smirk.

"Cheeky," said Cartruse.

"Don't you know it," said Charlie.

"And these two are for Louise, as is this," said Vera, holding up a large brown envelope.

She took the letters and the envelope, quickly scanning the addresses. Kate's service number was marked on the top of one envelope, and the other was from her father. They would wait.

The brown envelope had no markings other than her service number. Curious, she flipped it over, ripped open the top flap, and upended it onto the table. Letters fell out, spreading across the veneer, and Louise knew.

Her chest squeezed so tightly she could scarcely breathe. They were her letters. Letters she'd written to Paul. And they were unopened.

"Oh my . . . Louise, I'm so sorry . . ." Vera's voice trailed off as she and the other girls looked on in horror.

"It can't be," she whispered, picking up one of her envelopes and tearing at it. Her letter to him dated two weeks ago slid out, opening up just enough that she could see her usual salutation: *My dearest Paul . . .*

She ripped another open and another, pulling the sheets of thin paper free. Every single one of them was covered with her handwriting in blue ink from the fountain pen her father had given her on her sixteenth birthday. All of these letters, unopened and unread. For a month she'd been writing to him and he'd never seen a one.

"This can't be happening." The words came out on a sob that choked her. "He can't be dead."

"Maybe he isn't," said Mary, hopefully. She held up the large envelope. "Do you recognize this handwriting?"

Louise shook her head, unable to form words as grief swirled up to pull her down.

Cartruse held a loose sheet of paper and his mouth fell into a thin line as he read. He slid it across the table to Louise. "You need to see this."

Miss Keene,

I have been aware for some time that you are in frequent correspondence with Flight Lieutenant Paul Bolton, who has so valiantly served his country during this war. It is with my deepest regrets that I must inform you that on 11 November 1941 his plane was shot down over the Channel. I am told by his fellow pilots that he flew bravely to the end, taking two German planes with him.

I thought it best to return your correspondence to him unopened. I offer you my deepest condolences.

Sincerely,
Group Captain Gerald Reynolds

"He's dead," she said, numb to the core. "He was killed in action."

A hush fell over the entire NAAFI, servicemen and women she'd never met before instinctively knowing when one of their own was suffering a great loss. She wanted out of here. Out of this place, where everyone was staring at her. She curled her arms across her stomach, pulling in on herself as though that would keep the pain from radiating throughout her entire body.

She remembered the WAAF who'd received the telegram informing her of her husband's death in this same NAAFI. She'd felt so sorry for the woman but unsure what to do except sit in respectful silence. Now she was the one grieving, forced to share with all of these people the lowest moment of her life.

"Louise," said Vera softly.

She realized then that her friend was crouched down next to her, speaking quietly.

"I'm going to take you back to our billet," Vera said.

Dumbly, Louise nodded, but when she tried to stand, she found that her legs seemed to not be working. She stumbled toward the table, but before she could fall, Cartruse and Vera were at her side, each hooking a shoulder under her arms.

The walk to the billet was a blur—at once too slow and hazy, yet too fast to account for the blocks they'd covered. Nothing made sense. Paul was supposed to write her back, tell her he was worried about her because he loved her. He was supposed to promise her that they'd be together again soon. He was supposed to be as vital and alive as the morning he'd left her with a kiss at the front door of her billet.

"You can't come in," she heard Vera say. "There are rules."

"I don't care about the rules. She needs help," Cartruse said.

She lifted her head, suddenly aware again that she was propped up between her friends.

"I know you care for her, but the best thing you can do is let her be. She's lost her husband," said Vera, placing a light hand on Cartruse's arm.

Through the haze of her shock, Louise registered his shoulders drooping. "Then who will help get her upstairs?"

Charlie stepped into her view now—brash, fun Charlie, who had been there on her wedding day, her sole witness. In her hands she clutched the bundle of letters, meaningless words that Paul would never read.

"Vera and I will do it," said Charlie.

There was a bit of bustling around Louise as Charlie took Cartruse's spot, nodding to him as he held the door open. They were taking her upstairs. Up to her room. That's where she wanted to be. In her room. By herself. Maybe if she was in her bed she would wake up and find that this had all been a wretched dream.

Except dreams didn't hurt with such precise, searing pain that cut straight to the bone.

Somehow, Vera and Charlie made it up the stairs, carrying Louise most of the way. When they burst into their shared room, they quickly made up her bed and settled her down. Lovingly, they removed her boots and her tunic jacket before tucking her into bed as though she were a child.

"I'm going to get her some tea from the canteen," said Vera in a low whisper.

"Tea's not going to do a thing to make her feel better," said Charlie.

"It's the only thing I can think to do right now."

Charlie must've agreed, because Vera left without another word.

Lying on her side, Louise stared at a water stain just above the stack of Vera's mattress biscuits. Why wasn't she crying? She should be crying. She'd just lost her husband, yet she couldn't make the tears flow.

She must've said something, because Charlie stroked her hair and said, "You're in shock. That's why you can't cry. Just give yourself time."

"I don't understand how he can be gone."

"I don't either. I don't either."

Vera hurried back into the room, three cups of tea and a little tray of biscuits on a tray. "I told the girls in the canteen it was an emergency, and they scrounged up some biscuits."

"Can you sit up, Lou?" Charlie asked.

Putting her palm flat on the bed, Louise dragged herself up and took the cup of tea. She barely registered the warmth radiating from the mug.

For a few moments they sat in silence, until she said, "I don't understand."

"I know, dearest," said Vera.

She shook her head. "No. I don't understand how Paul can have been dead for so long and I'm only finding out now."

"It takes time for these things to make their way—"

"I'm his wife. I should've been informed by telegram. The eleventh of November was over three weeks ago."

Vera and Charlie both sat back.

"You're right. The RAF should've told you," Vera said.

"Maybe he didn't register the marriage," said Charlie.

"He told me he did in a letter, saying he was so proud that he could claim me as his wife. If the RAF knew, I should've been informed. Someone should've told me." She paused, something else getting through the thick haze of her mind. "And why did the group captain call me Miss Keene? He should've addressed me as Mrs. Bolton."

"I don't know," said Charlie, resting a hand on her knee.

"I can't speak to Group Captain Reynolds, but perhaps I can help find out what happened with the RAF," said Vera.

"How?" Louise asked.

"My uncle. He's army, but I would bet that with a few phone calls he could track down the right people to answer your questions. If that's what you want," said Vera.

"Of course that's what I want. Why wouldn't I want to know?"

"I just thought . . ." Vera's gaze fell to her hands twisting the blanket on Louise's bed. Flattening them, she smoothed down the fabric.

"I'm sure this is the matter of a clerical error and a careless commanding officer. Wasn't the man always denying Paul leave that was rightly due him?" asked Charlie.

Louise nodded, but a touch of doubt took hold. She was in the service. She knew the rules of leave well enough. What Paul's commanding officer had done was surely in direct violation of all sorts of practices. But what if he hadn't denied Paul leave at all?

A memory tugged at her. Reggie at her wedding breakfast, champagne sloshing in its flute as he gestured wildly, telling the story of Paul using his leave in Scotland. Paul insisting that it had happened last year, not this year.

Distrust broke through grief, and it made her wretched. She'd only just learned her husband was dead, yet she was already beginning to question his truthfulness, his honor.

She looked up at her friends and registered the quiet worry on Vera's face and the obstinacy on Charlie's. They'd row about Vera's implications when Louise wasn't there, thinking that she wouldn't know, but she would. She knew these women better than anyone in the world.

"I think that I would like some time by myself," she said, her voice hardly a whisper.

Charlie hesitated, but Vera nodded, tugging their friend by the back of her tunic.

"We'll leave you for a little bit," said Vera.

The door shut softly behind her friends. Louise slid down in bed until she was flat on her back, staring at the cracked plaster of the ceiling. She waited for the tears that should've come, but all she felt was empty. Hollow. Uncertain. Alone.

21

CARA

Liam knocked at Cara's door just before quarter past seven, as he'd promised. She took a moment to smooth her hair that she'd washed and blown out before adjusting the neckline of her dress and opening the door.

He had a ready smile, but when he saw her, he froze and blinked three times. "You look fantastic."

"Thank you," she said, fussing a hair behind her ear out of habit.

"I realized after my phone call that it wasn't fair to spring dinner on you without telling you. I worried you wouldn't have anything to wear. We didn't exactly talk about fine dining."

"Gran would disown me if she found out I didn't travel with something to throw on for an unexpected dinner invitation," she said.

"Well, we can't have that."

He held out his arm to her, and she took it gladly. He wore a thin-knit, deep-blue jumper over a white collared shirt and a pair of charcoal-gray slacks. As they walked, she could smell the faint, clean hint of the hotel's shampoo, and she let herself angle just a little closer to him, breaking off only when they reached the lift.

Downstairs in the restaurant, a maître d' led them through the half-full restaurant to a quiet table in one of the many bay windows.

She watched Liam under her lashes, trying to read any awkwardness or hesitation in his movements as the waiter doled out menus and wine lists.

"Do you think it's changed much since Louise and Paul came here?" she asked, when they were at last alone.

Liam looked up from his menu and smiled. "I'd hope not. It must've been quite something, even in the middle of the war, when it was requisitioned for officers."

"It really does feel like stepping back in time," she said, gazing along the rich light blue velvet banquettes that lined the back wall. Gold-leaf embellishment climbed up the walls in soaring swags, coming to meet in the five points along the ceiling like the church vaults she'd studied in her art-and-architecture class at Barlow.

"You meet Kate tomorrow," said Liam.

"*We* meet her," she corrected him.

He sat back, amusement in his eyes. "Yes, but you're the one who found the tin and set yourself on this journey."

"It feels strange to think that was just in September. It feels as though Louise has been a part of my life for a long time."

"You've lived with her story."

"And worried about her and wondered what happened to make her write that last entry. 'Everything is over.' It's so final," she said.

"We could be reading into it," he warned.

She shook her head. "We've both read the entire diary. Louise is a lot of things, but dramatic isn't one of them. If something went wrong, it went *very* wrong."

"Hopefully, we'll find out tomorrow," he said.

The waiter came and cracked open a slender bottle of sparkling water. "And would you care for wine tonight?" the waiter asked.

Liam tilted his head. "I'd be happy to order, unless you'd prefer to take a look yourself?"

She shook her head. "I trust you."

He ordered a 2014 Pouilly-Fumé she'd had before and liked, and the waiter bowed his head and slipped away.

"Do you know what I hope more than anything else?" she asked, turning her attention back to Liam.

"What?"

"That Kate tells us Louise wound up happy, Paul or no Paul," she said.

"We can only hope." He paused, eyeing her as though weighing something that had been on his mind. "Can I ask you a question?"

"Anything," she said. And she found she meant it.

"Why did this particular diary catch your attention?"

"It's a mystery and that's intriguing. Maybe I was drawn to the sadness of it." She shrugged.

"I think we know each other well enough that I can say it isn't everything," he said.

She sighed and sat back in her chair, searching for the words to explain the deep compulsion that had driven her on. Finally she said, "When you're young, you assume everything is going to last forever. Your friends will be your friends for the rest of your life. Once you decide you're in love with someone, you'll love them always. The idea of your parents dying is present but distant at the same time.

"In those days, it didn't bother me so much that Gran wouldn't talk about the war. Every family has things they don't talk about. This was ours. But as I grew older, I cared more. I think there's a natural, human compulsion to want to know where you're from. It gives us our ideas of ourselves."

"Identity," he said.

She nodded. "But then my parents died and suddenly I felt cut adrift. I lost a part of life that had grounded me. I thought I had all the time in the world to know them better and get to know myself in turn, but it was gone in an instant."

"And now you don't want to lose the chance to learn who Iris really is before she's gone," he said gently.

"Yes, and when she dies, that part of who I am will die with her." She drew in a breath. "And then, when I thought about it more, I realized there might be a family just like mine who doesn't know the full story of their loved one. I wanted to return the diary, but then Laurel said that Louise had died six years ago . . ."

"Maybe she'll still want to know," said Liam. "And maybe Kate can fill in the gaps for all of us."

"That's what I hope happens," she said. "There's always the risk that I'm opening up an old wound and causing new pain by stirring up things that happened more than seventy years ago."

"But you feel a responsibility," he said.

She nodded.

"Well, I for one am happy you did. Otherwise I don't know how long it would've been before I convinced you I don't bite," he said.

She cringed, thinking back to their first meeting. "Was it that obvious?"

He laughed. "You couldn't turn down my sister's idea that we have dinner together fast enough."

"I realized as soon as I said it that it sounded rude and standoffish," she said.

"Leah is always coming up with great ideas that she thinks the world should bend to. I'm her latest project."

"Project?"

He rubbed the back of his neck. "Yes, well, I'm single, and if there's one thing my sister can't stand, it's the idea of someone in her life not being matched up."

"She chose the wrong person then," said Cara with a laugh. "That day I'd had a phone call from my ex. I was feeling every inch the divorced woman, resigned to being alone forever."

His eyes lifted. "And now?"

Her breath hitched. "And now I'm feeling more like myself than I have in years."

"Good," he said. "I like this version of you quite a lot."

The waiter came back with the wine, pouring out generous glasses before cradling the bottle in a pedestal ice bucket. She ordered scallops and a lemon-and-thyme pork loin and Liam decided on the goat-cheese-and-beetroot salad and the duck, adding a bottle of pinot noir to be decanted for their meal.

"I might be overstepping, but will you tell me the rest of what happened between you and your ex? There's more, right?"

She sighed. "There's more."

Eyes fixed on a droplet sliding down the side of her water goblet, she paused. They'd opened a door between where they stood now and where they might be in the future. But before they could step through, she needed to tell him this. To unburden herself. It was time.

"I think I've come to terms with the fact that the divorce had a lot more to do with me than with Simon. Somewhere along the way, I got lost. To a girl who was never particularly popular in school, being with Simon was a revelation. He always had this roving, large group of friends, was always the center of attention. He was confident and funny and intelligent. I think I was dazzled."

"When did you stop being dazzled?" he asked.

"When I grew up." She cleared her throat. "We'd been fighting a lot the month before my parents were killed, and he was rarely at home. I found out later that he'd been staying with a friend who lived in South Kensington. When I got the call from the hospital, I called and texted him. He finally picked up after my third try, but when he eventually got home I realized he was too drunk to be driving."

"He drove drunk to pick you up to take you to the bedside of your parents who had been hit by a drunk driver?" Liam asked incredulously.

"Yes. I ended up having to call Nicole to drive me to Cumbria. I wouldn't have been safe on the road. I got to the hospital thirty minutes after Mum died on the operating table. I found out later that Dad had been killed on impact."

"And because you were delayed in going up there—"

"I didn't get to say goodbye to Mum. I knew I was never going to be able to forgive him for that. He fought the divorce for about a month, but then he was arrested for drunk driving himself. It was what eventually got him into rehab."

"And now?"

"He's stopped drinking, but he refuses to go to a program for his gambling addiction. He stayed away from the casinos for a few months after I filed for divorce, but then he relapsed. I don't know if he's still playing private games.

"It was a process working through the guilt of leaving, because he wasn't a healthy man but I couldn't do it any longer. I realized I didn't love him anymore. I ended up telling my solicitor that I'd pay off the more than three hundred and fifty thousand pounds in debt he'd accrued."

Liam gave a low whistle.

"It wiped out almost everything I had in savings, but I paid it because I had Mum and Dad's house to sell and I thought the settlement would make it better."

"It didn't, did it?" he asked.

She laughed. "Of course not. It just made all of the feelings more complicated. I finally found a therapist when Nicole put her foot down and told me it was time."

Liam's hand came over hers on the table.

"I'm sorry for everything that happened," he said.

She lifted her head and smiled. "Not many people get a second chance at building the life they want."

But looking across the table, she knew there was one area in her life that was missing, and that Liam could be right at the heart of it.

But before she could say anything else, their starters arrived and the conversation slipped back into easier territory.

∽

Full and a little sleepy from the wine, Cara and Liam made their way up to their floor, leaning against the mirrored wall of the lift.

"I think I'm going to be dreaming of that chocolate cake for the rest of my life," she said.

"The tart was good too," he said.

"That was definitely a chocolate meal. No sense in wasting precious dessert time on a bit of apple and custard."

He nudged her playfully. "You bake things. You should be more respectful of my tart."

She arched a skeptical brow, and he snorted as the doors slid open.

They spilled out of the lift, Cara tucked into Liam's side as he walked her back to their adjoining rooms.

"We're meeting Laurel at Kate's care home at eleven tomorrow?" Liam asked.

"That's right."

"Do you want to have breakfast together? I thought it might be good to see the Haybourne high street beforehand."

"That sounds like a plan," she said.

He rounded to face her as they stopped in front of her door and tilted his head in an unspoken question. She dropped her attention to her wristlet as she wrestled her key out, grateful for the moment to compose herself. When she looked up again, Liam's expression had changed from easy to serious.

"Is something wrong?" she asked.

"Cara, I'm going to say a few things, and I want you to listen."

"Okay . . ."

He grazed the sensitive skin on the back of her wrist and traced down to touch fingertip to fingertip. "You deserve to never be disappointed, and you deserve to be with someone who doesn't make you feel like your choices aren't the right ones."

A lump of emotion formed in her throat. "Liam—"

"And this is the most important thing: if I had been with you, I would've never taken you for granted no matter what was going on in my life."

They were simple words, yet they unlocked something deep inside her. The last piece of the puzzle. The little push she'd needed to once again feel whole again. She trusted this man implicitly, and she trusted herself to know what he could mean to her.

Slowly, he drew her closer to him, inch by inch, until their bodies were nearly touching. Then, he dipped his head and kissed her.

His lips were soft and patient against hers, but she knew that one sign from her would be enough permission for him to let loose all of his restraint. It was what she wanted that night. This man was it.

"Liam," she whispered, breaking away just as the kiss began to deepen.

"Yes?"

"Come with me."

And she unlocked her hotel room door and drew him inside.

22

LOUISE

Louise lay in bed for three days, hardly noticing the passage of time. Occasionally one of the girls from B Section would come in with water or tea, coaxing her to drink. She did numbly, but she refused every bit of food they brought.

There was no talk of her going back on duty. Vera or Charlie must've taken care of informing their superior officers that Paul was dead, but no one spoke to her about bereavement leave or reprimanded her for not being on the gun. They let her mourn, privately and deeply.

On the fourth day, before Charlie and Vera awoke, she rose from her bunk. Gathering up her wash bag, she made the long trek to the basement, where the showers stood. It wasn't her day to bathe, but when the orderly saw her, the girl just ducked her head. Everyone knew that she, Private Louise Bolton, was a new widow. No one would question her wanting something as simple as a shower.

The odd hours of a gunner girl meant that she had the showers to herself between shifts. Louises turned the spray up as hot as it would go and stepped under it. The hard stream of water beat on her back, stinging her scalp and scraping her skin raw. She scrubbed at herself, soaping her hair and her body longer than was necessary. She needed to be clean again, to let the purity of water wash away even the deepest hurt.

When she came back to the room, Vera and Charlie were dressed. They spun around, their eyes wide at the sight of her.

"We thought—" "You were—" they said at the same time, falling silent when she shut the door behind her and went to her bed as though nothing had happened.

Act as though nothing has happened. If they hadn't been deep into the war, she might have been able to give full purchase to her grief, but she was a gunner girl, and the longer she stayed locked up in this room, the harder it would be to remember that.

Her friends gave her space while she dressed. They were due in two debriefings that afternoon, so she pulled on her underthings, garters, skirt, shirt, tunic, and shoes. She checked that her buttons and shoes shone and pinned her quick-drying hair up in a simple roll that didn't rely on complicated pin curls slept in overnight. Settling her cap on her head, she took a deep breath.

"I'm ready."

Her friends followed as she opened the door. Mary, Nigella, and Lizzie waited there for her. How they knew she'd arisen when neither Vera nor Charlie had left the room, she didn't know, but she didn't question it. They formed a semicircle around her as they walked, protecting her in the only way she'd let them.

Their drills were conducted by Colonel Silhour, a tiny, thin woman with a lemon-sucking face. Silhour was unrelenting at the best of times, refusing to give quarter to any girls' complaints. The only acknowledgment she gave Louise was the briefest nod, and then she was shouting commands, drilling them as hard as ever.

The rest of the day was far from normal with all of the stares Louise earned as she walked through the teaching halls. Every time she caught someone's eye, she refused to flinch. She had a job to do, and she was going to do it no matter what had happened to her. Clinging to that, she just might survive.

However, her plan faltered when, leaving a debriefing on a new detection technology, she found Captain Jones waiting for her.

"Private Bolton," he said, his hands clasped behind his back.

She saluted him crisply. "Sir."

"It's good to see you back.

"Yes, sir."

His jaw worked as he searched her face. This was not a mere courtesy, she realized. He wanted something from her.

"Is something the matter, sir?" she asked, even though it felt like a silly question. Everything was the matter. Paul was dead. Her life, the one she'd hoped they would plan together, was gone.

"Come with me," said Captain Jones, turning hard on the heel of his boot and marching down the corridor.

He led her through a series of doors, deep into a part of the building in which she'd never been before. The offices of high-ranking officials lined the corridor, and through open doors she could see uniform-clad secretaries answering phones and typing up notes. No one laughed or jested. Everything here felt weightier, more important.

At last, Captain Jones stopped in front of a nondescript door and knocked. A moment later, a tall, slender man with a staff sergeant's badge opened it.

"You're expected, sir," said the man.

Captain Jones nodded to Louise.

"Through that door," said the staff sergeant, as she walked into the tiny reception space.

She hesitated and the man said, "It's all right. You can let yourself in. He knows you're here."

The question of who knew she was there leaped to her lips, but one look from Captain Jones stifled it.

Louise opened the door and found herself standing in the middle of a modest room, embellished only by a large map of Europe pinned to a wall. In the center stood a man with his back to her, so that all she could see was that he had perfect carriage and brutally scraped-back gray hair. It surprised her then that when he turned around, she found a man in his early sixties with features softened by fatigue and worry. Still, he wore a major general's stars, and that made her stand up a little straighter.

"Sir," said Captain Jones. "This is Private Louise Keene."

She slid a glance at Captain Jones, wondering at him dropping her married name, but the major general cleared his throat. "Thank you, Captain. What I have to say to Private Keene is a delicate matter."

Captain Jones saluted and retreated before Louise could even think to protest.

The door shut, and she was alone with the major general. He sighed and leaned a hip on the desk he stood in front of. "Private, do you know who I am?"

Her eyes narrowed slightly as she studied him. "Major General Garson," she said after a moment. "Vera's uncle."

"That's right," he said, pulling out a cigarette and tapping it on the packet. Then, as though remembering himself, he offered one to her.

"No, thank you, sir. We aren't allowed while we're in Ack-Ack," she said.

"Quite right, quite right," he muttered, striking a match. "Can't have shaky hands."

"No, sir."

Through a puff of smoke, he squinted at her. "At ease, Private. As you're probably aware, my niece asked me to look into the matter of your husband's death and why you were not informed."

Her throat constricted until she could hardly trust herself to form words. Instead she nodded.

"Vera is my only niece, and I'm not so hardened that I can't tell you there are some times when I wonder if she doesn't have me wrapped around her little finger." He sighed and scratched his brow. "I told her that the army rarely makes mistakes when it comes to informing families about a loved one killed in action, and I suspect His Majesty's Royal Air Force rarely does either. It's a delicate matter, and we take it very seriously. Still, she asked me to make some calls and find out what happened in the case of your flight lieutenant."

"And you've found something," she prompted him. She'd seen men do this too many times before. He was dragging things out, not wanting to tell her something that would upset her, when he didn't know the half of how tough she really was.

Major General Garson picked up a file off the desk and flipped it open. "Look halfway down the page."

She took the file and scanned until she saw what he was speaking of written in spiky black letters. *Married.*

"If it's recorded, I don't understand why I wasn't informed," she said, handing the folder back.

"Perhaps you would like to sit down, Private Keene," said the major general.

She swallowed. "I'd prefer to stand, sir."

"I spoke to a few of the men who knew Flight Lieutenant Bolton. As you can imagine, men thrown into close proximity during times of war spend a good deal of their days talking about their sweethearts. They said Bolton was indeed married. To a prominent barrister's daughter, a Lenora Robinson. Their fathers are in the same Inns of Court and have known each other for years."

Slowly, Louise sank down into a chair, her hand covering her mouth. "That's not possible. He can't have been married before."

"I'm afraid it is, my dear," said Major General Garson softly.

"But he could've been divorced. Maybe his men neglected to mention that." She looked up hopefully, but Vera's uncle shook his head.

"They were married just after he enlisted, when the war broke out. No one had heard of any divorce and there's no record of it. I asked," he said. "Mrs. Lenora Bolton is still living in London. She's a volunteer ambulance driver."

"But we were married." Her eyes brimmed with the tears she'd been waiting on for four days. "By Father Norwood. I have a ring. There was a wedding breakfast. We were husband and wife in every way."

The major general shifted uncomfortably. "There are stories about unscrupulous clergymen who've lost their parishes, looking for a way to make a few quick shillings. They perform a fast ceremony, no questions asked. Or the man may have been a charlatan of another breed, posing as a man of the cloth for his own gain. Despite the rosy picture of British togetherness you see in the papers, this war has driven people to do unspeakable things to one another."

"There were witnesses," she whispered. It had been a real wedding in every sense, but if Paul had been married before, the marriage was invalid. He was nothing more than a bigamist, and she was his unwitting victim.

All at once, rage filled her, as easy explanations for so many things began to present themselves. How it was almost impossible for Paul to secure leave. His refusal to allow her anywhere near his base. The way he'd written to her of his passion until she was certain she felt the same way, letting their letters stand in place of any real commitment. He'd proposed to her after a quarrel. Had he married her for fear that she would slip away from him, or had it just been part of his plan, another step in his quest for the love and adoration of the women around him?

It must have been so easy for him. He was a pilot, handsome and sophisticated. He could have had a woman in every single village he'd visited—more if he'd wanted to—and they would never have been any the wiser because by the time they were in love with him he would be gone.

So what had she been? A girl desperate for someone to give her permission to dream of a life away from home. A fool who didn't know how to see that the man she thought she loved was nothing more than a liar. An easy target. A conquest.

"You understand that my counterparts at the RAF are very concerned about Flight Lieutenant Bolton's behavior if any of this is true," said Major General Garson with a cough. "He was a decorated pilot and a war hero. If word were to get out . . ."

Louise shot to her feet, her fists pressed hard against the sides of her thighs. "The RAF need not worry about me. I am embarrassed, humiliated, and heartbroken. I have no desire for anyone else to know the reasons why."

"Right then. Well, my sincerest condolences, Private Keene."

Her maiden name was a slash across the heart as the major general showed her to the door. Mercifully, Captain Jones hadn't lingered. With a swipe at the tears that had pooled under her eyes, she gave a nod to the staff sergeant.

Her heels clicked hard and purposefully as she walked down the hall, back to the teaching wing of the building. But she didn't glance at the clock to check the time and gauge what briefing she was meant to be in. Instead, she walked straight out of the iron doors and onto the street.

∼

Louise had never jumped base before, because she knew the consequences. However, none of those crossed her mind as she walked to the bus. She had no money on her, but the ticket taker took one look at her uniform and waved her on.

She disembarked at Piccadilly Circus and took the tube to the South Kensington stop. Then it was a ten-minute walk to Cranley Gardens. Paul's street.

He'd told her often enough about his pokey little bedsit in the back of a nondescript building in Chelsea. He'd even listened to her say the address, amused as she let the glamour of the London street roll off her tongue. But standing in Cranley Gardens, she didn't see a run-down building at number 12. It was a mansion flat, and no buildings on the street had suffered a direct hit from a bomb. He'd told her lie after lie after lie, and she'd believed him, naive in her trust.

Mounting the steps, she leaned hard on the buzzer for the second-floor flat until she realized it was ridiculous to expect anyone to answer. Paul was dead.

A ground-floor window a few feet from the door squeaked open, and a woman with her hair tied up in a yellow cloth stuck her head out. "Ring it any longer and you'll break it, love."

"I—I'm sorry," said Louise, dropping her hand to her side.

The woman looked her up and down. "Are you trying the Bolton residence?"

"Yes."

"You knew the man of the house?"

Her wedding ring hung heavy on her hand. "Yes."

"Then you'd better come inside for a cuppa."

The woman disappeared back through the window before Louise could protest, and seconds later the door opened. The woman ushered her inside and through an open door on the ground floor.

"I'm Mrs. Fay. Now, you just sit there." The woman pointed to a sagging brocade armchair. "I'll put the kettle on."

Louise sat, at a loss in this strange flat, as she listened to the sounds of tea being made in the other room. The whoosh of water filling the kettle. The clang of metal on the stove. The clink of best china being pulled down from the cupboard.

After a few minutes, Mrs. Fay pushed back through the door, smoothing her lace-trimmed apron as she went.

"Now, that'll just be a moment to boil. How did you know Mr. Bolton?" Mrs. Fay asked.

Louise swallowed, readying herself to tell the lie she'd thought was the truth until just an hour ago. "He was my husband. I'm sorry if I'm the first person to tell you, but he's dead."

"Oh, I know he's dead all right. Husband, you said?"

Louise lifted her chin. "Yes."

"Well then, you just let me know if you need a drop of something stronger than tea. I have a bottle of sherry I've been saving. Seems to be useful these days."

Louise stared at the woman, but before she could ask what the woman knew about Paul, the doorbell rang.

"Just one moment, love," said Mrs. Fay, popping up rather merrily. She did not, Louise realized, poke her head out of the window to greet the visitor but went straight for the door.

An exchange of hushed voices preceded the shuffle of two pairs of feet on carpet, and Mrs. Fray reappeared accompanied by a tall, slender woman with razor-sharp cheekbones and elegant, molded curls that just swept her shoulders. Everything about her was elegance, from the cut of her navy wool dress—not a uniform, Louise noticed with envy—to the fine pearl clips that hung from her ears.

"Good afternoon," said the newcomer. "I understand that you were married to my husband."

Here she was, confronted with the living, breathing truth of Paul's betrayal. This was the Lenora Bolton Major General Garson had told her about. The barrister's daughter from a well-heeled, well-respected London family. Looking at her, it was easy to see why Paul had married her. She was beautiful and sophisticated. She made sense with him.

Louise stopped herself. It wasn't this woman's fault that Paul was a liar and a cheat and who knew what other number of things, any more than it was hers. They were the innocent parties in all of this. It was *Paul* who'd done them wrong.

Rising to her feet, she said, "I'm not entirely sure what to say except to introduce myself. I'm Louise Keene."

The woman looked at her outstretched hand with something akin to resigned amusement. "Lenora Bolton, although I'm considering becoming Lenora Robinson again, given the circumstances. I notice you don't use Paul's last name."

"I did, but given what I've learned today, I don't see how I can continue," Louise said.

Lenora nodded. "I can understand the sentiment. Perhaps, Miss Keene, you'd like to come with me."

She followed Lenora out of Mrs. Fay's flat and up the stairs. On the landing, Lenora pulled out a latchkey and unlocked the door.

The flat was nothing like what Paul had told her. It wasn't a simple bedsit for a student with just a gas ring for making tea. It was beautifully decorated in rich browns, reds, and creams. Books sat lined up on their shelves, waiting for some curious reader to pick them up and sink onto one of the two sofas before the fireplace. Oil paintings of landscapes covered the walls, and the entire place carried the faint scent of furniture polish.

"This is your home," Louise said.

Lenora nodded. "We were married the month after the war started. Paul had bought the place the year before with the inheritance from his grandfather."

"Then why did Mrs. Fay have to call you? I assume that's what she did."

"It is. I moved back to my parents' home just around the corner after the first girl arrived. She claimed that she and Paul had been engaged after meeting him in Devon. She'd heard that he was killed and came up here to be with his family as she grieved. Instead, she found me," said Lenora with a raised brow. "Now I ask Mrs. Fay to keep an eye on things for me and ring me if any other women come around."

"How many have there been?" Louise asked.

"You make the third."

Four women. Lenora, Louise, the girl from Devon, and another Louise hoped she'd never meet. Paul had deceived them all, convincing them that he loved them and only them. Making them feel special. Singular. Wanted.

"I don't understand," said Louise softly.

Lenora went to a carved silver box on a tiny side table, selecting a cigarette and snapping at the lighter until smoke billowed from her mouth. "Neither do I."

"Why would he marry me if he was already married to you? Why would he become engaged to those other girls?" she asked.

Lenora sighed. "Paul was a difficult man. He had a deep, almost compulsive need to be loved. You know, his parents thought they wouldn't be able to have children for the longest time until one day, miraculously, they became pregnant later in life. He was coddled and adored, more toy than child. I think it fed a desire in him to need that love constantly from all people, and what better way to get it than to charm any number of convenient women into falling in love with him?"

"But to lie like that . . ."

"Ah yes, well. It appears our late husband was also a compulsive liar and something I believe the psychoanalysts call a narcissist. Apparently it isn't uncommon among bigamists." Lenora tapped the edge of her cigarette against a cut-glass ashtray. "I've been doing quite a bit of reading in my widowhood."

Louise stared at Lenora. "That's what you've been doing since he died? Reading about bigamists and greeting his former lovers or wives or whatever it is we're meant to be?"

Lenora laughed. "No, of course not, but this helps pass the time between shifts at the volunteer ambulance corps."

Despite the woman's blasé attitude, Louise could hear the hurt in her voice. She had been Paul's first wife. His *real* wife. Now she was the one to tell the women he'd left behind the truth about him, illuminating the dark side of the man they'd all loved.

What he'd done was unforgivable. She could see now that he hadn't fallen in love with her that night in St. Mawgan, as he'd said. Instead, he'd seen her as a target. There was a girl who was simple and vulnerable and ripe for the picking. Except she wasn't any of those things. In the last few months she'd learned more about herself than she'd ever thought possible. She'd drilled and studied and fought, and now, after all this time, she was the woman she was supposed to be.

She would harden her heart against him, boxing up all the love she'd felt for him and shoving it into the deepest corners of her heart. She'd work and fight and sleep and get up to do it all over again until she was numb to Paul. Then, one day, her heart might heal enough that she stopped loving him.

"I'm very sorry this has happened to you," said Louise.

Lenora looked at her squarely. "Thank you, Miss Keene. I think you actually mean that."

"I do. Can I ask you something?"

Lenora inclined her head as Louise pulled out Paul's compass. All at once, the woman's strange composure fell.

"Where did you get that?" Lenora asked, brushing the ding in the side of the tiny compass with her fingertip while Louise balanced it in the palm of her hand.

"He gave it to me. He used it as a sort of engagement ring," Louise said.

"The bastard," Lenora swore softly. "It was my brother's. He was a soldier. He died early in the war and this was sent back with his effects."

"He told me it belonged to his uncle, and that he kept it as a talisman when he was flying."

Lenora's lip trembled. "I gave it to him to keep him safe."

"Then you should take it back," said Louise.

"I don't think I can." A long, shaky draw on her cigarette seemed to calm Lenora, and her next words were firmer. "Keep it or throw it away, you can do what you want with it, but I can't have it in this flat. Not anymore."

Not knowing what else to do, Louise tucked the compass back into her pocket.

Setting her cigarette on the edge of the ashtray, Lenora leaned down and scribbled something on a scrap of paper. Holding it out, she said, "This is the address of the family home in Barlow. If you ever need anything—someone to talk to or be gin-soaked with who will understand—they'll know where to find me."

"Thank you," said Louise, folding the scrap into her uniform's breast pocket. She couldn't imagine ever reaching out to this woman, when what she really wanted was to forget, but there was little else she could do.

"If you'll take a little unsolicited advice, Miss Keene, go on and live your life. Call this a wartime romance and put it behind you."

"And what of you?" asked Louise.

Lenora's gaze fixed on a point out the window. "I'll be here, greeting Paul's widows one by one."

∼

Louise made her way back to her billet, much the way she'd come. It was late, the sky already beginning to turn violet at the farthest reaches of the east.

In her room, she tucked away Lenora's note, pulled on her battle dress, and retrieved her tin helmet. The other girls would've already made their way to Woolwich Depot, and she hurried to make up lost time, her boots slapping loudly against the pavement as she jogged.

When she reached the building, she bounded up the stairs quick as she could. Nearing the top floor, she heard voices. The section hadn't yet taken to the roof, and were waiting instead in the relative warmth and dry of the indoors. She stopped before the door, pulling her shoulders back and shaking her hair from her face. Then, determined, she opened the door.

The room fell silent when they saw her. All of them, the girls, Cartruse, Hatfield, and Williams—even Captain Jones—searched her face. There was fragility there, she knew that, but her strength would hold her together. She would break in her own time, and she wouldn't be ashamed, but tonight she would show them who she really was. Louise Keene, Haybourne born, ATS trained. A woman in her own right.

Paul had stolen her past from her. He would not steal her future.

"My apologies for being late, sir," said Louise, addressing Captain Jones. "It will not happen again."

"Private Bolton," said Captain Jones, clearing his throat. "All of us would understand if you wished to take the bereavement time allowed to you."

Her fists clenched, nails cutting half-moons into her palms. It felt good. The pain grounded her, reminded her to stay focused on the present.

"I'm needed on the predictor, sir," she said.

"As you wish, Bolton," said Captain Jones.

"I think, Captain Jones, that given the circumstances, I should like to be addressed as Private Keene from now on."

A dropped pin could've rattled like a machine gun in the room. Slowly, Captain Jones nodded. "I will see to it that the RA and the ATS are informed of your decision."

"Thank you," said Louise.

She moved to an empty seat at the little card table they'd set up in the corner of the room. Sitting down, she looked each and every one of her compatriots square in the eye before picking up the battered deck of cards on the table. "Who has the scoring sheet?"

"I do," said Charlie, her voice cracking a little.

"Then let's play."

The cards whispered against each other as she shuffled and dealt. It took two hands of gin before the room relaxed a little. Four before Charlie hooted in triumph that she'd beaten Nigella badly.

Louise's focus was so intent that she hardly heard Cartruse pull up a chair next to her until he was close enough to whisper, "You're sure you're all right, Lou?"

She stiffened but kept her eyes on her cards. "No. But I will be."

And somehow, she knew it was the truth.

23

CARA

Cara woke up, curled up against the unmistakable heat of a man's body. She shifted a little, pressing back against Liam's chest as the arm thrown across her stomach drew her a little closer. Liam McGown was a sleep snuggler, a fact that hardly surprised her but made her smile nonetheless.

She lay there a moment, light spilling freely through the gauzy curtains because they'd neglected to draw the heavy cream-colored drapes the night before. This was the moment when any regrets she had about kissing him and inviting him into her room last night would surely surface, but there were none. Instead, she felt relaxed and loose, as though she'd been on holiday for a month.

Liam stirred behind her, pressing his lips to the back of her neck. His voice was all gravel when he said, "Good morning."

She turned around, careful to keep his arm in place, and kissed him. "Good morning."

"Weren't we supposed to meet for breakfast today?" he asked with a lopsided grin.

"At least now we know we won't be late."

"Don't be so sure," he said, rolling her on top of him as he kissed her deeper.

~

They made it down to breakfast just before the hotel stopped serving at nine o'clock, grinning at each other as the maître'd sighed and set his jaw before showing them to a sunny table.

They ate quickly and then climbed in the car to drive to Haybourne. It was still a small village, although there was an industrial park on the outskirts now that boasted office space with all of the modern business conveniences. Haybourne, it would seem, was growing.

Cara was glad Liam was driving, because as they rolled down the village high street, she found her hands had started to tremble just a little. They were so close to finding out the last pieces to the puzzle they'd been worrying over for weeks. They were going to finally meet Kate, the one person, it seemed, who might be able to draw together all of the disparate parts of Louise's story.

"Here it is," said Liam, pulling over into a parking spot in front of a real estate agent's office and killing the ignition. "This is where Bakeford's used to be."

They both looked at the storefront, but there was nothing to indicate that it had once been a grocer's. No charming painted sign, no wide, antique counters that the real estate agent's office had kept to preserve a sense of the space's history. It was just a building.

"It's a little disappointing," she said.

"Things change."

"Still."

"Hopefully Kate will be more helpful," he said, starting the car again.

Cara sat through the drive to the care home with her hands clasped together. She'd flipped through the last pages of the diary again at the hotel when Liam had been in the shower, thinking back on all she'd read. Paul was the kind of man who Cara might've fallen for when she was younger—had fallen for, if she was being honest. He'd swept Louise up off her feet in a whirlwind romance, just as Simon had done. Yet when

Paul was deployed, Louise hadn't sat at home and let the worry and waiting consume her. He and the fight with her mother may have been the push she needed to enlist and leave Haybourne, but the decision had been Louise's alone, and Cara admired her for that.

Liam pulled into the care home's parking lot and put on the brake. "Are you ready?"

"I think so," she said.

"Nervous?"

"More than I thought I'd be. I want to know the answers, but I'm also worried about what happened to Louise. I know that sounds ridiculous but—"

"You're invested," he said.

She nodded.

He took her hand and gave it a squeeze. "Well, there's only one way to find out."

The wind picked up Cara's hair as they walked to the front door hand in hand. She stole a glance at Liam, glad he was here with her. Glad Nicole had brought up the diary in an obvious bid to throw the two of them together. She owed her friend a phone call after all of this, or at least a text to say she'd snogged the professor.

A short, thin woman with a bob of silver hair rose from an armchair in the reception area. "Miss Hargraves, I'm Laurel Mathers."

"Please, call me Cara," she said, extending her hand.

"Then call me Laurel." Kate's daughter slid her gaze over to Liam with curiosity, no doubt having caught the two of them walking hand in hand into the building.

"This is Liam McGown," Cara said. "He's been helping me with figuring out who the diary belonged to. We're neighbors."

"How nice it must be to have such good neighbors," said Laurel, making Cara blush. "If you want to follow me, my mother's having one of her good days."

"Is her health very delicate?" Liam asked.

"As delicate as one can expect for a ninety-four-year-old. But the doctors tell me that her heart is strong and she's as lucid as she's ever been. She's excited that you're coming. She's been asking after you for the past three days."

Laurel led them through brightly lit corridors painted in soothing neutrals that gave one a sense of a being in a very calm hospital or hotel. Finally, they reached a door on which Laurel knocked softly and opened. "Mum, Cara Hargraves and Liam McGown are here to see you."

"There's a man too?" Cara heard a voice from the room inside. "If I'd have known, I would've put on a bit of lipstick."

Laurel pushed the door wide, revealing a big open room with a cluster of chairs around a hospital bed. In the middle of it, looking at them with blatant curiosity, lay Kate. Her hair had been curled in a set, and she had on a bed jacket tied with a pink silk ribbon over a plain white nightgown.

"Mrs. Mathers, it's a pleasure to meet you," said Cara, extending her hand.

"So you're the one who found my cousin's old diary," said Kate, her eyes sharp. "Where was it?"

"Hidden away in a house I was clearing out. I work for an antiques dealer and sometimes we go in and help families figure out what they can sell."

"Whose house was it?" Kate asked.

"A woman named Lenora Robinson," she said.

Kate's brows jumped. "Now *that* is a name I haven't heard in a long time."

"You know her?" Liam asked.

"I know *of* her, and the fact that the two of you don't makes me think that we might be here for a while. Why don't you sit down? Laurel, could you see if we could have some tea for our guests?"

They took two of the maroon upholstered chairs and pulled them closer to Kate's bed as Laurel went off to find a staff member.

"She'll be gone for a little while, because asking for tea at eleven o'clock in the morning is going to throw the staff into a tizzy. They'll have to find the matron and it will take an age, which is good," said Kate.

"You don't want your daughter to hear what you have to say?" Cara asked.

Kate shook her head. "Laurel and Margaret, my eldest, loved their aunt dearly, but because Louise lived so far away they rarely saw her and she became something of a mythic figure. I think it would be too painful to either of my girls to find out what really happened, so I'm going to tell you what I know as quickly as I can.

"You said there was a diary," Kate prompted.

Louise opened her purse and pulled it out of the plastic bag she'd put it in to protect it. Kate's eyes warmed as she took it.

"Do you know, I gave this notebook to Louise for her eighteenth birthday. It cost me one shilling and six pence," said Kate.

"She wrote that she started it at her father's suggestion, but also to spite her mother," said Liam.

Kate laughed. "That sounds like Louise. She was a quiet one when we were growing up, but there always a stubborn streak running through her. She and her mother never saw eye to eye. Aunt Rose could be a hard woman for anyone to love, but especially her daughter."

Cara watched as the old woman smoothed a hand gnarled with arthritis over the cloth cover. "If you open it, you'll find a photograph of her tucked in the front cover. It says it was taken on the Embankment," she said.

Kate did just that and held the picture up to the light. "Isn't she pretty? And so happy too. I've never seen this photograph before. One of the girls in her unit must've taken it when they were stationed in London." Kate cleared her throat. "Well, I suppose I should start at the beginning.

"You'll probably know that Louise ran off to register for the ATS. We were sent to training camp together in Leicester, but she was selected for special assignment."

"Yes, Ack-Ack Command," said Cara.

"It was hard to be separated, but we wrote so many letters to one another in those days that it almost felt as though I knew the other girls in her command. And then there was Paul. He'd swept through her life and, in the space of a month, I really do think she was in love with him."

"It seems so fast," said Cara.

Kate smiled. "Perhaps it was, but she was young and it wasn't a time for logic when it came to matters of the heart.

"At first I was as excited for her about Paul as she was. Louise never noticed the way the boys looked at her in school. I had a flair for the dramatic in those days and loved being at the center of everything, but Louise was more reserved. Somewhere along the way she got it into her head that she was quiet and shy, which couldn't have been further from the truth if you really got to know her.

"The ATS was good for her. It gave her purpose, and I think it was the making of her. She loved those girls in her unit fiercely, and I think it boosted her confidence to know that she was doing something that could actually help save lives in the war. But as all of this was happening, she began to mention gaps between Paul's letters. At first I didn't think anything of it. I knew firsthand how exhausting an army day could be, and he was hunting submarines with Coastal Command. All terribly daring stuff. But then Louise mentioned that she was frustrated he wasn't receiving leave and that made me sit up.

"They worked us hard in the ATS, but everyone knows that a soldier needs to blow off a little steam from time to time. I could believe that Paul's commanding officer was blocking longer requests for leave, but when he shot down Louise's suggestion that she come and see him, I became suspicious."

"She wrote about fighting over it in their letters," Cara said.

Kate nodded. "Then you know how angry Louise was. Paul must've sensed it too, because a few weeks later he showed up at her billet in London and proposed. I think he was terrified she was going to chuck him aside for a soldier or a sailor or another flier."

"But she loved him," said Cara.

"Yes she did, but Paul . . . Paul was a complicated man."

"We know they married, but after the wedding the diary becomes vague," said Liam.

Kate looked pained. "Then you don't know?"

For a moment Cara wondered if Kate would continue on, but then Louise's cousin said, "Paul died. He was shot down while flying a mission over the Channel."

It felt as though the air had been sucked out of the room.

"That's horrible," said Cara.

Kate shook her head, her mouth a grim line. "That's not all. Louise found out when a bundle of her letters was returned to her with a note from Paul's commanding officer. She was devastated, of course, but she was also angry. As his widow, she should've been informed properly. The branches of service had ways of doing this. It was only when her friend did some digging that she realized she wasn't Paul's widow at all."

"What do you mean?" Cara asked.

"Paul was already married."

"What?" Already married? Was that even possible?

"But they had a ceremony, didn't they?" Liam asked.

"They did. I don't know whether the priest knew, but as far as I could tell, the marriage was never recorded anywhere official. Things were chaotic then, and it was easy to pull off any number of scams. I doubt Paul was the only one. Lenora Robinson, the woman whose home you were in, was his first wife. His real wife, I guess you'd say."

Cara and Liam looked at one another, both of their mouths hanging open. Reaching for the diary, Cara opened it to the last page and laid it out on the bed as she read the last entry aloud, the sense of love and loss even more poignant now that she knew what had really happened.

"Oh, poor Lou. Paul was her first romance and the first man to make her feel special. If they'd been able to see each other for more than a handful of days, she would've realized on her own what he was sooner or later. She would've done what most of us have done and cried and raged and healed with time on her own."

"What happened to Louise after that last entry?" Cara asked.

Kate studied her. "You want a happy ending, don't you?"

"Yes, I do." Cara knew that life didn't always have happy endings, but she wanted it so badly for Louise. She wanted it so badly for herself.

"Louise stayed with her battery for almost the entire war. One of the girls, Mary, married her childhood sweetheart while he was on leave and became pregnant almost immediately. She was discharged—it was called going 'para eleven' because paragraph eleven was the part of the ATS handbook that dealt with pregnancy—but most of them stayed together. It was unusual, and I think that unit held Louise together in those early years after Paul's death."

"Do you know what happened to the other girls after the war?" Cara asked.

"I do, actually," said Kate. "Vera, the posh one, refused to move home and do the charitable work her mother expected of her. Instead, she got a job as the assistant to an architect and enrolled in the engineering program at Imperial College London."

"Good for her," murmured Cara.

"I always liked Louise's letters about Charlie the most," said Kate. "Charlie talked her way into a job at an advertising agency, and she'd write Lou with stories about martini lunches and the men who took her out dancing in London. It was all very glamorous.

"The quiet one, Nigella, married an American GI and moved to Illinois."

"A GI bride," said Cara. Just like her gran, except Granddad had stayed in England.

"What about Lizzie?" Liam asked.

"Well, Lizzie caused a bit of a scandal," said Kate. "She and one of Lou's section had a wartime fling. His name was Walker or Warner or . . ."

"Williams?" Liam asked.

"That's the one. When his captain found out, they all thought Lizzie would be reassigned, but it was Williams who was transferred. The gunner girls were too valuable to lose. She went back to Newcastle after the war and took over her mother's boardinghouse," said Kate.

"And what about Louise?" Cara asked. "She mentioned a man named Cartruse a lot."

"What a romantic notion, and one I had myself at the time," said Kate with a laugh. "She was always coy about Cartruse, and I think he would've been happy if she'd paid him any attention, but Louise wasn't interested in any man for a long time. It took her years to rebuild that trust.

"After the war ended, she stayed on as long as she could before the ATS demobbed her. Then she stayed with me for a spell in forty-six to help when I was pregnant with Laurel."

"Do you know why Lenora Robinson had Louise's diary?" Cara asked.

"Just before Laurel was born, I caught Louise on the way to the village post office where her father worked. She had a box all packaged up, and when I asked her about it she said it was just some unfinished business from the war. I always wondered what was in it," said Kate.

"And you think she sent Lenora the things in the tin?" she asked.

"I think it's entirely possible. Lou wanted a clean break, but I could see why it would be almost too difficult to just throw those things away. Plus, one of them belonged to Lenora," said Kate.

"What was that?" Liam asked.

"A compass. Lenora's brother was a soldier, and he'd been carrying it on him when he was killed. I guess Lenora gave it to Paul, and Paul gave it to Louise."

Jock had been right about the compass then.

Laurel bustled through the door with a tray for tea. "You haven't told them all the good bits while I was gone, have you, Mum? It took ages to order tea."

"I wouldn't dare, sweetie.I was just catching them up on what happened to Louise before the end of the diary they found. Now they're asking about after the war," said Kate.

"Ah, my aunt's great escape to America," said Laurel, pouring out cups and handing them around.

"She went to America?" Cara asked, her spirits lifting.

Kate's thin, birdlike shoulders drew back proudly. "Louise Keene became the first member of my family to graduate from university. She attended the University of California, Los Angeles, class of fifty-one."

"California," Cara and Liam said at the same time.

"Yes. She wanted to start over. All of us did, I think—Louise just went farther than most," said Kate. "She received her degree in maths— or math, I suppose they call it there. She went on to teach undergraduates at one of the local colleges."

"I remember she would call every Christmas and on Margaret's and my birthdays," said Laurel. "Long distance. It was so exciting having an aunt in the States, even if we didn't really know her."

"Did she ever come back to Haybourne?" Liam asked.

"Only for her parents' funerals in fifty-four and sixty-three. Her father passed first," said Kate.

"Do you think she was happy?" Cara asked.

Kate tilted her head as though considering this. "I don't really know. Louise changed after the war. She held her cards close to her chest, and we never talked like we used to, but I'd like to think she found something in California.

"There was a man. Tim. They met her first day at UCLA. I used to ask when she called the girls whether she and Tim were going to marry, but she always just laughed and told me to stop being so romantic. Knowing Louise, they might well have been married for years and never told us back in England."

"Why wouldn't she tell you?" Liam asked.

"We knew the old Louise," said Kate, shrugging.

"She wanted to leave that all behind and start fresh," said Cara, a deep understanding settling over her.

"And she did," said Kate.

Cara and Liam stayed only until they finished their cups of tea, because it was clear Kate was flagging. When they stood up to go, Kate beckoned Cara over to her bed. Cara stooped to lean in low.

"I hope that whatever you're looking for, you've found," said Kate.

Cara bit her lip. She had so many questions that were still unanswered.

Kate's eyes crinkled, and the old woman said, "My cousin rarely spoke of what happened during the war, but when she did, she never any mentioned any regrets. I think she made her peace with what happened, put it behind her, and made a new life for herself. All in her own time."

And just like that, Cara understood where Gran was coming from. Somehow this visit had given her a peace she hadn't known in a long time. It was wrapped up in Kate's reassurances about Louise's happiness, a promise that even when things seem the darkest, the light is waiting to shine again.

"Would you to keep like the diary?" Cara asked. "One of the reasons I wanted to figure out who wrote it was so that I could return it to its rightful owners."

Kate patted her hand. "You found it. It's yours now." Cara started to straighten, but the elderly woman tugged her hand again and said in a whisper, "If I were you and I had a man who looked at me the way your Liam looks at you, I'd be a very happy woman both in and out of bed."

Cara stepped away, blushing fiercely, as Kate gave a little tired laugh and said her goodbyes to Liam.

Out in the car park, Liam asked, "Do you want to walk a bit? There was a sign for the coastal path just before we turned off the road."

She nodded, and they walked in silence until the noise of passing cars was lost over the wind and the crashing waves against the cliff face below.

"How are you feeling now that you know everything?" he asked.

"I don't know," she said honestly. "Betrayed by what Paul did to Louise and hurting for her, but happy that she rebuilt her life."

"Do you know, I think she was lucky," he said, stopping at a bench along the path and sitting down.

"Why is that?" she asked, taking the spot next to him.

He squinted out to the distance. "It's the loneliest feeling in the world when someone betrays your trust, but she had her gunner girls. They helped her through it."

"You were lonely after your engagement ended."

"Yes, and I closed myself off to everything. I wanted to wallow. I was as pigheaded as they come."

And so was I. She'd left her life behind, cutting ties with London and leaving almost everyone except Nicole and Gran behind. She'd isolated herself, but Louise had helped her come back into the world. She was rebuilding her home, her career, her life. And now, sitting next to this man on a bench on the cliffs of the northern Cornish coast, she couldn't help the spark of belief that she was creating something entirely new.

"Cara, there's something I think you need to know, but I'm not sure I'm the one who should tell you," he said.

"Who should?" she asked.

"Iris. It's about her service. I don't think she's been honest with you about what she did during the war, but I don't know why."

She nodded.

"It might not be important, but I'm finding I don't like keeping things a secret from you," he said, taking her hand. It was an overture, an unspoken question of whether she trusted him or not. She shifted closer to him on the bench until they sat leg to leg.

"If it's not your secret to tell, I understand," she said, resting her head on his shoulder.

He blew out a breath. "Thank you."

"We'll go see her when we get back. It feels like it's time for all of this to end," she said.

They sat there like that for a few minutes, enjoying the weak, late-autumn sunshine in silence, until Liam stirred. "It's nearly time for lunch. Shall we head back?"

She nodded and pulled out her keys. Her thumb brushed over the raised letters of Granddad's dog tags. She glanced down at them, just as she had countless times before, but this time something made her pause. Maybe it was Liam mentioning secrets, or maybe it was just that, with Louise's mystery solved, she could see things clearly now. Either way, her brain clicked over, more puzzle pieces slotting into place.

"Liam, we need to get back to the hotel," she said in a rush.

"What's wrong?" His hand went to her waist as though to steady her.

She shook her head. "I need to see Gran's medical records. The ones we found in the safe."

He didn't question her, just hurried back with her to the car park and drove straight to the hotel. In the lift, she fidgeted, running her thumb over the dog tags over and over again. When the doors dinged open, she already had her room key out of her pocket.

As soon as she unlocked the door, she went to her purse. Liam had teased her the day before about the size of it, but she'd felt compelled to bring everything they'd found with her—including Gran's files and the wooden box.

She spread the paperwork out on her bed. There, printed innocuously at the top of the medical record next to Iris Warren's name, was her blood type. B. Cara laid Granddad's dog tags on top of the records. The single "B" that recorded Granddad's blood type shouted out the truth to her.

"What are you seeing that I'm not?" Liam asked.

A little breathless as her whole world shifted, Cara said, "Gran's blood type is B. Granddad's blood type is B."

"Okay . . ."

"When Mum was in the crash, the surgeons at the hospital tried to save her. They transfused her. She had type-A blood. I don't remember much from my biology classes, but I do remember being made to do Punnett squares to figure out possible genetic combinations for a child. Two B-type parents can't have an A-type child. It's impossible."

He stared at her for a moment. "So you're saying . . ."

"Mum wasn't Granddad's daughter. At least not biologically. Liam, I need to go see Gran."

This was what the fight between Mum and Gran had been about. Cara knew it with absolute certainty.

"I'll go tell the hotel we're checking out early," Liam said.

She was already moving to her suitcase when he stopped and came back to her. He cupped her jaw, tilting her face, and kissed her. Her whole body buzzed with the reassurance of that kiss.

When he pulled back, he nodded and without another word went to sort things out with the hotel.

24

CARA

It was after eight when Cara and Liam arrived, unannounced, at Widcote Manor. No one was at the front desk, so they walked straight through to the lifts.

Now, standing in front of Gran's door with the weight of decades of secrets on her shoulders, Cara hesitated. Liam stroked a hand down her spine, letting it rest on the small of her back. "It's going to be okay."

"I'm about to accuse my Gran of having an affair and passing off my mum as Granddad's daughter," she said.

"No one's family's perfect," he said.

When Gran answered the door she was dressed in a pair of silk lounging trousers and what looked like a modified man's smoking jacket.

"Well, this is a lovely surprise! I thought you were both in Cornwall," said Gran.

"We were. We just drove up," said Cara.

"Well, come in, come in! You two must be exhausted," Gran said, ushering them in. "Claire from down the hall baked a cake today, and she left the entire thing here after tea. She said she didn't want to calories tempting her, even at eighty-one. I'll just put on some tea."

It was strange, Gran pottering about happily while Cara knew that she was about to change everything.

Cara slanted a glance at Liam, and he nodded. She closed her eyes, willing herself to be strong enough to do this, because she needed to know. Needed to hear Gran tell her the truth.

"Gran, could you come back for a moment?" said Cara.

"I'm just putting the kettle on, dear," Gran called.

"Gran, please."

Gran's low-heeled mules clattered from kitchen tile to hardwood as she reappeared. "What is it, Cara?"

"I know."

For a beat, Gran stood still, a tea towel hanging from her hands. Then, slowly, Gran sank down onto the sofa. "How?"

"Your medical records and Granddad's dog tags," she said.

"I don't understand," said Gran.

"You and Granddad both had type-B blood. Mum was type A."

Gran shook her head in disbelief. "I can't believe after all this time—"

"I'm not angry," Cara said softly. "And I'm not going to judge you."

Gran gave a strangled laugh.

"I'm not," Cara insisted. "I just want to know what happened."

She wanted the full story, just as she had with Louise and the diary. But with Louise's story it had been about the mystery and the responsibility to another family. With Gran it was deeper, more personal. This was Cara's own family history, and it was time to pull the secrets from the dark into the light.

"I've never told anyone," said Gran with a shuddering breath.

"I can leave if that makes it easier," said Liam.

"No, you might as well stay. You know this much already," said Gran, hugging a pillow to her stomach.

"Why don't you start with telling us what you really did during the war," Liam said.

Gran looked up sharply. "How did you find out?"

"I recognized the name Fenny Stratford. If you were billeted there, it was a logical jump that you would've worked in the area. I had a friend look into your service record, which confirmed it."

Gran rolled her shoulders back as though preparing for a speech. "Cara, when I joined the ATS, we were required to undergo a series of aptitude tests. I tested as having a high aptitude for word puzzles. I was requisitioned by the Government Code and Cypher School and made to sign something called the Official Secrets Act. Do you know what that was?"

"I've heard of it, but I don't know why," she said.

"Yes, well, it was in the press a few years ago because of that film about Alan Turing. The Official Secrets Act meant that I had to promise I wouldn't talk about my war work for my entire lifetime. People took it very seriously. I never told anyone. Not my parents, not your mum." Gran cleared her throat. "I was one of the women working at Bletchley Park. I was assigned to one of the huts taking down intercepted radio signals from German operators."

"You were in intelligence?" Cara asked.

"I was."

"The files of those in Bletchley Park were declassified in the seventies. You've been allowed to talk about what you did for decades. Why remain so secretive about it?" Liam asked.

"Is it so hard to believe that I felt it my duty to keep a secret that won us the war?"

"Gran . . ." Cara said softly.

"I'm sorry, Liam." When Gran lifted her chin, her eyes shone with tears. "The Official Secrets Act was also convenient for me because I had another secret to hide. While I was at Bletchley, I had an affair with my superior officer."

"The man in the photographs," Cara said.

"Edwin was extraordinary. He was plucked out of Oxford as soon as it looked as though there would be a war and was trained to manage teams of brilliant minds. He was charismatic and we were all devoted to him, but I was the one who went a step too far. I knew he was married. I knew that what we were doing was wrong, but I didn't care. I was young and silly and thought I deserved my own happiness."

"You did. You do," said Cara.

"Not at the expense of another woman's. He'd been married for nearly seven years when I met him, and he had three children. And still, I thought I could give him something that his wife couldn't."

"What was that?" she asked.

"Adoration. Youth. Take your pick. It's foolish, but I was hardly more than a child at that point," said Gran. "The affair lasted almost a year, until the spring of forty-five."

"What happened?" Cara asked.

"I became pregnant. I thought he would leave his wife when he found out—all of us other women always think that. I told him on VE Day."

"Oh, Gran . . ."

"I know," said Gran with a little laugh. "I don't think I can even blame it on the excitement of the day. I was so madly in love with him, but he was never going to leave his family or his position. It would've meant serious consequences for his career.

"So I did the only thing I could think of. I turned to a sweet American soldier who'd been hanging about for months."

"Granddad," said Cara.

"We'd met in London at a NAAFI dance—that part of the story was true—and he spent most of the autumn of forty-four coming up whenever he could to see me. I think I knew Edwin was pulling away, and I liked the attention Steve gave me but I was never really invested until I needed him."

"I thought your courtship was just four months?" Cara asked.

"It suited us later to make the timeline a little hazy," said Gran.

"When did he propose?" Liam asked.

"Three days after VE Day. Three days after Edwin turned me away."

"Did you tell Granddad that you were pregnant when you accepted his proposal?" Cara asked.

Gran hugged the pillow tighter. "No."

"When did he find out?" she asked.

"We were married two weeks later, because he didn't know where he was going to be sent after the Germans surrendered. He wanted to make sure I would have some rights as his wife," said Gran.

"When did you tell him you were pregnant?" Cara asked.

"After I'd reached four months and couldn't hide it any longer. We'd been married for a month," said Gran.

"What did he say?" Cara asked.

"He walked out of our flat and I didn't see him for three hours. When he came back he asked me if the affair was over. I told him it was, and he promised me that he would love our son or daughter as though it was his own. He wanted me and a child more than anything else in the world." Gran wiped away her tears. "He was a good man."

"He was," said Cara.

"I don't think I fully believed him until your mother was born, but he fell in love with her the moment he saw her. I used to wake up at night and find he'd gone to her nursery just to watch her as she slept."

Tears burned in the back of Cara's throat. "I miss her, Gran."

Gran opened her arms, and Cara went to her, kneeling on the floor next to her chair. "I do too, dear," Gran said into her hair. "I do too."

They held each other for a moment while Liam quietly retreated to the kitchen.

When at last Cara pulled back, she asked, "What did you tell Mum when she found out?"

"The truth. I married Steve knowing I didn't love him, but that I came to love him in the end. I think she's what saved our marriage and made us stronger."

"But you and Mum still fought," Cara said.

"It was too much to much to think she would take it anything but poorly. I just wish . . . I just wish I'd had time to try to fix it," said Gran.

"She died knowing that you loved her and that Granddad did too. I have no doubt about that." And as she said it, Cara found that she believed every word of her reassurances.

"I just can't help but wonder—"

"Don't," said Cara. "I've spent too much time worrying about whether I made the right decisions or not. I'm learning it's time to move forward."

Gran nodded toward the kitchen with a smile. "Is that what you're doing?"

Cara smiled. "Yes. In more ways than one."

Gran laughed. "Was the hotel snowed in?"

"No snow needed."

Gran covered Cara's hand with hers, the gold of her wedding ring catching the light. "The one thing I wish for you more than anything else is that when you love again you'll love with your whole heart."

"If you'd asked me to do that a few months ago, I don't think I would've believed you that it was possible. But now . . ."

Gran smiled. "Then that's a start."

"I love you to the moon, Gran."

"And back."

~

Cara was quiet during the final car ride home, happy to let Liam drive. The roller coaster of a weekend had left her drained, and now the real world would close in around them.

He parked in her drive, and they climbed out and retrieved their bags. He handed her back her keys and hesitated before kissing her on the cheek.

"Get some rest," he said.

Then he turned and retreated to his house, Rufus barking at the sound of his steps.

Inside her cottage, Cara dropped her overnight bag and purse in the hallway and went straight to the kitchen to put on the kettle. She prepared tea, glancing out the window as lights came on in Liam's house.

The kettle clicked off just as music began to pour from his windows. It was loud and guitar-filled, and thinking how Mrs. Wasserman down the road would hate it made her smile.

She poured the hot water over the leaves in her teapot and pulled down a mug. The music switched now. Jazz maybe, with a saxophone hitting a series of high notes. She listened closely, trying to catch the tune, but couldn't.

There was so much to do before the workweek. She should get a load of laundry on—neglecting to do that before leaving had been a mistake. She'd all but ignored her email, and she still owed Nicole a call. But as she went to pull out her phone, she realized there was only one person she wanted to talk to that night.

Pulling down another mug, she poured out the tea with a dash of milk and carefully opened her front door. She picked her way down her front path and around to his. With the toe of her shoe, she rapped low on the front door, sending Rufus into a spurt of barking.

She stood there, knuckles turning red from the heat, for nearly thirty seconds before Liam ripped open the door.

"I brought you tea," she said, holding the mugs up.

He rubbed a hand over his face, and she thought for a moment than she'd miscalculated things in her own excitement. But then he said, "Thank God. I was worried I'd screwed it all up."

"How?" she asked.

He took the mugs and set them down on the ground. Then he pulled her to him, his hands framing her face. "By not doing this."

He kissed her, her entire body going weak as he slid his lips along hers, drinking her in. All of the passion and comfort of the weekend was back. But this time they were standing on his front doorstep, not in a hotel far away, and somehow that made it matter more.

"I didn't want this weekend to end because I didn't want this to end," he whispered against her mouth.

"Then let's not let it. I'm tired of being cautious and waiting to start my life over again. I want it now, with you," she said. What she'd told Gran was true. She was moving on, and she'd do it just as Louise had: without regrets.

"Me too, Cara. Me too. Do you want to come inside before we shock half of Elm Road?"

"Yes," she said, glancing down. "And we might need more tea. It looks like Rufus got to ours."

He laughed as the dog stared up at them, tea dripping down his chin. "Come on. I'll make you another cup."

It would be, she knew, the first of many.

Acknowledgments

Writing my first book about World War II was a deeply satisfying, daunting task, and I'm grateful to several authors for their excellent work on the time period. In particular, *The Girls Who Went to War* by Duncan Barrett and Nuala Calvi, *Girls in Khaki: A History of the ATS in the Second World War* by Barbara Green, and *The Secret History of the Blitz* by Joshua Levine proved invaluable in my research. I am also thankful for the women who served and have since shared their stories.

I am eternally grateful for the generosity and enthusiasm of my support network. The HBICs in my life: Alexis Anne, Alexandra Haughton, Lindsay Emory, Mary Chris Escobar, and Laura von Holt (who danced through the Village with me when I told her this book was going to be a reality). Sonia, Jax, Ben, Tamsen, Nigel, Sarah, Aidan, Kather, Christy, Sean. My wonderful agent through thick and thin, Emily Sylvan Kim. My incredible editor, Marla Daniels. (We're going back to that restaurant and ordering champagne next time.) Jennifer Bergstrom and the entire team at Gallery Books, including Polly Watson, Christine Masters, [TK Gallery Team].

Mum, Dad, Justine, and Mark, thank you the most for putting up with a writer on deadline for months. You helped me figure out character, didn't say anything when I plastered my bedroom with Post-It notes to figure out plot, and have been asking "When can I read it?" for ages now. I love you all and couldn't be more grateful that you're my family.